STRICTLY NOT YOURS

CARRIE ELKS

CHAPTER
ONE

BLAIR

As soon as I walk through the door, I feel that something's wrong. Call it intuition. Or superstition, maybe. Although it's more likely a combination of the lack of sleep from pulling an all-nighter on my latest college assignment, combined with the shock of having my six-year-old nephew ask me first thing this morning if it's true that babies come from a hole between your legs and that daddies have planted them.

I sent him packing to his mom to answer that one.

And now I'm standing right inside a swanky apartment in New York's Upper East Side, cleaning supplies stuffed into my oversized backpack, trying to work out what's out of place.

And nothing is.

Dr. Holden Salinger has to be the cleanest client City Slickers – the cleaning company I work for – has ever had. I've been cleaning his apartment for two years and there's never anything out of place. Not even the photographs of his All-American family move an inch between my visits.

I know. I measured them once.

Putting my pack down on the floor, I close the front door behind me and slip off my shoes. We have to wear slippers while cleaning, though Georgie – my boss – has never specified what type of slippers we should wear. So I'm wearing Tigger ones that my sister bought me last Christmas. They clash with the pink cargo trousers that Georgie supplies, but I kind of like that.

It's as rebellious as I get.

With a Tigger-like bounce in my step, I walk across Dr. Salinger's highly polished wooden floored hallway to the living room, where I shrug off the laptop bag I'm carrying and put it beside the desk. Then I take another good look around. His cream leather sofa looks untouched since last week, though I think there may be a new medical magazine on the black onyx coffee table that separates the huge sofa from an even huger TV.

The kitchen is just as untouched. Sometimes I wonder if Dr. Salinger actually eats anything. The touch sensitive halogen stovetop shines like a mirror and when I open his refrigerator, there's very little in there.

I've never seen a half-eaten takeout carton in there, let alone the mouldy fruit or expired milk I've found in the shiny appliances of my prior cleaning clients. This is why Dr. Salinger is my favorite.

Even if I've never met him.

That's the strange thing about being a cleaner to Manhattan's richest and most successful. I probably know more about them than their closest friends. I know all their bad habits, their secret addictions – drugs, sugar, and otherwise – and I know all about their families from the photographs on the walls and the angry voicemails filling the quiet as I clean their spaces.

But they know nothing about me at all. They could pass

me in the street and wouldn't know who I am. I kind of like that. Being anonymous makes me feel safe.

And I'm all for that.

It's only when I reach the main bedroom that I realize my intuition was right all along. The bed isn't made. The white thousand thread count covers are half on the bed and half on the floor. And there's something on the pillow. Wait. Is that blood?

I swallow hard and do something I rarely do when I walk in this house.

"Hello?" I call out, staring at the thick black door that separates the main bedroom from the huge bathroom that I've always envied. Is he in there? Is he hurt? Or has he hurt somebody else?

Protocol says I should call Georgie if something is wrong. She takes our safety seriously. Instead, I pad across the thick cream rug that covers his bedroom floor, my heart thudding against my chest.

"Dr. Salinger?" I gingerly push on the door, but it doesn't give. "It's your cleaner," I say. "Blair."

There's no response. So I take a deep breath and grab the handle and push it down, half ready to run if some feral criminal who specializes in kidnapping doctors rushes me.

But there's nobody in the bathroom. And yes, for a minute I feel envious all over again as I take in the shiny black floor tiles and the white marbled walls and the bathroom fixtures that cost more than I can ever dream of earning.

And though there's nobody there, I fixate on the counter. There is used medical equipment. Sutures. And wipes with blood on them. Like he's cleaned somebody's wound and dressed it.

Again, I know I should call Georgie. She has a strict no-blood policy. We're supposed to report something like this right away and leave. She'll throw Dr. Salinger off her client list. Which is concerning because I need this job.

This one, I mean. In this apartment.

Because it takes less than an hour to clean his already-spick and span home. Then I get to use the rest of the three hours to catch up on my college work. If I didn't have this apartment to clean, I won't pass my degree.

And I have to pass my degree.

"Dr. Salinger," I murmur. "You're in luck. This is going to stay between the two of us." I press my lips together and walk back to the hallway to grab my cleaning supplies and in less than a minute I'm pulling on my gloves, ready to attack the scene of the crime.

Not that I think he's committed a crime. From what I can tell, he's too busy for that. Never here, never eating, never making a mess. Still, as I pull out a trash bag and put away the mess he's left, I can't help but try to work out what's going on.

Once the empty suture packets and wipes are in the bag, I spot a small black card nestled against the mirror. Lifting it up, I read the words on the front.

The Black and White Club.

Interesting. There's an address there – it's near my college, I think. I've definitely been down that road before. Although, I don't remember seeing a swanky club there. The area where I study is definitely more down to earth than top notch.

Putting it in my pocket, I clean the bathroom with gusto, feeling proud of myself once it's restored to its usual pristine state. Then I do the same with the bedroom, changing the bedding and taking the sheets down to the laundry, then vacuuming the rug before making sure there are no specks of blood on it.

There aren't, thank goodness.

By the time I've done the same to the rest of his apartment, a little more than an hour has gone by. I have two and a half more hours before the laundry is finished so I head back to the living room and slump down in Dr. Salinger's leather captain chair, taking in the photograph of six men propped up on the mahogany desk which I suspect he also doesn't use.

They're all standing in a field by a lake, their arms around each other, laughing as they look at whoever's behind the camera. They have to be related, brothers maybe, and all of them have the kind of perfect smiles you only get with expensive dentistry and good meals. They're tall, muscled, healthy, and they make me yearn for something, though I'm not sure what.

All I know is that any photographs of me and my sister aren't like this at all. We've never even been near a lake as pretty as that one.

I linger on it a moment more, wondering which of the six muscled, dark-haired men is Dr. Salinger.

And then I pull my eyes from the photograph and grab my bag to take out my laptop, opening it up and connecting it to my phone's hotspot. I might be cheeky, but I'm not cheeky enough to use Dr. Salinger's Wi-Fi to do my homework.

Funny thing, he has no idea who I am, and yet if it wasn't for him, there's no way I could graduate this year at the age of thirty-four.

Maybe one day I'll be able to tell him that.

————

HOLDEN

It's only four o'clock in the afternoon, but I'm already yawning. Something to do with being called into the emergency room at the ass crack of midnight to consult on an eight-year-old girl who was rushed in with a headache causing vision issues but had a suspected brain tumor.

And now I'm sitting across from two people who are looking at me like I'm the worst person in the world. Because at this moment I am. I'm the person who's just told them that their world has changed. That their child's scans are showing dark shadows and though we still need to run some more tests, they need to be ready for the worst.

The mom – Alice – is crying. The dad is trying to look stoic but his bottom lip is trembling and he won't look up from his hands. Next to me, Carter, our intern, is taking loud whooping breaths. I kick his shoes with mine because he knows better than this.

"It can't be," Alice whispers. "We're going on vacation next week."

I can't tell you how many times I've had this conversation since I finished my pediatric oncology fellowship, but not once has it ever been the same. Sure, there's a similar vein to the movement from disbelief to anger to possible hope, but every parent's response is different.

"You can still go on vacation," I say. "We'll give you some advice on what to do and what not to. We can start the treatment once you're back."

I don't tell them it'll probably take that long to get authorization from their insurance company to go ahead with whatever course we decide to follow, but it's true. I spend half my life on the phone with goddamn insurance companies, fighting for the treatment plans. But that's my problem, not theirs.

And we will make it work.

"What about her hair?" Alice asks. "She loves her hair. Please tell me she won't lose it."

Carter whimpers next to me. I nudge him again, but dammit, I can tell he's on the edge. My jaw tightens. And then I wince because I still need to properly clean up the wound I got last night. The sutures I put on right before I was called out need redoing. It was a ham-fisted attempt and I'm annoyed with it.

"Shut up about her hair. She has cancer, dammit." That's the dad. He's already at the angry stage and I don't blame him. I'd be furious if it was my kid.

Which is one of the many reasons why I don't have any.

Still, if it was one of my nieces or nephews, I'd also be furious. At the doctor, at the world.

I speak softly to them both, trying to reassure them as much as I can, before they go to see their daughter who's on the ward, while I turn to Carter and lift an eyebrow at him.

There are tears pouring down his face. He looks at me and it reminds me of how I used to feel years ago when I first started doing this.

"Wipe those away and shut the hell up," I tell him, keeping my eyes narrowed, mostly because one of them is swollen from last night. And the bruising is coming out too. "What did I tell you?"

"That we shouldn't cry." Carter sniffs. He looks at my swollen eye and opens his mouth as though he's going to say something else, then closes it again.

Good.

"That's right." My voice is tight because I'm annoyed with him. He knows this already. "And why shouldn't we cry?"

"Because..." Carter sniffs again. "Because I'm stealing their emotions."

"And?" I lift a brow. Shit, that hurts.

"And they need to believe in me. That I can help."

"That's right. So what aren't you going to do next time?" I ask him.

"Cry."

"Good."

Carter stays silent for a moment. And I don't take my eyes off him. He's not a kid, even if he looks like one. He's a medical student, and he needs to harden up. The same way I did.

The way all of us have.

"When does it get easier?" he finally asks, wiping his eyes with the back of his hand.

"It doesn't," I tell him. "And it shouldn't. The day it gets easier is the day you should quit your job."

"But you don't blink an eyelid. You just told those people their kid has a brain tumor."

"I know. And I fucking hate it, but you know what? I've learned to deal with it. Go get a hobby, Carter. Kiss your girl, go running, do whatever it takes to work through the pain, but don't you ever.. and I mean ever… cry in front of a patient or their parents again."

Carter looks like he's going to cry again, but somehow he stops himself and nods, then sniffs loudly and runs out. That's when I see Rose, our senior ward nurse, standing by the door. She gives me one of her looks – the kind that scared me shitless when I first joined the team here.

"You're too hard on them," she says.

"He'll thank me later." He probably won't, but I'm not sure I care. I'm trying to harden him up for a reason.

She steps inside my office and passes over some papers. "These need signing. And maybe you should take some of your own advice."

I read each paper and scribble my name across the bottom. "What advice?" I murmur.

"Kiss a girl. Rather than doing whatever it is you're doing to get an eye and lip like that."

I look up. "I tripped."

"Sure. And I won the lottery. That's why I'm here, working my guts out."

A smile slides across my lips. Rose gives me hell, but I don't mind. She's the best damn nurse I've ever met. Smart, hardworking, tough, yet she makes our patients feel special. I don't know what it is about her but I wish we could bottle it and spread it throughout the rest of the team.

"You'd still come to work even if you were a millionaire," I tease, because I seriously suspect she would. "There you go." I pass the papers over – mostly orders for tests and lab work – and then pick up my coffee cup full of dark liquid that's gone cold but I drink it anyway, because I probably won't get another coffee for hours.

"And you need to find a new hobby," Rose says. "That one's going to kill you."

She's probably right, but it's also the only thing that keeps me sane. Not that I feel very sane for the next two hours as we all run ourselves ragged around the ward.

It's only at seven o'clock, when the next shift has come on, that I realize I haven't slept for almost forty-eight hours, and I really should head home for bed.

But first I walk into the private room at the far end of the ward. It has posters on the wall, not of boy bands, but of Penguin classics. The same kind of books are stacked on the table next to the bed.

And the patient sitting on that bed – Mabel – has her earbuds in and her nose in a book as always. It's not until I touch her arm that she realizes I'm here, almost jumping out of her bed.

"You scared me," she says, frowning. At sixteen, she's one of our oldest patients, though we treat some all the way into adulthood. She's also one of my favorites. I don't know why. She just has this grit about her, even though she's been in and out of the pediatric oncology ward for the past year.

"What are you reading?" I ask her. She passes me the book and I'm careful not to lose her place, sliding my thumb between the pages. *A Tale of Two Cities* is written across the front, with Charles Dickens at the bottom. The front image shows a man standing on wooden gallows with white buildings behind him.

"You get bored with *The Hunger Games*?" I ask her. The last time she was in, she was on some kind of post-apocalyptic kick.

"I finished them. But now I'm onto the classics," she says, taking the book back from me. "Have you read it?"

I laugh because it's a running joke between us. I don't read. I can't remember the last time I opened a book. Or watched television or went to the movies.

"Is it the one about the hungry kid?" I ask.

Mabel rolls her eyes. "That's *Oliver Twist*. And what did you do to your eye?"

I reach up with my free hand to touch it. I'd forgotten about that. "I fell on the sidewalk." And that's when I remember I left the bathroom in a bloody mess. "What day is it today?" I ask her.

She gives me a look only a teenager can. "You're the doctor, you tell me."

"It's… Thursday?"

Another eye roll. "It's Wednesday."

Shit. Shit. My cleaner comes on either Tuesday or Wednesday, depending on her working pattern, and I'm pretty sure this is a Wednesday week. And I know I left crap everywhere in the bathroom this morning. And if I had any energy I'd be worried because I'm a doctor and I know better than to leave human waste out for somebody else to touch.

Actually, I *am* worried.

I hand her the book back and tell her to get some sleep.

"You too," she says. "That eye thing looks nasty."

"It's fine," I reply. "I'll see you in the morning."

And for the first time she smiles. It feels good because I haven't seen too many of those today.

The rest of the day shift has already clocked out by the time I head to the locker room to grab my things and head into the cool night air.

And for a minute I consider heading east, to The Black and White Club. But it's a bad idea, I know that.

So instead I go home, grabbing a pizza on the way, then pretty much stumble into my apartment.

It's only later when I go to throw the empty box out that I realize that it's clean and tidy and somebody else is responsible for that.

And yeah, that makes me feel like a bit of an asshole.

CHAPTER
TWO

BLAIR

Early mornings in our apartment always resembles that moment in a movie when everything goes to hell and all the characters begin running in different directions. I'm trying to upload next week's half-written assignment to the cloud so my stupid, old laptop won't magically delete everything I've written between home and school. Annie, my sister – younger by four years – is trying to make a brown bag lunch for her son, Evan and pack her own bag for work, all while she has a phone wedged between her ear and shoulder because she's on a conference call since she should have been at the office an hour ago.

And Evan – actually, where is Evan? Our apartment is tiny. Two bedrooms, if you can call them that, plus a kitchen- dining- living room that always looks like a hurri- cane has passed through on the way to something more exciting.

Then I hear it. The wheezing. It's only light, but it makes me wince.

Annie looks at me and frowns, taking in my pinched brows and pressed-together lips.

"What?" she mouths.

"Evan."

She pulls the phone from her ear and listens. "Shit." She scrambles through his Spiderman bag that's open on the kitchen table and pulls out his inhaler. I grab it from her, motioning for her to go back to her call because she needs this job and they're already murmuring about her not showing the 'appropriate level of commitment.'

Evan is in the bathroom when I find him. He looks at me like I'm an idiot when I hold his inhaler up.

"You're wheezing," I tell him and he wrinkles his nose because he hates the inhaler and he hates having asthma.

I hate it, too. But I give him the albuterol anyway, and his breathing returns to normal. He grabs the gel he likes putting in his hair and slicks it back.

"Do I look cool?" he asks me.

"As a cucumber." I wink.

He grins. And I know he's fine to go to school – if we kept him home every time he wheezed he wouldn't graduate until he's sixty – but I still hate it.

"Everything okay?" Annie asks, a worried look on her face as she walks into the bathroom.

"It's all good," I tell her. "Go."

She leans down to kiss Evan. "Be good for Auntie Blair. I'll pick you up from Emma's, okay?" Emma is the babysitter who picks Evan up on the evenings I have late classes and can't be to his school by three pm.

"Okay." Evan nods. He's such an easy going kid. Doesn't complain, doesn't ask much of anything. I have this dream of getting him out of New York, away from the congested air and the lack of trees and the cost of living that means we don't get to do much more than survive here.

Take this apartment. The only way we can afford to pay

for it is because I'm currently studying under the GI bill. And yes, it's kind of ludicrous that I'm a student at my age, but once I get my degree, everything's going to change.

I'll get a job somewhere different. Somewhere that we can afford a house with a backyard that's green and air that doesn't taste like a mixture of gas and dust.

The front door slams and that leaves me and Evan to finish getting ready. I keep a close eye on him as we pack everything up and head out of the apartment. As we hit the streets his breathing is still fine. But it doesn't stop me from reminding him that if he has another attack he needs to tell his teacher right away.

And I know Annie will have phoned the school on her way into the office.

The next eight hours are taken up with lectures and tutorials and study groups in the library. I'm studying for my masters in library science, and our current project revolves around creating digital archives, which is pretty much as dry as it sounds.

But it's all part of the plan.

———

It's raining by the time I leave just after six that evening. My stomach is rumbling but I ignore it and head for the bus stop. Before I get there I pass a building with a sign outside that I must have passed a thousand times before without looking.

But now I look. Because the sign has words that interest me painted in silver across a black-and-white striped background.

The Black And White Club.

Without thinking, I turn around and walk back toward the club, taking in the faded sign and the peeling letters. It looks nothing like the swanky club I imagined a man like Dr.

Salinger would visit. The ones that have VIP rooms and guest lists and sell Patron by the bottle.

Instead, it looks almost boring. Nondescript. And because I'm an idiot I push at the door, almost jumping when it gives and immediately swings open.

One day curiosity is going to kill this cat.

The rain is getting heavy, so I step inside, closing the door behind me, and my eyes take a moment to adjust to the gloom of the club. Blinking, I look around the empty room. It looks normal, like the bars I used to go to in a different lifetime.

On one side is a counter that stretches the entire length of the wall. Bottles and glasses neatly arranged on the shelves, along with some television screens that are turned off. There are wooden and leather bar stools neatly pushed against the counter – and even from here I can tell they've seen better days.

The main floor is filled with black tables, white chairs stacked on them like somebody has been cleaning the wooden floor. In the corner is a stage and speakers, with a little space where I assume people can dance.

It's clean enough. Not City Slickers standards, but as I walk across the floor my shoes don't stick to it.

The far wall is full of photographs. I can't tell who's in them from where I'm standing but they look like the ones that have celebrities in them who've visited the joint and then sign them as a favor to management.

"Hello? Who's there?" An older man walks through a door at the far end of the bar, his eyes landing on me. He must be around fifty. Wearing black pants and a white shirt that's tucked over his pot belly, his hair is gray and sparse. From the way it's slicked back I can see the pinkness of his scalp.

"Oh, sorry." I grimace, embarrassed at being caught snooping. "I was just going."

He tips his head. "Wait? You here about the job?"

I open my mouth to say no, but nothing comes out.

"Come on over here so I can see you," he says, and for some stupid reason I do.

Maybe it's because I owe him an explanation for why I'm standing in his empty bar when I should be on the bus heading home. Or maybe it's because I'm still wondering what the hell Dr. Salinger was doing in a place like this – where I assume he ended up either bleeding or meeting somebody who was.

"Yeah, you'll do. You have any experience?"

"I'm sorry?" I blink. And hold back a gag because this guy must be wearing an entire bottle of cologne. It's not bad smelling but it's so strong that it's filling my nose up.

"You worked behind a bar before?" he asks me.

"Yes." That's the truth at least. I've done pretty much every job imaginable to supplement the money I get from the government to pay for my education. "A few times."

His eyes scan me. "You know what this place is, right?"

"The Black and White Club," I say and a smile pulls at his lips.

"You don't, do you?"

I have absolutely no idea what he's talking about.

"It's okay. We'd just need you behind the bar anyway. Three nights a week. Seven until one. Twenty dollars an hour plus tips. Most of the team makes at least three hundred a shift on the weekends."

"You mean a week," I say.

"No per shift."

My mouth drops open. Three hundred a shift, for six hours' of work. That's... yeah, above minimum wage for sure. A minute ago I was planning to tell him this was a mistake before apologizing and running out, but holy hell, the things we could do with that kind of money.

And then I feel a little tingle on my neck. If there's one

thing I've learned during my time scrimping and saving and working all the hours I can, is that there's no such thing as a free lunch.

If something sounds too good to be true, it usually is. Like the time I started working as an assistant to an older gentleman who needed help to get up in the morning. Turned out he liked to pretend to be a baby and wanted me to change his diaper.

Hell to the no.

"Your bartenders earn three hundred for a six-hour shift," I say, my voice disbelieving.

"We have some very high tipping customers."

I look around the bar. "In here?"

"No. Mostly in there." He inclines his head at a pair of double doors on the other side of the room. "You'd only need to deliver drinks. And take payment. That's it."

"What's the dress code?" I ask, because if it's a bunny suit or a bikini I'm out of here.

He shrugs. "Whatever's comfortable. Jeans. T-shirt."

Okay, I'm going to ask. Even though I'm not sure I really want to know. Part of me just wants to say yes. Take the job whatever's involved.

But Momma brought me up to be a good girl.

"What's behind the door?"

His smile widens. "Finally. Come on." He walks around the counter, pulling a ring of keys from his pocket, and strides across the bar. I follow him slowly, calculating the distance between me and the front door. If I need to, I could outrun this guy. Yes, it's been a while since I did daily PT but I still keep my fitness up despite having left the Army years ago.

He doesn't seem to notice my hesitation. Or that I'm hanging back as he slides the key into the lock. It clicks open and I swallow hard, wondering what I'm going to see.

A strip club? Women in cages? What?

When he pushes the door open and flicks some lights on,

I'm more confused than ever. There are chairs and tables – black and white again – and then just chairs closer to the center of the room. But the thing that draws my eye is right at the very center.

It's a boxing ring. All in black and white, with the club's name written in the center. The ropes are white, too. Though much like the rest of the club, it's tatty and has seen better days.

But still.

It's not a strip club or a human trafficking ring or anything like that. The Black and White Club is a fight club.

And though I hate fighting with a passion, if they want to pay me three hundred dollars a night while people smash the bejeezus out of each other, hell, I'm all in.

HOLDEN

It's Friday night as I'm walking out of my office, nodding at Rose who is talking to the parents of one of the new patients, showing them where the kitchen is and explaining that they can bring their own food in or use what's in the community fridge when one of them stays with their five-year-old son, who's been diagnosed with a malignant bone tumor.

I leave them to it and walk down the corridor, checking in on a couple of patients who had procedures today, and once I'm satisfied that all is well I pop my head into the last room on the left.

Mabel is out of bed, sitting on a chair, her feet propped up on a little coffee table. And of course she's reading again.

"How's Dickens?" I ask her.

She looks up and wrinkles her nose. "I finished that one. I'm onto *Wuthering Heights*."

I smile because at least I know something about this. "Heathcliff, huh?"

"Have you read it?" She looks almost hopeful. And part of me wants to lie and say I have. But I made a pact with myself long ago that I'd never once lie to my patients.

"No, but I might have seen the film. He's the handsome angry guy that everybody falls in love with, right?"

She makes a gagging sound and for a minute I go into doctor mode. But then I realize she's pretending to vomit.

"He's not handsome and nobody should fall in love with him," she says. "He's an asshole. And so is she. They all deserve to be miserable."

I smile. "I'll take your word for it."

"You really should try reading a book sometime," Mabel tells me. "It'll expand your mind."

"I'll just watch the movies, it's quicker."

She sighs. "That's cheating."

"Good night, Mabel."

"Night, doc. By the way, your eye is looking better."

"Thanks. Sleep tight."

When I get to the parking lot and into my car, I know I should head home. I've worked non-stop all week and I actually have a chance to sleep for two days. But instead of turning left at the exit, I hit the right indicator and head east, driving for twenty minutes to the one place I know I shouldn't be.

There's only a couple of spaces left in the parking lot. I pull in between a Bugatti and a Ford and climb out, then walk to the front of the nondescript building that houses The Black and White Club. One of the security guards nods at me and opens the door, and as soon as I walk inside it feels like my whole body is relaxing for the first time in days.

I've been coming here since I moved to New York and started working at the hospital. Before that, when I was in Chicago, I used to mostly box in a gym. But my hours here are always erratic, and joining a gym that kept the same hours was almost impossible.

That's when I heard about The Black and White Club. A normal bar with a jukebox and the occasional live music in the main room, and then at the back there's a boxing ring where they hold fights most evenings. All amateur, all levels of ability, and all kinds of men who like to fight. I've exchanged blows with bankers, lawyers, shop workers, and teachers.

But we all have the same aim. We relieve our stress by fighting in a controlled manner. And yeah, it's not something I exactly broadcast across the hospital. But if I didn't come here I think I'd end up losing my mind. Or drinking too much. Or taking drugs like I've seen so many of my colleagues do.

Coming to the club and fighting under their rules – seems like a better option.

"Hey, Salinger."

I look up to see Jimmy, the owner, walking toward me.

"Jimmy." I nod at him.

"Your eye any better?"

I reach up to touch it. The bruise is mostly yellow now. Not exactly looking great but it's on the way to healing. "It's fine," I tell him.

"I threw the other guy out. He's not coming back."

I nod, because Jimmy likes a clean fight. The guy hit me after it was over, when my headgear was off. He had a grudge and he used it.

"You fighting tonight?" he asks. "I got a couple of slots."

I shake my head. "Just watching."

"Well if you change your mind let me know."

I nod and walk over to the bar, feeling the fatigue of the week finally wash over me. I'll grab a drink, watch a fight, and go home. Katrina is standing behind the counter and her eyes follow me as I reach the bar.

"Hey handsome," she gives me a wide smile. I'd take it personally but Katrina flirts with everybody. "The usual?"

"Please."

She grabs a glass and a bottle of water, pouring it in. "Ice?"

"No thanks." As she passes it to me I become aware of another woman behind the bar. She's talking to a customer, but all I can see is the back of her head as she nods.

"New girl," Katrina says, following the direction of my stare. "Pretty sure she's not going to last more than one night. She hates the fighting."

My lips twitch. "Then she came to the wrong place."

Katrina shrugs. And I look at the new girl again. Or woman, because that's what she is. I can tell that much from the way she holds herself. The natural color of her dark hair and the smoothness of her shoulders tells me she's younger than me, but not a kid.

Her hair falls over her shoulders in waves, shining beneath the dim bar lights. She's wearing a black tank tucked into her jeans, and as she leans forward I can see the upper part of her hips, where they flare out from her waist.

"There ya go," Katrina says, passing me the water. "On the house."

I put a tip down for her anyway and grab my glass, taking one last look at the back of the new girl.

It's weird how a sense of familiarity washes over me. Maybe she's a past patient or a family member.

And as I head over to the backroom, walking through the doors, I push her out of my head because it doesn't matter. I'll watch one fight, head home, and get some proper sleep for the first time in forever.

But of course, I'm lying to myself.

Because I don't.

CHAPTER
THREE

BLAIR

The night goes past fast, filled with drink orders and deliveries. According to the security guard, who came in to intervene in an argument between a drunk woman and her husband, there's now a line of customers halfway around the block.

I can't believe I didn't know this place existed. I must have walked past it a hundred times on my way home from class. But I guess it was the wrong time of day, and maybe I'm the wrong woman.

One thing I know is that my tip jar is almost empty and Katrina's is stuffed with tens and twenties and even some fifties and I'm beginning to think that Jimmy was full of it when he said I would earn three hundred dollars a night.

"We don't share tips," Katrina says, catching me eyeing her jar. She's been nice to me since Jimmy introduced us half an hour before the club opened, but she's also keeping her distance. I kind of appreciate it, to be honest.

"I know, you told me." I flash her a smile. I'm not going to steal her tips.

"Good."

I take a deep breath, because either I ask this question or I probably won't come back tomorrow. "How did you earn so many tips?"

Katrina stops what she's doing and looks at me. A band has set up on the stage and they're playing that country song about a Traveling Soldier and I kind of like it and kind of hate it because it reminds me of my time in the Army.

"If you want to make tips you need to serve in the fight room," she tells me. "Nobody's gonna tip like that in here."

Oh! I'd asked not to serve in there. I really don't like fighting. Not for its own sake. Another hangover from my previous career, I guess.

I pull my lip between my teeth because I'm torn. The line between money and morals is at its thinnest when you're at your most desperate.

"Why don't you take these in?" Katrina says, sliding a tray full of whiskeys to me. "Try it. They don't bite. They're mostly too busy watching the boxing to even notice you."

"I hope they notice me enough to tip," I say wryly.

For the first time all night she smiles at me. She's very pretty, with long blonde hair and eyes that beg for that slanty eyeliner. I'm kind of impressed by how steady her hand has to be to draw such perfect lines on her skin.

"They'll notice you enough for that, honey."

Shaking my hair over my shoulders, I take the tray, glancing down at the check to see it's for table twenty-four. I carry the full tray across the main room, dodging the few people dancing on the floor, then use my shoulder to nudge open the left side of the double doors, stepping in as it gives.

It's like stepping into a different world. The atmosphere feels thicker, on edge. It's like the bar out there doesn't exist.

And Katrina's right, nobody pays me any attention as I weave through the tables all angled toward the boxing ring. They're mostly full of men, some in suits, others dressed more casually, and all of them are facing the ring as two men beat the hell out of each other inside the ropes.

I try not to look, instead I lay the tray on table twenty-four, and pass out the whiskeys. When I slide the check on the table a tall man dressed in a black suit and black shirt takes it, then passes me a hundred and fifty dollars.

Sixty more than the cost of the drinks.

"I'll get you some change," I mutter, even though my inner-Katrina is screaming at me.

"No need, sweetheart," he murmurs. "Keep it."

Okay then. I exhale a thick breath and take the empty tray, muttering something about wishing them a good evening, but they're not paying attention to me at all. They're watching the game, laying money down on the table.

Are they gambling on the result? I'm not sure I want to know.

I'm kind of relieved when I reach the doors back into the bar. I've been in barracks and guard rooms and once in a strip club, and not one of them felt as full of testosterone as this place.

Before I can walk out there's an enormous cheer, and I look to see one boxer slumped against the ropes, the other in the middle of the ring, the referee holding his arm up.

He doesn't look too beaten up. Neither of them do. And for the first time, with that tip in my hand, I wonder if I can actually make this work.

If I'm here until graduation, I could build up a good nest egg. I'm still thinking about it as I walk back to the bar and pass the money to Katrina.

"Nice," she says, putting it in the register then pulling sixty back out and putting it in my jar. "How was it?"

"Okay. There was a knockout."

"Was it Dickie?"

I blink. "I don't know."

"Short guy. Looks like Joe Pesci," she says.

"Yeah, I think it was," I nod. "I'm not sure."

She grins. "If you stay around you'll get to know them all." She passes me another tray. This one has a bottle of Dom Perignon and some glasses on it.

"Ready for another?" she asks.

"Don't you want to do it?" I blink, because she's being way too nice. And I bet she wants these tips as much as I do.

Katrina shrugs. "We can share tips if you like."

Of course we can.

"Starting now," she says, when she catches me eyeing her jar again.

And because she's been here a while and I need her help – and because the tips are already better than I'd hoped for – I agree. And for the next hour we take turns serving the fight room, sliding bill after bill into our jars.

I find out she's a single mom to two boys, that her ex is a junkie who only comes around when he wants to steal something. That she lives with her mom who babysits every night so she can work here to make enough money to keep the four of them with a roof over her head.

I warm to her. Especially when she shows me the trick to changing the vodka optic without spilling it everywhere, and points out the customers I should avoid because their hands always go where they shouldn't.

By the time midnight comes around, I'm carrying trays across the bar with ease, sliding them onto the tables, and handing the drinks out so smoothly that I usually get an appreciative nod along with the tip.

I'm mentally calculating how much I'll be taking home tonight when the emcee breaks through my thoughts.

"Ladies and Gentlemen, for our last fight of the evening, we have a couple of old favorites," he says, his voice thick like he's been chain smoking. "Please put your hands together and give a warm welcome to The Medic and The Mechanic..."

Loud voices erupt as two men climb into the ring. The first one has a shiny robe on, his name emblazoned on the back. He shrugs it off and gives it to a woman standing next to the ring, then leans down to give her a passionate kiss.

He's the mechanic. I know because it said it on the back of his robe.

But it's not him I'm looking at anymore. It's the tall, muscled man in the center of the ring, wearing a pair of low slung shorts that cling to his defined hips. My eyes slowly rise up his body, taking in the perfectly chiseled stomach muscles and the flat thickness of his chest, along with the scruff on his chin that frames his perfectly straight lips.

There's a tattoo on his arm, but I can't quite tell what it's of. And to be honest, I don't even care. Because all I really want to look at is his eyes. They're strikingly blue. Almost unreal. I'd say he was wearing contacts but even I know that would be a foolish thing to do in a fight.

The other thing about those eyes? I recognize them from a photograph. And they're looking right at me.

Warmth suffuses my body.

For a moment there's nothing else. Just him and me standing there, the two of us staring at each other.

And then the noise around us rushes in. The Mechanic pulls his headgear on, and piercing blue eyes does the same.

No, not piercing blue eyes. Holden Salinger. My client. My boss. I have no idea what to call him. All I know is that I can't watch him fight but I also can't look away.

"He's hot, huh?" Katrina whispers in my ear. I turn my head to see her smiling.

"I guess."

"Word from the wise, he's definitely one to avoid," she tells me.

"Why? Is he a groper?"

She shakes her head. "Worse. He's a commitment-phobe. Avoid him at all costs."

They're pulling on their gloves now, and the noise of the crowd is reaching a crescendo. Katrina has to lean closer to whisper in my ear.

"You know why they call him The Medic?" she asks.

I turn to look at her. "Because he is one?"

She blinks. "How did you know? When I found out I thought it was wild. His job is supposed to be saving peoples' lives. Then he comes here and beats the shit out of them. And he always wins."

I swallow hard, because I know way more about Dr. Salinger than she does. But I'm not supposed to. Sure, a few hours earlier I was thinking about walking out of this job after tonight and not coming back, but now that my tip jar is stuffed full I'm reevaluating.

And I'm thinking that if this guy finds out who I am it could all be in danger.

"It was a lucky guess," I say, then I turn and head for the double doors, because I'm here for one thing. Make enough money to make our lives easier. Mine, Annie's, and Evan's.

Those two are the only ones that matter. And I need to remember that.

There's a thud and a cheer and I can't even turn around to see who landed on the floor and who is still standing.

It's none of my business.

But somewhere deep in my heart I know exactly who's won. Mostly because I can feel the warmth of his blue-eyed stare on my back as I walk out of the fight room.

———

"Okay, new girl, you can go home," Katrina tells me right after last call. "I'll finish up here."

The band has finished and there's a slow song playing from the jukebox. The bar is half-empty, two couples sway drunkenly on the dance floor, clinging to each other like one of them could fall at any moment.

"How long will I be the new girl?" I ask Katrina, kind of amused. She's still got a little frost to her, but she's definitely warmer than she was earlier. Probably because I worked like a demon tonight and ended up making more tips than she did. We split them, the way we agreed though.

"Until I think you're planning on staying," she says. "Most don't."

"I'll be staying," I tell her. At least for a while.

"We'll see."

I grab my jacket from the hook and pull it on, then stuff my half of the tips into my purse.

"You should get a cab home," Katrina tells me. "I'll call you one."

"I'll take the bus."

"With that money?" she asks, eyeing my stash. "You should take a cab, honey. That way you won't get robbed."

I shrug. "Okay, sure."

She gives me a half smile. "See you tomorrow?"

"You will." That's one thing I'm sure of.

"Good," she says, nodding. "You did good."

I say goodbye and wind my way through the chairs. I'm too busy thinking about what to do with the huge wad of cash in my pocket to notice a shadow passing over me. It's only when my body slams into six feet two inches' worth of steel-grade muscle that I realize I've walked straight into him.

The Medic. Holden. My boss that doesn't know it.

My chin catches the bone of his clavicle, making me bite into my tongue. "Ow!" I step back, wincing as I taste blood in my mouth.

Just my luck that I've been perfectly balanced all night until now. I haven't spilled a drop of whiskey or champagne despite all the hazards in this place. And now I've spilled my own blood.

His eyes sweep over me.

"You okay?" His voice is deep. Deeper than I expected. I can't quite tell whether it's laced with concern or amusement.

"I'm fine." I glance at his chest again. How does somebody punch that without breaking their knuckles? No wonder they all need to wear gloves.

Those pretty blue eyes of his catch mine. "Does it hurt anywhere?" he asks.

"No," I croak. "I don't think so." Apart from my pride. And my tongue. But I'm not telling him that. I rub my chin, because that took a bit of a beating, too.

Okay, it hurts. But I'm not going to admit it.

"Did you bite your tongue?" he asks. He definitely looks concerned now.

"No. Why?"

"Because you're sucking at it."

I immediately stop. "I might have caught it inadvertently."

He's so close and I'm so tired and a wave of dizziness washes over me. I might sway a little. Enough for him to suddenly reach out and steady my shoulders.

What kind of reflexes does this man have? And I'm really trying not to notice how good he smells. Like the rain had a baby with a forest and it grew up to be a strange doctor who likes to hit people.

When I focus on him his eyes are narrowed.

"What's your name?" he asks.

"Why?" I ask genuinely. Why would he want to know that?

His lips twitch. "I'm trying to find out if you're concussed."

Oh. I could see how you could get concussed against his chest. "I'm Blair."

"Blair, do you know what year it is?" he asks. His voice has a softness to it. Must be part of his bedside manner.

"Nineteen seventy-four. Nixon just resigned over Watergate. Somebody should make a movie about it with Redford and Hoffman."

He smiles and I have to swallow hard, because somehow an amused, boyish Dr. Salinger is way more attractive than the muscled hard ass fighting one.

"I think you're okay. Sarcastic, but fine."

"Thanks, Doc."

He lifts a brow. "How do you know I'm a doctor?"

Oh shit. "I saw you go into the ring." I didn't say his last name, did I? Please God tell me I didn't.

Luckily he doesn't look suspicious. "It's Holden," he says.

"Hi Holden."

He's still half smiling. "Hi Blair."

It's only when my cheeks ache that I realize I'm smiling at him, too. And that neither of us have said a word for way too long. "I need to go," I say. "But thank you."

He tips his head to the side, watching me. "You need a ride?"

My cheeks flush again, because I'm imagining a whole different ride to the one he's offering. What the hell is wrong with me? "No thank you. I've got a ride."

He nods. "Well take it easy, Blair."

"I will."

And my stupid heart pounds rapidly against my chest as I walk toward the doorway. When I get to the door I turn to look at him again. He's at the bar, talking to Jimmy. I hadn't noticed earlier, but he's wearing a pair of jeans and a gray t-shirt, his hair slightly damp like he's taken a shower.

Before he can catch me staring – *again* – I walk resolutely through the front door and into the cool night, heading straight to the bus stop despite my promise to Katrina.

When it arrives I take a seat at the back and lean my head against the cool glass of the window, and all I can think about are blue eyes and powerful hands.

Damn, I'm in trouble.

CHAPTER
FOUR

BLAIR

"There you go," I say early on Sunday morning, passing my sister two hundred dollars. It's mostly made up of twenties and a singular fifty. She stares at the bills then at me.

"What's this for?" Her brows pinch together and she looks weirdly concerned. "Where did you get this money, Blair?"

"Some tips from the last two nights." The rest will go into our escape fund.

"You got two hundred dollars in tips?" Her voice lifts an octave. "What the hell kind of bar is it?" Evan runs in and her face immediately turns blank. "Did you brush your teeth, honey?" she asks him.

"Oops." He runs out again. The kid hasn't learned to walk when he can run. I kind of miss having that exuberance. Once upon a time I couldn't wait for the next thing to happen.

Nowadays I kind of dread it.

As soon as she hears the faucet running Annie leans in. "Seriously, why did you get this much in tips? You're not stripping, are you?"

I look down at my body then back up at her with a withering look. She gives me one just as good back.

"You've got a hot body, so shut up," she says. "People would definitely pay to look at it."

"For medical purposes," I joke and she rolls her eyes. She folds her arms across her chest and a rush of love for her flows through me. For so long it's been just three of us. First Annie, Mom, and me. And now the two of us and Evan.

His dad left Annie before Evan was even born. He never sends any money but we're used to that. Our own dad did the same after he left our mom.

"Okay, it's not what you think," I tell her. "It's a bar. With a fight club."

"A what?" She blinks.

"They box in the back room. People pay to watch. I'm pretty sure there's some illegal gambling going on too but that's it. Rich guys come in and they tip well."

"And they don't ask to look at your chest?" she asks, looking puzzled.

I laugh. "No. Seriously they're all about the fighting." I find it hard to believe myself. All that testosterone was fogging up the room, but they were all more intent on the boxing ring than the people serving them.

"So what am I supposed to do with this?" Annie asks, looking down at the pile of bills.

"Put it toward Evan's next doctor visit. Or his prescriptions. And use the rest for his swimming lessons."

The swimming pool is where they're heading this morning. Evan loves the water and the doctor says as long as the chlorine doesn't trigger his asthma it should be good for him. Annie found a local gym that has a saltwater pool and offers lessons, but it's much more expensive than the local YMCA.

She shakes her head. "Those things aren't your problem. You should spend the money on yourself."

She's as stubborn as I am sometimes. We both get that

from our mom. She never accepted help, never chased after our dad when he left. The same way Annie never mentions Evan's dad.

We don't enjoy taking help. Not even from each other.

"I made over two hundred," I tell her. "I'm putting the rest into our escape fund."

She looks up again. "Blair..."

"What?"

"Don't do anything stupid, okay? We've got this. Evan's fine, we both have good jobs. Don't risk what we've got."

"Have you ever known me to take any risks?" I ask her.

Her eyes lift to mine. She has the most perfect lashes. Thick and glossy, just like Evan's. "You joined the Army."

"To get the benefits. And to pay for my education." It was the most calculated decision I've ever made. And if I'm honest, I hated most of my time there. But I pushed through to get here. "It's part of the plan," I remind her. "And this money's going to help. We can get out of here in a few more months if we're lucky."

Annie presses her lips together. "I don't know..."

My sister has never left New York City, apart from a couple of school trips and a vacation in the Adirondacks one year when Mom borrowed a tent from a friend. And I know she's scared. She likes the idea of Evan having fresh air but hates the idea of the unknown.

I'm not going to force her to leave. If she wants to stay here, I'll find a job in the city once I graduate. But man, I hope for Evan's sake that we do.

"It'd be nice to have a backyard though," she whispers.

"Yeah. Real nice," I say. "We could get Evan a swing set."

"And you won't have to work three different jobs," Annie says.

For some reason that makes me think of piercing blue eyes and warm gentle hands. The kind that can knock a man out cold but then take care of people at the same time.

"It's going to be so good," I tell her. But I'm still feeling weird. Like somebody's walked over my grave.

"When are you working there again?" she asks.

"Wednesday night." It's weird how my stomach tightens at the thought.

He probably won't be there. Katrina told me weeknights are quiet. Sometimes they don't even have fights. And the tips are bad, too, but since I'm also on the schedule for Friday and Saturday I don't mind that.

"Just don't do anything I wouldn't," she says. Evan runs back in before the words have left her mouth and she turns to him and starts talking about their plans for the day.

"I won't," I promise, but I keep my fingers behind my back. She must know I'd do anything for the two of them.

———

HOLDEN

It's ten o'clock by the time I finally finish working on Wednesday night. Even Mabel's light is out – although she's been known to sneak a flashlight under her sheets to read, according to Rose who knows everything that goes on in these rooms. I stop at the nurses' station to talk with them before I leave, making sure they know what to monitor overnight, then head out into the night, where it's started to rain.

Not a torrent. Just that soft, in-the-air kind of drizzle that gets you wet even though it's not bad enough to put on a jacket or use an umbrella.

Sliding into my car, I check my phone. There are some missed calls from my brothers, but that's not unusual. It's too late to call them back now. Two of them have kids and the rest are probably either in bed or out somewhere.

And I should be in bed, too. So I start up the engine and reverse out of my space, fully intending to turn left at the exit to the parking lot.

Instead, ten minutes later, I'm pulling up outside The Black and White Club.

I'll go in for one drink and leave. Just to see who's there tonight.

It's stupid, but I've been thinking about the new girl since the weekend. Wondering why she feels so familiar. I tell myself that once I find out I'll lose interest. It's just this nagging gut-like feeling that I can't quite shake off.

The bar is quiet when I walk inside. The doors to the boxing room are closed, and no light is spilling out through the gap between them and the floor. Which is kind of a relief. Definitely one drink and then I'll go home.

I walk over to the bar and lean on it, waiting for the new girl to turn around.

But she doesn't. I take a minute to realize she's writing something in a book. The big kind that I remember using when I was in school, back when dinosaurs walked the earth.

I clear my throat and she jumps then turns around, her eyes wide. They get even wider when she sees me standing right in front of her.

"What are you writing?" I ask.

"What?" She grabs the book and the pen and tries to hide them behind her. I try not to smirk but from her expression I've failed.

And now I feel like a jerk. "You all recovered from the other night?" I ask, because for some reason I want to have a conversation with this woman.

"The other night?" she repeats, frowning.

"When you tripped."

"Oh." A look of relief washes over her, making me wonder what the hell else happened the other night. "Yeah, I'm fine. Thanks for helping me."

"No big deal."

She tries to slide her book beneath the counter without me noticing but I get a look at the front. Blair Walsh is written across it, and below that is a course name.

"You a student?" I ask.

She pulls her lip between her teeth and nods. Fuck, she's pretty. I'm not sure if it's the hair or the way she looks at me with those wide doe-like eyes.

For a second I imagine wrapping that hair around my hand and jerking her head back.

"I'm studying for a masters in library science," she says. "Final year."

She's gonna be a librarian. Suddenly I'm imagining her wearing glasses. And naked.

Jesus, I really need to get a life.

"Impressive," I say.

"Shut up." She rolls her eyes but she still looks pleased.

I smile. "Why shut up?"

"Because you're a doctor. *That's* impressive." The door to the bar opens and a couple stumble in, the guy trying to put down an umbrella and failing miserably. In the end he props it by the table.

"So, what can I get you?" Blair asks me.

"Just a soda water."

"Coming right up." She turns to grab a glass and I get a good look at her. She's wearing a denim skirt and a black t-shirt with *Book Nerd* written in silver across the chest.

"Nice T-shirt," I tell her.

"My sister bought it for me." She gives me a half smile as she passes me my drink. I put ten on the counter and shake my head when she tries to give me change.

"My brothers bought me a t-shirt with *I'm A Doctor and I'm Never Wrong* on it," I tell her.

"And are you?"

"A doctor? Yes?"

She smiles and it lights up her face. "I meant never wrong."

Her eyes catch mine and I'm hit with that weird feeling again. "Do I know you?" I ask.

Blair blinks. Then shakes her head.

"Then I'm sometimes wrong. Because I feel like we've met before. Maybe at the hospital?"

"I don't think so." She runs the tip of her tongue along her bottom lip. "You said you have brothers?"

"Five of them." I lift a brow. "Mostly assholes."

She grins. "Does it run in the family?"

"Probably." I take a sip of my soda then look at her again. Okay, so I don't know her. But I want to.

"Can I ask you something? About books?"

She looks surprised. "Okay."

"One of my patients, a kid, she's reading *Wuthering Heights*. Have you read it?"

Blair nods. "Sure. A few times."

"Can you tell me something about it? Something that will surprise her. She thinks I can't read and I want to call her bluff."

Blair tipped her head to the side. "What kind of doctor are you again?"

"I didn't tell you." I respond, but I kind of like her interest. "I'm a pediatric oncologist."

"Cancer."

I nod.

Her lips part and she exhales softly. And I know that look. Somewhere along the line she's been part of my world. I don't know how but I know it.

I wait for her to ask the usual questions. How do I get through each day? How hard is it to lose a patient? Doesn't it drive me up the wall?

But instead her eyes catch mine. "There's a scene in *Wuthering Heights*," she pauses, her brows pinching. "Chapter nine, I think. Where Catherine, she's the heroine, talks to her maid, Nelly, about Heathcliff. She's just got engaged to another man and says it's for the best because even though she and Heathcliff are like twin souls, he's below her."

There's a passion to her words that I haven't seen in anyone before. "Okay."

Her gaze flickers up. "And they don't realize, but Heathcliff is listening. And he leaves before she confesses she loves him. She tries to find him but gets sick and he disappears for three years."

I say nothing. She looks almost enraptured.

"And this chapter, to me, it was the most important one. It felt like the end of innocence. Of childhood. The beginning of the end, really. It was beautiful and sad and I don't know…"

"Okay, I'm back. You can take your break now." Katrina walks in, her long blonde hair tied into a braid. "Oh, hey Holden," she says to me.

From the corner of my eye I see Blair slide her book into her bag. Her cheeks are pink again, the way they were when she ran into me the other night.

She puts the strap over her shoulder then looks at me once more. She's going to head to the staff room for her break. I've been in there a few times. There are old rusty lockers, a central table, and a mini kitchenette with a kettle and a coffee machine that's seen better days.

Flashing me the smallest of smiles she turns away.

"Thanks for the lesson," I tell her.

"Anytime."

"What lesson?" Katrina asks, once Blair has walked through to the back.

"Nothing important." I have no idea if Katrina knows Blair studies when she's working. Or rather that she was doing it when she was supposed to be working.

"Okay." Katrina shrugs. "What are you doing here on a Wednesday night?"

"Just stopped by for a quick drink." I tap my half-empty soda. "I'm going to head home now."

She glances at her watch. "We close in an hour. If you wait, I can come with you."

It's not the first time she's made an offer. It probably won't be the last. But she doesn't seem to mind at all when I shake my head and finish off the last of my soda and head for the door.

I climb back into my car, hearing the purr of the engine as I start it up, and then I frown because I feel the fizz in my veins again.

I'm interested in her. And a woman like Blair could be a dangerous addiction if I let her.

Only problem is, I already have too many of those.

CHAPTER
FIVE

BLAIR

As soon as I hear the key in the dead bolt the next week I know the gig is up. I've been cleaning Dr. Salinger's house for an hour. And to be honest, I've been feeling guilty, because it almost feels like I'm violating his privacy now that I've met him in real life.

So I've been scrubbing extra hard. Seriously, the man won't know what's hit him when he walks in. Every surface that can shine does, the place smells like a mixture between a pine forest and a floral glade.

But now it's for nothing. Because this is it. Of course now would be the first time he comes home when I'm here.

I'm in the kitchen, my gloves on, a soft cloth in one hand, and I look at the gleaming oven door, seeing my reflection staring back at me. She looks almost as scared as I am.

"Oh, hi," he says, sounding confused.

I swallow and slowly turn around, explanations running through my head.

But instead of Dr. Salinger standing in the door way,

there's another man. Just as tall, not quite as muscled – but with the same dark hair and blue eyes.

He looks like one of the golden boys in the photograph in the living room. A brother. Younger than Holden, I think. He gives me an easy smile.

"Sorry, I didn't realize anybody would be here."

I open my mouth to say something then close it again.

"I'm Linc Salinger. Holden's brother. You must be the poor woman who has to clean up after his dirty ass."

He walks forward, holding his hand out like we're about to go into a business meeting. And I'm so surprised I hold my own – yellow rubber gloved – hand out. And then I shake my head and pull it off, letting his fingers wrap around my own.

"Blair," I say. "The person who cleans up after your brother's dirty ass."

He smirks and damn if it isn't exactly the same as Holden's. "I hope he pays you well."

Oh, you wouldn't believe.

"Of course." I run my tongue along my bottom lip because not once in the two years I've worked here has anybody walked in. It's a good thing I felt guilty and didn't do any studying today. That would have been hard to explain. "Um, can I get you a drink?"

His face softens. "I'd kill for a coffee if you have time."

"Sure." I grab a cup from the cupboard that's as clean on the inside as it is on the outside and take it over to the shiny silver machine that has a place of pride on his counter.

And stare at it.

"Um, I just need to Google how to work it."

The brother starts laughing. "It's okay, I can do it." He puts the cup beneath the spout then grabs a little capsule from the caddy next to it. "You want one?"

"I'm fine, but thank you."

"How often do you clean here?" he asks, making conversation as he also makes his coffee. It's funny because he seems so much more relaxed than Dr. Salinger. I look at his knuckles and wonder if he's a fighter, too.

"I clean once a week," I tell him.

"Seriously?"

"Yeah." I nod. "That's what he pays for."

Linc turns around and looks at me carefully. He's wearing a pair of expensive and strategically ripped jeans and a black t-shirt that perfectly molds to his body. "Go figure," he says. "Holden's the most anal guy I know. Like a neat freak. You should have seen him when we were kids. If I moved something slightly to the left he'd scream at me."

"Dr. Salinger screams?"

His lips twitch. "Do you always call him Dr. Salinger? That sounds so weird. Like..." He wrinkles his brow. "Like Daphne in *Frasier*. Yeah, that's it. She calls Frasier Dr. Crane."

"I don't exactly have the British accent," I point out.

"Yeah, but it sounds just as weird. Do you call him that to his face..." His eyes widen. "Wait, please tell me he doesn't insist on you calling him that."

I take a deep breath. Does this guy have an off button? I get the feeling he could make talking an Olympic sport. "Um, I've never actually met him."

"What?" He does a double take. "Seriously? You like clean all his crap up and you've never actually seen the guy?"

"I thought we established he doesn't have a lot of crap to clean up."

"Yeah, true." He runs his thumb along his jaw, still looking at me. "So tell me, have you found his secret porn stash yet?"

My cheeks pink up. "No."

"Damn. I was so sure he'd have one. I guess that's the problem with the digital age. It's probably all on his phone."

My face is even hotter now. Just thinking about Dr. Salinger watching porn is... Oh God. Thankfully Linc's coffee seems to be ready. "I should get back to work," I say.

"Sure." He nods. "Actually, wait. Can I get your help with something?"

"I'm not looking for porn with you," I say.

He laughs and it lights up his face. "What about his sex dungeon?"

"I only clean that once a month," I tell him, deadpan.

"I like you, Blair." He grins at me. "But really I just need your opinion about something. Holden's lending me a dinner suit. Apparently, he has a few. If I try them on will you tell me which one you think is the best?"

So that's why he's here. I hadn't thought to ask. I was too taken aback to wonder why somebody like him was in his brother's apartment at this time of the morning.

"I don't have a lot of experience with dinner suits," I tell him.

"Even better. A fresh eye." He winks at me. "Stay here, I'll be out in a moment."

He rushes down the hallway and then I hear the click of the bedroom door, and I make myself busy, cleaning up after his coffee making. I'm washing out the little reservoir at the bottom of the machine when I hear Linc clearing his throat.

"How about this one?" he asks.

Linc walks into the room wearing a black jacket and dress pants along with a crisp white shirt. He looks devastatingly handsome. Like GQ worthy. "You look good," I say.

He tips his head to the side. "But do I look great?"

"You want me to give you all the superlatives?" I ask.

"The what?"

I hide a smile. "You want me to talk you up?"

"Yes please."

"You look amazing. Breathtakingly manly. Like some kind of dinner jacket god has just walked into Manhattan and taken control of the city. I can barely look at you because I'm blinded by your absolute charisma and charm."

He lifts a brow. "It's okay then?"

"The jacket is a little loose," I confess.

He looks down and pulls at the lapels. "Yeah, I thought that. Don't go anywhere, I'll try on the next one."

I'd ask how many dinner suits Holden Salinger has, but I already know that. Five. Each one perfectly hung, the cleaner's packaging still covering them. It could take some time if Linc tries them all on.

Luckily, he's back in a couple of minutes. His hair looks mussed but he's still smiling. "This one's better, right?"

I tip my head to the side. The jacket is one of those slim cut ones that makes a guy look like it's been designed exactly for him.

Really, it's been cut for Holden Salinger. I wonder where he wears it. To galas, maybe. Don't doctors go to a lot of those?

"It's the kind of dinner jacket that could set the world on fire," I tell him.

"Thanks, Blair. But I'm gonna need more." There's a teasing note to his voice.

I take a deep breath. "You look amazing, Linc. As soon as you walk into the room all the air gets sucked away. I can't look at anybody else but you. I'm dazzled, entranced. You're the God of dinner jackets for sure."

"Yeah." He nods, smiling. "I think I might be."

He tries on another two anyway. And with the last one he calls out my name from the bedroom, sounding almost panicked.

"What's up?" I ask, walking in.

"I pulled a button off," he whispers, as though we're being monitored. He's standing in another pair of tailored pants, open to reveal his black shorts. His t-shirt is still clinging to him like a lover. But his eyes are wide. He looks almost fearful as he holds out his palm, a black button at the center.

"Holden's going to kill me."

"It's just a button," I tell him. "No big deal."

"He hates me messing with his things. I borrowed his Game Boy once and kind of scratched the screen and he screamed at me for three days."

"I can sew it back on," I tell him.

Linc looks at me as though I'm some kind of angel sent to save him. "You can?"

"Yes. Give me a second, I just need to find a needle and thread." We search around for five minutes, but of course Dr. Salinger doesn't have a sewing kit.

"He's gonna whoop my ass good," Linc groans. "I should have told him I was coming this morning."

"Wait!" I say. "He doesn't know you're here?" He said he did. Didn't he? I can't remember. My heart almost stops.

Linc shakes his head.

"So I let you in and you're not supposed to be here?" That's one of the biggest no-nos in my job. Never let somebody in unless the owner has given strict permission. I've heard tales of thieves cleaning out entire houses. One cleaner even got tied up as they did it.

"Technically, I let myself in," Linc says. "But the rest.. yeah. Sorry."

I let out a lungful of air. "Just give me a minute." Dr. Salinger's bedroom looks like a bomb has hit it . There are clothes everywhere. The perfectly made bed has dents in it from where Linc has been throwing things on it. And there are tiny pieces of black cotton on the cream carpeted floor that must have come from Linc's socks.

"His spare medical kit," I say. "That should have a needle in it."

"Yes!" His face lights up. "Where does he keep it?"

"In the bathroom."

He runs in and starts rifling through the cupboards that line the bottom half of one wall, pushing things to the side and letting out grunts when he doesn't find exactly what he needs. And for a moment I find myself sympathizing with Dr.

Salinger. The man's a neat freak with a bull in a china shop for a brother. If this was my stuff, I'd kill him.

"Here it is."

I run into the bathroom and pull the box from him. If he messes up the first aid kit I'm not sure his life will be worth living. "Why don't you leave this to me," I say. "Get dressed and go drink your coffee." That he left on the counter without a coaster, and that I've already cleaned up once.

"You sure?"

"Positive."

I take two minutes to sew the button back on, though I'm not happy with the clear medical thread I'm using, so I remind myself to re-do it next week with some black silk thread that I have at home. And then I tidy up the bedroom – again – making sure everything is as perfect as Dr. Salinger likes it.

By the time I get back to the kitchen, Linc is putting his coffee mug in the dishwasher. He turns around and smiles at me.

"Everything okay?" he asks.

"He'll never know," I promise him. Especially if he doesn't wear a tux between this week and next.

"Thank you. I owe you one." He gives me a crinkle-eyed smile, and I marvel at the genetics of this family. One handsome brother is normal. Six? Dammit, where are my lucky genes?

In Evan.

Yeah, that's where they are.

When he leaves – thanking me again – I take his coffee cup out of the dishwasher, wash it, then clean the inside of the dishwasher for good measure.

When Dr. Salinger gets home, he won't know what's hit him. In a good way, I hope.

It's the least I can do.

HOLDEN

Mabel stares at me for a minute, her brows pinched like she's trying to work me out. Her lips are pursed and she's holding her battered copy of *Wuthering Heights* in her hand.

"What?" she finally says, still looking at me like I'm an alien that landed in Manhattan.

"I said it's my favorite part. The part where everything changes."

She looks down at her book and then up again. "So let me get this straight. You've read *Wuthering Heights*."

"Yep." I give her a dazzling smile. This is more fun than I thought it would be.

"And your favorite part is in chapter eight."

"Nine."

She lets out a grunt, and I know she was testing me. "Okay, nine. You like the part with Catherine and Bella."

"Nelly," I correct. "The maid."

This is one good thing about having a photographic memory. I only have to be told something once. The bad thing is that my head is full of useless crap. Now I get to add some over-emotional Yorkshireman to it.

"When did you read it?" she asks, looking exactly the same way our moms used to when all six of us would go quiet in the house as kids.

"The first time?"

"Yes." She doesn't take her eyes off me. When we get her into adulthood she's gonna be one scary woman.

"Last night."

"Bullshit."

"Mabel," I say. "Inside words, please."

She rolls her eyes. "Cow… Crap…"

My lips twitch.

"You haven't read it, have you?" she says.

I decide to stop teasing her. Not just because I know when she's reached her limit, but because it's taken me years to build this trust between us. I'm not about to jeopardize that for some book.

"No. I haven't."

"I knew it!" She shakes her head. "What did you use? Sparknotes? Google?"

"I asked a friend." I'm smiling at her. "She helped me out."

"You have a friend?" Mabel looks skeptical.

"Yes." Though I'm wondering if Blair is actually a friend. We've only met twice. Whatever.

"A girl?"

"A woman. Yes."

"Is she your girlfriend?" Mabel asks.

"No."

"Do you want her to be?"

I roll my eyes at her and she gives me a sassy head tip. "What?" she asks. "You can't come in here and try and get one over on me and not expect me to have questions."

"She's just somebody I know who's into books. She's studying to be a librarian."

Mabel's mouth drops open. "You know somebody into books?"

"I know two people." I look at her pointedly.

"And she's going to be a librarian? That's so cool." Mabel leans forward. "Does she live in the city?"

"Yeah. I think so."

"Can I meet her?"

Whoa. Alert, alert! I wrinkle my nose. "I'm not sure…"

"I'd love to be a librarian." Mabel's expression turns dreamy. "All those books. All those facts. The smell…" She sighs.

Fuck it, if it makes her happy then so what? "I'll ask her if she can come in some time," I tell her. "No promises, though. She's a busy woman. She studies and works at a bar in the evening."

"What's her name?"

"Blair."

"Blair what?"

I frown because I can't remember. So much for my photographic memory. "Um…"

"You don't know her last name?" Mabel asks, looking annoyed. "What kind of boyfriend are you?"

"I'm not her boyfriend," I say patiently. "Just a friend."

"Okay. Whatever. Just make sure you find it out before I meet her."

I look her in the eye and nod solemnly.

"And Dr. Salinger?"

"Yes?"

"Chapter nine is my favorite part, too."

CHAPTER SIX

BLAIR

The atmosphere in The Black and White Club is thick and electric the following Friday. It tastes like expectation and stress and we try our best to keep up with the orders but even Katrina is looking frazzled.

"Jimmy wants another round," a man in a dark suit says, having pushed through the people lining up at the counter. Katrina and I are trying to stick to table service, but it's mayhem and we're doing whatever we can.

"Can he wait?" Katrina asks.

The guy in the suit turns back around, not bothering to answer her. He has one of those black earpieces in. The kind that used to have curly black wires that led to the inside of the lapel of a security guy's suit, but nowadays they're all wireless.

"I'm gonna kill him," Katrina mutters. "I told him we didn't have enough staff for this."

I shoot her a sympathetic smile and start loading up the order. Four whiskeys – G. Scott Carter gold label, two

Manhattans, and a vodka tonic. Plus a bottle of sparkling water.

Jimmy's entertaining some big cheese from Vegas tonight. Plus a congressman from the district. According to Katrina, who growled it out when she stopped bitching for a second, Jimmy's looking to open a second club and he needs them on his side.

"Can you take this?" Katrina asks. "If I see him again I'm gonna strangle his scrawny neck."

"But you're his server." She's been taking drinks in to Jimmy and his pals all night. First to the fight room, then to Jimmy's private room where they're playing cards while they wait for the last fight of the night.

"I'll be his jailed server if I have to go in there again," she tells me. From the look on her face she isn't kidding. She has a withering expression that could make a grown man cry.

She's almost certainly pissed because neither Jimmy nor his guests have given a single tip all night. So although our jars are half-full, they don't reflect the usual income she expects on a Saturday night, or of the work we've been doing to earn the tips.

She's already serving somebody else by the time I think about protesting more, so I pick the tray up and head over to the fight room.

Jimmy's office is on the far side so I have to weave my way through the tables. There's nobody in the ring right now so most of the customers are talking amongst themselves. Some tables are empty where people have gone out for a smoke.

Somebody else – possibly Jimmy – put some music on, some slow jazz, and it somehow sounds sultry as I finally reach the door to the backrooms.

There's a corridor first. Bare brick walls, no frills. On the left are two metal doors – leading to two changing rooms where the fighters prepare. On the right is the door to

Jimmy's office. I somehow center the tray in one hand and rap my knuckles lightly on the other.

"Come in," he yells out.

Using my elbow, I push down the handle then use my ass to maneuver the door open. When I step inside there are five men sitting around Jimmy's table, cards in hand, cigars in mouths.

"Just here, sweetheart," Jimmy says, not looking up.

"Who's having the whiskey?" I ask.

A dark haired man with pocked skin nods. I think I recognize him as the congressman. I pass him a glass, then look around for the next whiskey drinker.

Once I've handed those out, I give Jimmy his Manhattan then lean across to hand the other to his brother, who I've met exactly once.

And then I feel a hand on my ass.

No. Just no. Nothing pays enough for that.

"Get your hand off me," I say, because I've had enough people touching me to last a lifetime.

Pock mark looks up at me, a drunk grin on his face. Then he squeezes again.

Oh no you don't.

My tray clatters to the floor as I reach behind me to grab his dirty hand and turn, twisting it over the asshole's head until he lets out a high-pitched squeal.

"What the fuck?" Jimmy finally looks up from his cards. Pock mark is screaming. His security guy jumps up from his seat in the corner and runs over but all I can hear is the blood rushing through my head.

"Do not touch my ass," I tell him, my breath tight. He's still yelping, but the guard grabs me and the high-pitched noise lessens. Jimmy is shouting, then suddenly I'm pinned against the wall, my hands behind me, a muscled body making sure I can't move.

I try to pull out of his hold, because I really don't want to be touched.

Then suddenly I hear a soft voice in my ear.

"Blair, it's me. Holden. Stop struggling."

But I don't, because I'm in fight or flight mode, and when it comes down to it, I'll fight. He loops his arms around my waist, still whispering. "He's a congressman. You'll lose. Now let me get you out of here."

He pulls me away from the wall. Jimmy's staring at me like I'm some kind of alien entity, pock mark is frowning, rubbing his arm, and the suave guy next to Jimmy is laughing.

"Did you see that?" he says, to nobody in particular. "You should put her in the ring. I'd put all my money on her."

Holden's grasp is unyielding as he turns me away, walking me out of Jimmy's office and into the hallway. I feel myself shaking as he leads me into his dressing room, his arm still wrapped around my waist. And then I'm sitting on a bench and he's crouched in front of me, urging me to breathe slowly, doing it with me, his gaze concerned as I get control of my breathing.

And finally mortification washes over me.

"Oh God." I put my hands in front of my face. Did I really put a congressman into an armlock?

"You okay?" Holden asks, prising my fingers down so he can get a look at me. I don't resist him.

"No." I'm annoyed and I'm embarrassed and I hate that he saw that.

I take a moment to focus but then I see what he's wearing. A pair of shorts and nothing else. Up close I can see every rise and fall of his chest muscles. The hard curve of his shoulders. The thickness of his biceps. And that tattoo again. Two snakes wrapped around a pole, wings at the top. Etched in black.

"Where'd you learn to do that?" he asks me.

"The Army." I don't tell him any more than that. I don't

want to. But I didn't just learn to protect myself for the fun of it. From the first month there, I'd learned that a few men in the Army saw women as fair game.

It was ironic that I had to learn to protect myself from my own side. And traumatic, too. I'd learned to protect myself but tonight the congressman took me by surprise. He shocked me.

And I don't like that at all. I don't like that I'm having to think about any of my past.

"Impressive."

"You didn't see it," I say, because I'm pretty sure he wasn't in the room when I got felt up.

"No, but I heard the screaming. Takes a lot to make a grown man squeal like that."

"I almost broke his arm," I say, groaning at the realization. "I almost broke the congressman's arm."

Holden looks like he's trying not to laugh. But it's no joke. "I'm gonna lose my job."

"No you're not. Jimmy's a fair guy."

"He didn't stop me from being felt up," I point out.

Holden's eyes flicker. "Yeah, I know." His voice is gruff. "But he'll make sure it doesn't happen again. Believe me."

For some reason I do. And now that I can breathe again I'm feeling calmer. A little stupid, truth be told. "Aren't you supposed to be fighting?" I ask him.

"I got twenty minutes. It's good." His eyes catch mine and I feel a weird pull in my stomach. Like somebody has lassoed a rope around it.

"I don't think dragging a violent woman out of an office is the best pre-fight preparation," I say.

He's full on smiling now. "Librarians aren't violent."

"I'm not a librarian *yet*," I say, not able to pull my gaze from his.

"Yeah, and you're not violent either. A guy touched you, so you made sure he doesn't do it again. Which is good, because if I'd been in there he probably wouldn't have an arm left."

He sounds serious. And it's both concerning and strangely erotic. That he'd pull a guys' arm off for touching a woman.

"I don't like violence," I whisper.

"Then why were you in the Army?"

It's a good question. With a simple answer. "So I could study without getting into debt." That's the short story. There's a longer one but I don't feel like sharing it with him right now.

He nods, looking like he understands. "A couple of doctors I worked with did the same thing."

And that sparks up my own question. The one I've been thinking about since I found out what he does here. "Why do you fight when you're a doctor?" I ask him. "Aren't you supposed to preserve life, not hurt it?"

As soon as the words come out of my mouth I regret them. I look down at my hands, wanting to slap myself with them. When I finally look up at him again, there's a strange expression on his face.

"It doesn't matter," I say. "Forget I said anything."

"It's a fair question. I asked you one, you get to ask me one."

My breath catches in my throat. He's so close, still in front of me, his huge hands on either side of my thighs, holding the bench lightly. I can smell him – pine and something else. Testosterone maybe. It makes my heart pound too fast against my chest.

"I fight so that I can go back to work the next day without wanting to hit something I shouldn't," he says slowly, as much to himself as to me. "I fight because it's the only way I can deal with my emotions, which I know isn't a good thing. But it's a thing."

"Okay." I nod.

"This is where you tell me I should go running instead,"

he says, looking at me with that half smile. Then he lifts his hand up from the bench and runs his thumb along my cheekbone, wiping the final tear that escaped before I calmed down.

"You can do what you like," I say, honestly. "It's not my business."

There's a knock at the door and Holden calls out for them to come in. A second later Jimmy walks in, running his hand over his scant, brushed back hair.

"You okay?" he asks me.

I nod. "I'm sorry. I shouldn't have…"

He holds his hand up, palm in front. "Yes you should. He's gone. Not coming back."

"You want me to leave, too?" I ask him.

Jimmy's brow pinches. "Why would I want that? I just came to see how you are." Holden stands and looks at him, and for some reason Jimmy's cheeks pink up. "Though, ah, if you want to go home you can. You'll be paid for the night, of course."

I try to picture Katrina's face if I left. And if I'm being honest, I'm feeling fine now. The panic attack came out of nowhere, and it's gone into nowhere, too. Now that the handsy guy is gone I feel okay.

"I'll get back to work," I say.

Jimmy catches my eye. He looks almost… impressed. "What Craig said… I don't suppose you fight, do you?"

"No." I shake my head. "Definitely not."

"Shame." He turns to leave, then glances back over his shoulder. "Anybody touches you again, you tell me, okay?"

I nod. "I will."

"Good."

———

HOLDEN

. . .

I'm fighting a new guy tonight. We're toe to toe and he's looking at me like I'm a piece of shit and it's riling me. Everything is tonight.

It was the screaming that had pulled me into Jimmy's office. At first I thought it was a woman, it was so high pitched. But then I'd seen the congressman and the goon with the security earpiece who was heading straight for her and I'd acted without thinking.

Carried her across the room and pushed her against the wall, putting my body between her and the assholes, because otherwise I had no idea what they were going to do to her.

And if I'm honest, I'm mostly riled because she's a strong woman who can hold her own but people like the congressman try shit with her. And she has to deal with it because she was born with two X chromosomes and somehow that makes her easy game.

The bell rings and I push every thought out of my head. A fist flies my way and I feint to the left, dodging the blows as the other guy dances around me. I dance back then get a couple of blows to his ribs. Enough to put him off his rhythm for a minute.

Blood pumps through my veins. It's not about me and him, it's just about me. Feeling the rush, moving my feet, landing a punch where I know it's gonna hurt the most.

He moves back and I try not to smile because I know he's on the retreat. He narrows his eyes, lunges, and I dance to the left, turning to watch him run head first into the ropes before volleying back.

That's when I see Blair. Standing with an empty tray, watching me. And that momentary lapse is all it takes. There's a fist to my stomach. Hard. Winding. Her eyes widen as I feel myself reel backward.

The back of my head hits the ring and for a second I'm

frozen. I turn my head and her eyes are still on me. She's frowning, and I realize that I've bit my lip, because I can taste the blood.

Then I wink at her and she frowns deeper.

Before any count can begin, I'm up. Wiping my mouth with the back of my glove. I want this over now. I'm bored. It needs to be done. There's a roar in my ears – the sound of my pulse mixed with the cheers for my recovery – and I launch myself at him, landing a volley of blows that sends him to his knees.

He doesn't get up. The referee counts him out and then the noise is deafening as he grabs my hand and holds it up. I look for Blair but she's gone, and for some reason I'm disappointed. I climb over the ropes, ignoring the people who surround me and walk back to the changing room.

I want to get out of here. I want to go home. I want to sleep for a hundred years. But first I need to find Blair.

CHAPTER
SEVEN

BLAIR

"He wants you to *what*?" Annie asks me.

"Go to the hospital and talk to one of his patients," I tell her again, though less patiently because she obviously heard me the first time. "She's into books and he thinks it would be good for her to have another bookworm to talk to."

"To an oncology ward."

"A pediatric oncology ward," I correct her. "With kids."

"So what did you say?"

It's Tuesday morning and we're running late *again*. I'm trying to finish my reading for this afternoon's tutorial and she's trying to eat a bagel, make Evan's lunch, and fill out a form online for Evan's prescription.

"I said yes." And if I'm honest I don't even know why I did. Maybe because he helped me out and I have a thing for paying people back. Plus, when he cornered me after the fight he'd taken a shower and had that Holden Salinger good smell thing going on.

It wasn't a fair fight. I lost.

"Seriously?" Annie looks up from her phone, her mouth full of bagel. "But you're so busy. Can you really fit this in?"

"It's just a visit." I shrug. "I'm not doing brain surgery."

"I don't get it is all," she says, shaking her head. "You hate connecting with people. And yet this guy is everywhere. You work for him, you work in the same place he frequents. Now you're going to his workplace."

She's not saying anything I haven't thought about all weekend since I agreed to meet Mabel, his patient. If I'm being honest, I can't work it out either. I should avoid him. But I can't.

But I don't have time to think about that right now.

———

It's my turn to take Evan to school today, so we head left and Annie heads right after she's given him a hug and a kiss. He's in a fairly good mood, talking to me about dinosaurs and how scientists built their bodies wrong when they first discovered them, and how he wants a Lego dinosaur for Christmas because his friend Olly has one.

"Not a little kid one, a *Jurassic Park* one," he says. Then he blinks. "Can I watch *Jurassic Park*?"

"Ask your mom," I say, which really means no, because the nightmares this kid would get from that are too horrific to imagine.

The usual group of parents are standing around when we reach the school gates. I nod at them – Annie knows them all better than I do – and go to leave but then one of them calls my name.

"Blair, isn't it?"

"Uh, yeah." I ruffle Evan's hair and remind him to see the teacher if his breathing gets tight, then turn to look at the woman next to me.

"I'm Susan. One of the class moms. I was wondering if I could ask you for a favor." She smiles widely at me.

Maybe Annie's right. I'm losing my touch. It's so rarely that people ask me for anything. It's one of the reasons she prefers me to do the school run. She has this pretty, open personality that means she always gets ganged into volunteering for bake sales and fundraising.

"Um, okay?" As in I'm not sure. Hit me with it and I'll decide.

"Mrs. Springer, the kindergarten teacher, has asked me to gather some names for career day. I was wondering if you'd be able to take part."

I tip my head and look at her. "You probably want to talk to Annie. She's the one with a career." I try to picture myself doing a cleaning demonstration to a classroom of kids. Nah. Not going to happen.

"Actually, it is you I want. You were in the Army, weren't you?" Susan asks.

I have no idea how she knows that. "I was, but it was a long time ago."

"Perfect." She claps her hands together. "I want to put a big emphasis on women doing non traditional jobs." She gives a little chuckle. "So don't talk about being a librarian, okay?"

I mutter something and shuffle off, annoyed as I head back home to grab my cleaning supplies. Annoyingly, I don't have any clean City Slickers polo shirts – damn our intermittently PMS ridden washer – so I put a plain white one on and hope to hell that Georgie doesn't pop in on me unannounced.

I'm still feeling grumpy when I get to the tall brownstone building that contains Dr. Salinger's apartment. So grumpy, in fact that, I don't see him walking out of the door until I bump into him, the air escaping from my lips with an oof.

Shit.

More dirty words rush through my head as his eyes blink with recognition.

"Blair?" he says, looking bemused.

In eighth grade I auditioned for a part in our school play. *Speed the Plow*. The drama teacher pulled me aside and suggested I paint the set.

But my audition was master acting compared to how I'm trying to rearrange my expression right now.

"Oh, hi! What are you doing here?" I say. I can't keep my voice even. It's lifting up and down like a Wurlitzer.

He's wearing a suit. *A suit!* It's dark blue and fits him perfectly. Beneath the unbuttoned jacket he has on a crisp white shirt, unfastened at the collar, no tie. And I think I'm about to melt into a pile of goo.

Seriously.

He glances behind him at the door he's just come out of and then at me again. "I live here."

I've seen this man in jeans, in shorts, and half naked. But this suit… it's doing stupid things to my insides. They need to stop.

"Sorry?" I say, because I only half heard him.

"I live in this building." He clears his throat. "What are you doing here?"

My backpack is pulling at my shoulder like a bitch. I want to take it off but then it'll thud onto the ground and he'll wonder what the hell is in there.

Cleaning supplies. Cloths. Brushes. Everything pretty much.

"Oh, I have a study session," I say, not quite meeting his pretty blue eyes.

"In here?"

I try to think quickly. And fail miserably. If I say yes, he'll ask who. And what apartment number. If I say no then why the hell am I about to walk into this apartment building?

As though the *God of Cleaners who Really Need to Keep Their*

Jobs is listening, his cellphone starts to buzz in his pocket. He's still looking at me, his lips slightly parted, as he pulls it from his pocket.

"Yeah?" he says, clearing his throat. "Okay. Ten minutes. Tell them to hold off until I get there." He disconnects and gives me the softest of smiles.

Seriously, I could wrap myself in it.

"Gotta go. You still okay to come in to see Mabel this week?"

I nod. "Yep. I'll be there Thursday afternoon." And I'll do the best damn job I can to make his patient happy because seriously, the guilt is getting to be too much.

"Great. Thanks, Blair."

"No problem, Dr. Salinger."

He runs his hand through his hair. "Can you do me a favor?"

"Sure." I'm pretty sure I owe him a few.

"Call me Holden?"

I swallow and nod.

"Thanks. See you on Thursday, Blair."

Yeah, he will. Hopefully by then my heart rate will be out of the danger zone.

HOLDEN

My head is pounding. Like some tiny boxer has got in there and beat the hell out of my cranium. I can't remember the last time I had something to eat, but my stomach feels like I'm about to be sick. I watch as our palliative care specialist takes over the meeting with the parents of an eight-year-old girl who has come to the end of the road with treatment.

We've tried everything. Some things twice. And now I want to punch something, because life is so damn unfair.

Jan, the palliative care nurse, talks through what to expect in the next few weeks. They talk about quiet rooms and hospice and Make A Wish. The mother talks softly, the father – who has flown in from Florida where he lives with his second wife – is silent.

And so am I. I can't look at them without wanting to apologize. It's a failure. I'm a failure.

I'm supposed to save lives, not talk about them ending.

When the meeting is over I go in search of painkillers, getting somebody to write me a script so I can take the good stuff. And then I have a talk with one of our fellows who got a drug dose wrong last night and could have endangered the patient if a nurse hadn't double checked.

And then to top it all off, I have to spend an hour on the phone to another fucking insurance company who demands a peer to peer before they will consider paying for life saving treatment. By the time I hang up all I can think of is going to the club and smashing the hell out of something.

Someone.

Okay, yeah, someone. But at least that person will be a willing victim.

When I walk out of my office Rose is waiting. She takes one look at my expression and wrinkles her nose.

"You were hard on Luke about the dosage," she says.

"He's a doctor. He knows better."

"He's still learning. That's why you're here. To teach him."

I'm not in any mood to talk about teaching right now. "I got off the phone with Amy Riley's insurance. They should email through the go ahead."

"Great." She smiles big. "That's fantastic news." Then she inspects me. "Are you okay?"

"Migraine." I pinch my nose because it's getting worse.

"Have you taken something?" she asks.

"Yep."

"You should go lie down."

I shoot her a withering look and she shakes her head. There's too much to do and way too little time. Still, she follows me like a mother hen as I storm down the corridor, then come to an abrupt halt outside Mabel's door.

It's open. And she's inside, but she's not alone. Blair is sitting on the chair next to her bed, and the two of them are laughing.

Is it Thursday? Fuck, I think it is.

"She arrived an hour ago," Rose says softly. "You were in the meeting so I checked the notes. Her parents agreed to the visit."

"Yeah." I nod. "I spoke to them on Monday."

"They've been talking non stop. I haven't heard Mabel laugh so much in weeks," Rose continues. "I went in to see if they wanted a drink but they were too busy talking about Darcy and how swoony he is."

"Darcy?" I ask.

"*Pride and Prejudice*. You must have heard of it." Rose sounds almost sweet.

"Yeah, probably." Blair's wearing a pair of jeans and a t-shirt with writing across the chest, though from the way she's sitting I can't read it. Her hair is down, glossy and wavy. And even though I'm fifteen feet away from her I swear I can smell the floral notes of her shampoo.

"You should try reading more," Rose says to me.

"You sound like Mabel. When would I get the chance to read a book?"

She gives a little huff. She sounds like a baby dragon, except less cute. "Maybe if you fought less, you'd have more time for other things."

I freeze. And then once I'm kind of used to the shock I turn to look at her.

There's the strangest expression on her face. Its the facial equivalent of Bite Me.

"What?" I say, stalling for time.

"Oh come on, do you think I'm an idiot? I know what you do. And I know how bad it is for you. That headache – don't you think it might be a result from being punched around on a weekly basis?"

"We don't punch heads," I say.

"Yet your lip was cut to hell and your eye was swollen the other week."

We hear Mabel laugh again. And then looks up, her lips curling into a smile as she sees Rose and me standing outside her room. "Hey, Dr. Salinger."

Blair's head snaps up. She's holding a book – I can't see the title because my eyes are hurting and I can't focus that hard. The large lettering across her chest is easier to read though.

I Have No Shelf Control

"Nice t-shirt," I say.

The corner of her lip quirks. "Thanks."

"Mabel, your hour is up," Rose says. "You should probably let Blair go now."

Mabel's face falls. "Seriously? She just got in here."

"Actually I need to go," Blair says, giving Mabel a soft smile. "I'm working this evening."

"Just ten more minutes…" Mabel's voice takes on a wheedling tone.

"Mabel." I lift a brow. And she does that teenage thing of rolling her eyes and slumping at the same time. It's weird, but this is the best part of my shitty day.

Seeing Mabel act like a normal kid.

"I'll come back next week," Blair promises her. Then she stands and stretches her arms above her head and I try really, really hard not to watch as her breasts lift.

I fail.

"I'll walk you out," I tell Blair, because I want to ask her about how it went. And maybe a mouthful of fresh air might cure this fucking headache.

"Sure." She slides a book back into her bag and pulls out another. "Read this one," she says to Mabel. "We'll talk about it next week."

Mabel's face lights up and she's so busy reading the back of the book that she doesn't even protest as Blair leaves. Rose walks into the room and closes the door, leaving Blair and I in the hall.

"Thank you for coming in to talk to her," I say, stepping to the right so we can both walk down the hallway. When we get to the door at the end of the ward, I press the release button and we head toward the elevators.

"It's a pleasure. She's fun."

"Yeah, she is. When she's not being a teenager."

Blair laughs. "I guess you have more experience with kids than most single guys your age."

"Pretty much." But only sick kids. I don't tell her that but the fact hangs in the air anyway.

"Are you coming to the club later?" she asks.

A knife stabs me between the eyes from the inside. "I don't think so," I say, because if I go into the club I'm going to collapse on the floor. "I'll probably be there this weekend though."

"I'm working Saturday so I'll see you there if you do."

"Yeah. Sounds good." I wish I could say more but I'm trying not to vomit.

"Are you okay?" she asks, tipping her head to the side.

"I'm fine. I gotta go." I flash her what I hope looks like a smile but it's too fucking painful to know. "Thanks again."

"Sure." Her voice trails off as I almost run back into the building.

As soon as I get to the ward I head for the bathroom and throw my guts up. Rose gives me one of her looks as I walk out, having washed my face and hands until the top layer of my skin turned raw.

"Go to bed," she says.

"I'm going to. Ten minutes," I promise.

Before I do, I check in on a few patients, then on Mabel, who's laying on her bed, the book that Blair gave her in her hands.

"Another Dickens?" I ask her. "Or Bronte?"

"Nope. More modern." She holds the book up and through the haze in my eyes I read the title.

The Catcher In The Rye.

Funny, Blair. Real funny.

"The author's got the same name as you," Mabel says. "Salinger."

Yeah, and the hero – if you can call him that – has the same first name as me, too. I might not know a lot about the classics but I know that much. My parents had a sick sense of humor. "You have a good time with Blair?"

Mabel grins. "She's fab. I love her. Did you know she used to be in the Army?"

"Yeah, so I hear."

"You know what else?" Mabel asks, lowering her voice.

"No, tell me."

"Every time I said your name she blushed. I think she has a crush on you."

"Shut up. You've been reading too many romances," I tell her.

She shrugs. "I know lust when I see it."

"You do?" Now I'm a little weirded out. "Well okay then. I'm heading out for a bit. Be good for the nurses."

"I'll try." She shrugs. "But I also might fail."

"Night Mabel."

She shoots me a warm smile. "Night Doc."

I close her door softly and walk down the hallway. And then I find the nearest empty room and collapse on the bed.

CHAPTER
EIGHT

HOLDEN

I wake up on Saturday morning to the rhythm of a fist hammering against my bedroom door. There's only one person I know who gets up this early in the morning, and sadly I'm related to him. I groan and stretch my arms – then I shake my head because the migraine was still lingering yesterday evening, forty-eight hours later, but thankfully it seems better now.

"Holden?" Linc yells. "You here?"

I guess he let himself in. I should probably feel lucky he didn't just wander into my bedroom but I don't feel lucky right now.

"Yeah." My voice sounds rough as shit. I spent Thursday night trying to sleep off the worst of my headache which meant by Friday a million issues had built up at work. I didn't leave the hospital until almost eleven. Thankfully, I now have two days off to catch up on my sleep, which is good because I feel exhausted. "Coming."

When I walk out of my bedroom and into the kitchen Lincoln's already started helping himself to my food. He's got a bagel in one hand and a jug of orange juice in the other.

"Use a fucking glass," I tell him.

"I'm just trying to save you on some cleaning." He shrugs and lifts the jug to his lips and drinks straight out of it. And I know for sure – and from too many years of living with him – that some of that bagel is now mixed in with the juice.

"What do you want, Lincoln?" I say, grabbing a glass and pouring some water into it.

"Be nice." He pouts. He has the best lips out of all of us. He once broke the world record of the most lip flaps in ten seconds. Seriously, look it up in the *Guinness Book of Records*, his name is there.

"This is me being nice," I mutter. My stomach growls. When did I last eat? Thursday was a mess, and yesterday I was still feeling ropey. I take another mouthful of water and open my refrigerator.

And it's empty. Linc has taken the last bagel.

"I came to check on you," Linc says. "You haven't been answering our messages."

"I've been working."

"I know. You also haven't returned my calls." He sounds like a whiny teenager. He could give Mabel a run for her money.

And then I remember that tux I promised him. Shit. "If you want to try on the dinner jacket you can."

"The gala was last week," he tells me. "And I already borrowed it."

"You did? When?"

"Two weeks ago."

I blink because I could swear he only asked me the other day. Time does weird things when you're constantly holed up in a hospital. "Really?"

"Yeah." He nods.

I turn to look at him. He's got half a bagel hanging out of his mouth. "But you didn't leave a mess." And Linc always leaves a mess. He's like that kid from Charlie Brown with the dust constantly hanging around his head.

"Your cleaner was here." He shrugs. "She made sure I didn't."

"You made my cleaner tidy up after you?" I frown. "That's not her job."

He smirks. "She was happy to finally have something to clean. You're such a neat freak. The poor woman must be completely demoralized working for you."

I roll my eyes. "I'm not a neat freak. I'm just not walking chaos like you."

He finishes the last of the bagel and drinks some more orange juice from the carton. "Do you want me to summarize the group messages or what?"

"Sure." I don't, but he's going to do it, anyway. I busy myself making a coffee – black because I forgot to buy cream.

His voice is like a low buzz in my ear as I start thinking about all the things I need to get done before my next shift. Plus I need to check in on some patients.

"Shall we say about eight?"

"What?" I turn to look at him.

"Tonight. When Liam and Myles get here. Shall I make the reservation for eight?"

I've clearly missed something. Okay, a lot of things. "Myles and Liam are coming to New York?" I ask. My two oldest brothers live in West Virginia with their families. Once upon a time they both lived here in the city, but then they kind of fell in love with best friends and moved southwest.

"Yes. They have meetings on Monday and thought it would be a good chance for us to catch up. We barely see you, bro."

"I know. I know." I pinch my nose. "I'm sorry." And now I'm going to make things worse. "I can't meet you at eight."

"Why not?" Linc sounds annoyed. And it takes a lot for him to get like that.

"Because I have something to do."

He gives a long sigh. "Is it that thing that you're not supposed to do?"

Here's the thing. My brothers and I... we have a don't ask don't tell policy. It worked perfectly when Myles had a thing for the woman he was supposed to hate – the woman he ended up marrying, and equally well for Liam, my second oldest brother who used to have so many women we all lost count.

Until he met the one.

And yeah, I'm aware there's a pattern here. But it's also one I've broken. Because there is no one. I wouldn't subject anybody to my life.

"Message me at ten and tell me where you are. I'll catch up with you."

"We'll probably go to a club."

"Cool."

"And pick up women," he adds, his eyes flicking to mine. He hates that I don't go out on the prowl with him. But I'm just not interested.

I start to laugh. "With Myles and Liam? Good luck."

"You're such an asshole," Linc says, shaking his head at me.

"Yep," I readily agree.

He holds his hand out and I stare at it for a moment, like I'm supposed to be reading his palm or something. A long lifeline. Shitty heart line. Whatever.

"Give me your phone," he says, while I'm still staring.

"Why?"

"Because I'm going to put an alarm on it. One you can't silence. That way you can't forget to meet us."

"I thought you were going to message me," I say.

"And you'll say you had your phone on silent and couldn't respond." He gives me a look that reminds me so much of his mom – my stepmom – it makes me want to laugh.

But because I actually want to get rid of him from my kitchen at some point today I unlock my phone and pass it to him, letting him do his thing while I drink my coffee.

"See you tonight, loser," he says.

"Sure," I agree. "Looking forward to it."

"You'd better be. We're gonna have a Salinger Brothers' night this city won't forget."

―――――

BLAIR

"You look nice," Annie says as I grab my purse, ready to run out of the door. It's Saturday night and I'm running late, mostly because I spent way too much time trying to decide what to wear.

And no, not because a certain doctor is going to be there tonight. I just decided it was time to look pretty for myself. Working with Katrina, the golden haired beauty, always makes me feel like I'm starting from a disadvantage. So I put on my best, tightest jeans and a halter top that makes my boobs look good.

"Thank you." I kiss her cheek. "I'll probably be back after one. Make sure you lock the door."

"Yes, Mom."

I give her a look. "Not your mom, just somebody who loves you."

"I know, I love you too," she tells me. "Now go."

Thankfully, it isn't raining tonight. Instead the evening air is almost sultry, a reminder that summer is around the corner and that we may be leaving spring behind. There's a spring in my step, too, as I walk around the corner to the street where The Black and White Club stands proud. And I'm so caught up in my thoughts that at first I don't see the guy on the ground.

He's old. Homeless almost certainly. His beard is dirty and his fingernails are black. He looks up at me with hooded eyes, and I can see the wrinkles pulling at his face. "Got some money I can have?" he asks.

I shake my head. "No, sorry." But I stop and hunker down next to him. "Do you need something to eat? Maybe a drink? I work at the club over there." I point at the nondescript building across the street. "I can bring you something out."

"What kind of drink?" he asks.

"A soda? Juice? I can make you a sandwich too."

He nods then clears his throat. It's full of phlegm. "You look like my daughter," he says.

"Do you want me to call her?" I ask him. Because if this was my dad I'd want to know he was homeless.

Okay, I'd probably leave my dad in the street. But anybody else and I'd be there.

He shakes his head. "She's in Florida. Doesn't want to know me. Don't blame her, I'm an asshole."

"Aren't we all sometimes?" I ask him and he tries to chuckle but ends up coughing again. I look down the street and there's a gang of kids standing at the corner. "What's your name?" I ask him.

"Sam."

"Sam, will you come with me? There's a little courtyard at the back of the club where you can sit and wait for some food." He'll have to wait outside because the security guards won't let him in. Not looking like this. "And then maybe later we can find you a hostel or something?"

"Don't want no hostel but I never say no to food." He lets

me help him up. His skin is surprisingly warm. He has this half-shuffle as we cross the road and I point at the alley down from the club. "Second gate. It's unlocked while the club is open," I tell him. "Give me half an hour and I'll sneak out."

He pats my face with his hot hands. They smell but I try not to wince. "You're a good girl."

"I try." I shoot him a smile and wait for him to walk to the alley. When he's disappeared from sight I run into the club, pulling off my jacket as I walk behind the bar counter.

"Hey," Katrina says. "You'll be pleased to hear there's no politicians in tonight." She flashes me a smile and I flash one back because I think we're friends now. She also thinks I'm Kick-Ass because I can defend myself when needed.

There's a sheet behind us showing the fights tonight. Holden's name is on it. I swallow hard because I still can't watch him.

But I can't *not*, either.

It's aggravating. I want to ignore the way my body feels every time I watch his muscles tense. I hate the way my insides respond to the sheer power of his punches.

Because I hate violence.

But I like him. Too much.

I take a deep breath because I don't need this emotion now. I blame my inner damsel in distress – very inner, because she's never been here before – for being grateful to him for saving me.

Talking of saving, I have my own kind to do. "Can you cover for me for a minute?" I ask Katrina. She glances at the massively full bar and back at me.

"I'll owe you one," I promise her.

She beams. "Sure. And I'm going to take you up on that."

I head straight for the staff room, where there's some basic food and drinks, and quickly make up a salami sandwich and fill a plastic jug full of juice. I have to sneak it past the security guard at the back of the bar. He looks at my food stash and I shrug. "I'm feeling as hungry as an ox," I say sweetly.

He nods like he understands and I slide past him. He's used to people doing this. Katrina goes out every time she either wants a smoke or to talk to one of her boyfriends. I only come out here when I need to throw something in one of the over sized wheeled trashcans at the back.

As soon as I walk through the emergency door – wedging it open because it's one of those that you can only get through from the inside, I take a deep breath and look around. The pungent aroma of days old meat and vegetables from the restaurant next door fills my nose.

"Sam?" I call out, looking around. He's not here. "Hello?"

I hear a groan. Not from here but from the alley itself. Putting the food and cup down I run to the gate and push it open, finding him slumped against the wall, his hands clutching his chest.

"Sam? Are you sick?"

"They kicked me."

Oh shit. Those kids. I swallow hard. "Do you think you can stand up?"

"Hurts." He sounds like a little boy. It touches my heart the same place that Evan touches it.

"Okay, don't move. I'm going to call an ambulance."

"No ambulance," he grunts. "Please."

His lips look blue, like he's not getting enough oxygen. I have some basic first aid training, but this man looks bad. And then an idea hits me.

"What about a doctor? I know one," I tell him. "He could help."

"Can't afford no doctor."

"I know. He won't charge." I'll pay him if I have to. Not that I'l have to, I'm pretty sure. "Don't go anywhere."

There's a a ghost of a smile on his pained face as I run

back into the club, ignoring Katrina's call as I weave through the customers on the dance floor and into the fight room.

There's a fight already on, but it's two young guys I haven't seen before. I take a left, pushing through the door to the offices and locker rooms, my heart doing a little clenching thing because Jimmy's door is open and the office is empty but I can remember exactly what went on in there last week.

I rap at the first locker room, but when I'm called in Holden isn't there. "Do you know where the Medic is?" I ask the guy winding tape around his hands.

"Other room," he grunts.

When I hammer on the second door, Holden opens it right away. He has an expression on his face I can only think of as murderous. Like he wants to punch anybody and it might just be me. But then his gaze softens as he takes me in, his head tipping to the side.

"Blair? You okay?"

"I need your help."

He doesn't hesitate for a second. "Okay, what do you need?"

It's stupid but that simple response makes me feel all gooey inside. It's not a maybe or what can you do for me in return? It's just a yes and he's ready to help.

I haven't had many people like that in my life.

"There's a homeless guy outside and he's been kicked in the stomach. I think he might be sick, too. He's very hot. Feverish."

"I don't have my medical bag with me," Holden says.

"I'll get the first aid kit."

He nods a 'that'll have to do' kind of nod and follows me back through the club, neither of us looking at the ring as we half-walk half-run. He hasn't asked me why I'm the one getting him and not security and I appreciate that too much. I point at the door to the outside. "He's in the alley against the wall," I say. "I'll get the kit and be right behind you."

By the time I've grabbed the first aid kit from the cupboard and run out into the night, Holden is squatting in front of the old man, talking softly to him as he touches his neck for a pulse.

He's so gentle again. It's mystifying how a man like that could hit people and enjoy it. "I've got the kit," I say, joining him.

"Can you get me some wipes and gloves," Holden says. He murmurs to Sam again, and has to lean forward to hear Sam's response. I pass him the wipes and he cleans his hands before he snaps on the gloves. Then he slowly pulls Sam's top up and I can see the redness of his stomach.

Holden touches it tenderly, his fingers moving over Sam's abdomen. He's still talking, and Sam's nodding and looking like he's getting some breath back again. "I'd like to admit you for a scan," Holden whispers. "To be completely sure there's no internal bleeding."

"I'm fine," Sam says roughly. "Just got surprised, that's all."

The gate opens and Katrina's there. "What's going on?" she asks.

Shit. I turn to look at her. "Nothing. It's all good, just go back in."

"Jimmy wants you inside," she tells me. "I can't keep telling him you're in the bathroom. He's going ape because people aren't being served fast enough."

"Go back in," Holden says. "I've got this."

"I can't leave him here," I say. "And you're supposed to be fighting."

Did I really just say that? From the surprised look on his face I think I did.

"Tell Jimmy I had to call it off," Holden says. "I'll square it with him later."

"Are you coming or what?" Katrina says. I'm about to say no, because this is my mess and I can't have other people cleaning it up for me, when Holden looks at me, and mouths 'go'.

So I do. And immediately get swallowed up in the backlog of orders, running around like a blue assed fly in an attempt to catch up

CHAPTER
NINE

BLAIR

"Is there something going on between you and Holden?" Katrina asks when I walk back into the bar, having looked everywhere for Holden and not found him.

"What do you mean?" I reply, trying to sound surprised. "I barely know the guy."

"Looked like you knew him pretty well in the alley," she says pointedly.

I open my mouth to reply but thankfully a customer demands her attention, and she sighs as she grabs a shot glass and some tequila while I take the tray that's already full of drinks for the fight room. I have to do three more runs before things start to calm down – mostly because the next fight has started and the bar room itself is getting quieter.

And then Jimmy bustles in.

"Where's the Medic?" he asks, looking behind the counter as though Holden is crouching there, hiding from him like a kid.

"Ask Blair," Katrina says, and it's my turn to shoot her a narrow-eyed look. *Thanks, friend.*

"Do you know where he is?" Jimmy asks me.

"There was a guy outside who looked sick," I say, because all Jimmy has to do is look at the security cameras to know what happened.

"And?" Jimmy questions.

"And I asked Holden to help him."

"He's due on in ten minutes. Find him," Jimmy instructs, his eyes meeting mine.

"I need her here," Katrina protests. "Come on, Jimmy. Holden's a big boy. In so many ways." Her lip quirks and she looks at me from the corner of her eye. "So many," she breathes.

Despite the fact I know she's trying to get a reaction I still blanch.

"I'll go find him," I say, because this is all my fault. And I pretty much run past the security guard who pays me little attention to the emergency exit, and back out into the yard. I cross it quickly, making it to the alleyway, but it's empty. There's nobody out there at all, including Holden and Sam.

Confused, I walk the length of the alley to the road, wondering if Holden persuaded Sam to get into an ambulance after all. But it's empty save for the occasional cab. Then I walk back up it, as far as I can go, my eyes sweeping the ground in the gloom for clues.

And finally, because there's no other way and I have his number – even if I don't want to use it – I message Holden.

Hi. Everything okay with Sam? Let me know if I can do anything. – Blair.

. . .

I take a second to hit the send button. Mostly because it makes me feel weird. We only exchanged numbers in case I needed help getting into the hospital to see Mabel and it turned out I didn't. Will he think I'm overstepping the mark?

After a minute there's no reply, and that sends my stupid thoughts into a tailspin. Either there's something really wrong with Sam, or Holden is annoyed at me messaging him. Both make me feel a little sick.

Jimmy's waiting for me as soon as I walk back into the bar. "Well?" he asks, his thick arms folded across his barrel chest.

"He's not there," I say.

"Find. Him." Jimmy's eyes narrow.

I let out a mouthful of air. Not just because this is futile but because I can feel the heat of Katrina's annoyed gaze on my back. I'm absolutely certain we won't be sharing tips tonight.

I nod at Jimmy and rush to the locker room I dragged Holden out of, opening it up in case some kind of miracle has occurred and he's there.

But of course it's empty. Feeling defeated, I slump down on the wooden slatted bench and try to think straight.

"Blair?"

Looking up, I see Holden standing in the hallway. He's still wearing the gray sweatpants and black t-shirt he was in when I grabbed him from here, though they look more crumpled now. The t-shirt still clings to his chest though, revealing the plains of his deltoids.

And I'm a stupid gooey mess because he came back and even though I have no need for a knight in shining armor he looks like one right now.

"How's Sam?" I ask standing.

"I think he has some kind of flu on top of the stomach injury. He wouldn't go to a hospital, though, so I called a friend who runs a shelter. She's found him a place for the night. Promised to keep an eye on him."

Warm air escapes my lips. "Thank you."

"Do you know him?" he asks.

I shake my head. "I just found him outside earlier. Offered to bring him some food. And then..." I wave my hand. "I really appreciate your help."

He gives me a half smile. "No problem."

And it's stupid but I want to put my head against his chest. I want him to hold me like he did last week when he got me out of Jimmy's office. He looks at me again, his brows pulled down, his lips half-open, and there's this electricity in the air.

I feel it tingling on my skin. And I know it's because he helped me without question. And maybe also because he's this intriguing combination of violent and gentle. Or maybe I'm just tired of pretending I'm not attracted to this man.

Even though he's the last person I should be feeling this way about.

"Can you tell me which shelter? I'll go see him tomorrow."

"He'll be gone by then, Blair. He's not the kind to stay anywhere for long."

"What do you mean?" I frown.

He shrugs. "I mean he's a homeless guy for a reason. He'll get chucked out from the shelter in the morning and head somewhere else. Wherever he thinks he can find food and roof. So there's no point telling you the name of the place because it'll be a wasted journey."

"But he's sick."

"I know." His eyes don't leave mine.

"If they let him go he could end up dying somewhere."

"I know that, too." His voice isn't soft but it isn't hard either.

I feel annoyed at the world. "So that's okay?" I ask him. "It's okay that he could crawl away somewhere and die alone. Like an animal? It's okay that because he has no money he doesn't get to have the dignity we'd give to our own pets?"

"It's life, Blair," he says thickly.

"Well it shouldn't be. Nobody should be treated like that. And you might be able to live with it, but I can't." I go to storm out of the locker room. Our shoulders brush and I feel it again. That stupid chemical reaction I have to him.

Before I can stomp the rest of the way out, his fingers close around my wrist. "Blair."

I snap my head up at him. "I'm sorry. It's not you I'm angry at. It's..." I wave my hand because right now it's the whole world. My nephew can't breathe properly because people love their diesel engines more than they love kids' lungs. Sam can't be treated because someone along the line decided insurance company profits are more important than treating fellow humans with kindness.

And now I'm treating Holden badly and it isn't his fault.

He's looking down at me and I can feel the heat of my face reflected in his eyes. They're dark. Unmoving. His lips part.

My heart hammers against my chest. He lowers his head, his nose brushing mine. And I realize the person I'm most angry at is myself.

"I'm sorry. I'm a mess up," I whisper.

"You're the most together person I know." I can feel the warmth of his words as he breathes against my skin. He hesitates for a second. And then our eyes connect again and a single word escapes my lips.

"Please..."

He takes my words for what they are. Consent. I want his mouth on mine. I want to feel the hardness of his body against the softness of my own. I want him to kiss me until I forget why I'm angry and only remember the way his lips feel against mine.

I want him. More than I think I've wanted anything.

"There you are." Jimmy walks in, not even noticing how

close we are. Within a millisecond Holden steps back, leaving me staring at him, my mouth half-open, my body full of desire that I have no idea what to do with.

"Hey." Holden nods at Jimmy.

"We've been looking for you all over. Had to delay the fight. You gonna be ready soon?"

"Give me five," Holden says, already pulling his t-shirt over his head. And I'm subjected to a close up view of the kind of muscles I've only seen a few times. His biceps contract then lengthen as he throws his shirt on the floor.

"Blair, you need to go serve," Jimmy tells me.

I duck around him and scurry out, hearing the low level of the two of them talking as I head down the hall. What the hell was I thinking almost kissing him? Maybe Jimmy is my fairy godfather, looking out for me.

Making sure I don't do things I'll regret later.

I join Katrina at the bar just as she's taking another tray. "You back for good or are you planning on running off again?" she asks.

"I'm back."

"Good. Go take this tray." She shoves it at me, clearly pissed. "And for the record, I'm not sharing my tips tonight."

I nod. "Got it."

———

The atmosphere in the fight room is electric as I run around picking up empty glasses from the sticky table tops. I'm still feeling edgy, and not just from Sam and his injury and then my confrontation with Holden, but because Katrina is still being bitchy every time I step behind the bar and I'm so over it.

Yes, this job pays a lot. And yes, I need the money. But the minute I get my masters and a job offer outside of New York City I'll be gone.

It's the only thing that keeps me feeling sane as Jimmy's voice booms through the microphone and he announces the next match of the night – and music starts to blast through the speakers.

My lips twitch because Jimmy's obviously annoyed about Holden's disappearing act. He's switched up Holden's entrance song.

"Bad Medicine" by Bon Jovi echoes through the room as the Medic comes out, his expression completely blank as cheers erupt from the watching customers.

"Dear God," a woman at the table in front of me says. "I'd pay good money to try out his bedside manner."

"No need for a bed," her friend replies. "I'd get down on my knees for him in the ring."

My teeth grind a little, but I'm too busy watching Holden easily jump into the ring and shuck off his robe.

I think every X chromosome in the place explodes. Along with more than a few Ys.

Nobody pays much attention to his opponent as Holden puts on his headgear and turns, his gaze hitting mine.

And I'm a damn puddle of goo. This man has the finest body I've ever seen, but it's his stupid eyes that get me every time. I'm literally clenching here, as he continues to stare at me, I'm breathlessly staring back.

He mouths one word.

"Stay."

I nod imperceptibly, because I owe him for taking care of Sam. If he wants me to stay and watch him knock himself to pieces I will

Even if Katrina is going to kill me. *Literally.* She's already feral and she scratches.

I'm going to go home ripped into bits.

I hold the tray full of empties as the two fighters face up to each other, toe to toe. I can't hear what the referee is saying – and frankly I don't care. I'm too busy looking at him.

This man saved a life a few hours ago. Now he's about to hammer the hell out of one. It's wrong. It's bad. It's completely sexy.

I'm so confused I can't think properly. So I don't think. I watch as Holden circles his opponent – a man two inches shorter than him but built like a juggernaut. And then it's like something switches. Holden swings and I hear his glove connecting with the man's chest. I can feel the heat of my blood pumping through my veins.

He punches again, and again, and instead of the revulsion I want to feel, I feel desire. I want to punch something, too. Hard and fast until the anger at the world stops.

Is this why he does it? Why they all do it? Because to keep the anger in would be so much worse?

The bell rings signaling the end of the first round and Holden goes to the corner and takes a drink, then turns to look at me. My hands feel unsteady, and the empty glasses shake on the tray. I put it down on the table beside me, and luckily nobody seems bothered.

The second round is harder than the first, in every way. Punches land harder, spittle flies, there's blood but I'm pretty sure it's not Holden's. But it's the sound that gets me. The grunts sound like sex. The thuds sound rhythmic. And I feel like I'm on fire.

"Can I get a whiskey, sweetheart?" a voice whispers in my ear. I turn to see a suited guy who smells like money standing next to me.

"Sure. What's your table?" I ask, my attention only half on him.

"That one. And what's your name?" He has a dimple. And one of those sheens of self assurance only the really rich can get.

And then I feel a shiver snake down my spine so turn to look at the ring. Holden is staring at me and the guy next to me. Then he turns back to his opponent and lays him out.

I watch as he hits him again, hard enough for the man's body to ricochet off the ropes until he face plants on the floor. The referee goes over, counts him out, and my heart thuds against my chest with every number up to ten.

People jump up, shout and cheer, waving their arms and chanting Holden's fight name.

He pulls his headgear off and turns to stare at me once more.

"Stay," he mouths again. And I now know what he's asking. He wants me to stay at the end. Meet him.

I nod and the smallest of smiles pulls at his lips.

I'm not stupid. I know he's not asking me to stay for a chat. To shoot the breeze about earlier or his fight or anything else.

He's asking me to stay because there's part of him that has the primal urge to fight and fuck every time he's at a low.

God help me, I'm feeling that urge, too.

"That whiskey?" the suit next to me asks, pulling me out of my stupid sexual haze.

"On it," I say, grabbing the tray of empties and turning on my heel, preparing myself for Katrina's wrath.

But she's weirdly chirpy when I join her behind the bar. So chirpy, in fact, that she smiles at me.

"Everything okay?" I ask, still feeling stupidly breathless. The clock above the bar says it's eleven, but I feel like I've been here for about a week.

"All's good." She puts three whiskeys on a tray. I move to take it but she pulls back. "This one's mine," she says, lifting a brow as she glances over my shoulder. I turn to follow her gaze and I can see exactly why she's calling dibs.

There are three guys sitting at the table in the center of the bar. All handsome as hell. They're laughing about something, and there's a family resemblance between them all. Dark hair, blue eyes, winning smiles.

The one at the far end of the table looks like the oldest.

He's wearing what looks like an expensively cut suit, and when he lifts his arm up I can see the glint of a watch that I'd bet is a Rolex.

The guy next to him leans over and whispers in his ear and it's like someone has doused me in a tub of cold water. Because I know exactly who he is – and now I know exactly who they all are.

Holden's brothers. They're here. And one of them knows I'm his maid.

————

HOLDEN

I shower and change in the locker room then pull on my jeans and gray t-shirt. A glance in the rusty mirror on the door reveals shadows under my eyes from way too much work and not enough sleep. I probably shouldn't have come here tonight. I almost didn't.

But there's a draw that I'm finding it increasingly harder to ignore. I think she is, too.

I know she is. And I'm aching to explore it with her.

Running my fingers through my still-damp hair I walk into the fight room. A few people come up to congratulate me, shaking my hand, but I'm half-assed in my replies because I'm looking for Blair.

She's not here.

So I push my way through the doors that lead to the main bar and look over at the counter, expecting to see her waiting for an order.

Instead I hear my name being called.

I look over at the table and see my brothers.

Linc, Myles, and Liam are all looking at me as though I've just walked off of a spaceship.

I groan because seriously? I just want to go home. Take her home.

And that's when I remember I was supposed to meet them.

For a minute I try to work out if I can just grab Blair and we can run out of here. But Linc is walking toward me, looking annoyed.

"I called you," he said.

"Yeah." I run my thumb along my jaw. "Sorry. I got caught up in something."

"You were fighting," he says. "That's what this is, right? A fight club?"

My mouth feels dry as tinder. My last hope, that they didn't see anything, disappears. I run my tongue along my bottom lip. "Listen, I need to talk to somebody. Can you go back to the table and wait for me?"

He pouts. "Are you going to run out on us?"

I was thinking about it, but no. "Just stay there and I'll be right back." I need to talk to Blair. Tell her there's a situation.

But I'm still taking her home tonight.

Katrina looks up when I approach the bar. "Are those really your brothers?" she asks.

I guess one of them has been talking to her. "Yep." I still can't see Blair. Maybe she's on her break.

"Are any of them single?"

"Linc, the youngest."

"Which one is he?" She glances over my shoulder.

"The one with the blue shirt."

"Oh, he's cute."

"He's really not." I shake my head. "Where's Blair?"

"Why do you want to know?" She tips her head to the side. I think she's trying to be funny but it's just annoying.

"Is she in the break room?"

"No, she had to leave."

I blink. "What?"

"She asked if she could leave early. I said yes." Katrina shrugs. "Is there something that I can help you with?"

No, there isn't. This night is turning into shit. First Sam, then my brothers, and now Blair disappearing.

A wave of annoyance washes through me, because she's run away. From me. But I don't have time to think about that right now.

Taking a deep breath I turn to look at my brothers. They're still sitting around the table. Still looking at me.

Okay then. Time to pepper them off with excuses and go home. It looks like I'll be sleeping alone tonight.

CHAPTER
TEN

BLAIR

"I told you so," Annie says, lifting a brow at me. "You never should have taken that job."

I look down at the picnic that last night's tips paid for – and no, Katrina didn't share her tips, but I still made enough on my own to pay for this week's food and Evan's copay for his prescription for the next three months.

"How was I supposed to know his brothers were going to show up?" I ask her. "They never have before. And from the way Katrina reacted to them it was their first time there." Not that I watched too closely. I was too busy trying to figure out what to do.

And the only thing I *could do* was get the hell out of there.

"I hate that you have to work so hard," Annie says. "You look constantly tired."

I like working hard. I always have. Maybe it comes from our mom. She was the same way after Dad left her. I can't remember her ever having less than two jobs, often three, to keep the roof over our heads.

She prided herself on that. The same way I'm proud that Annie and I are keeping things together. I think Mom would like where we are now. We're both college educated. Annie got her degree in business while I was in the Army, sending money home each month, and then I came back and the Army funded my education, too.

It was the only reason I joined. We had a plan then, and I have a plan now.

These two jobs are part of that. I can't take the risk of losing either of them, let alone both of them in one fell swoop.

We're sitting on a blanket in Central Park, underneath the shade of a tree. I met them after Evan's swimming lesson and we took the bus here.

Evan has gotten bored of listening to Annie and me talk and has made friends with a group of kids who are running around playing tag on the grass. The sun is warm and the mood is bright and I should feel better than I do.

I haven't told Annie all the gory details about Holden. Like the way I turn into some kind of puddle of desire every time I look at him. Or how I was moments away from going home with him in an attempt to scratch that very hot, deep itch that I get every time our eyes meet.

I should be grateful that his brothers were there. It made me act the way I should have, if I had any common sense. But now I owe him an apology and explanation and I've never been a good liar. I have no idea what to tell him.

Tell him you're not interested.

I exhale heavily, watching as Evan and another kid laugh at something. It's so good to see him running around in the grass. Enjoying life.

I can still remember the day Annie told me she was pregnant. She was so scared to tell me. She started crying, saying sorry, and I couldn't understand what she was apologizing for.

"You paid for me to go to college and I've ruined everything," she'd wailed and I couldn't understand it at all. We were a team then and we're a team now.

And Evan is the best thing that's happened to us all. Sure, we've had to up our game, working harder than ever.

But watching him laugh and have fun is worth it.

Annie lifts a carrot stick from the bowl and chomps into it. "So you're into him, huh?"

"What?" I frown as I look at her, pulling my thoughts away from the past.

She gives me a sneaky smile. "Come on. Every time you mention his name your cheeks get all flushed. You like him."

I will my cheeks not to heat. "He's my customer."

"You went to the hospital to meet his patient," Annie says, lifting a brow. "And you never do something like that."

"He's a nice guy. He asked me to help and I did."

"A nice guy who beats other people up for the hell of it," Annie says, lifting a brow. "And you like it."

"I don't. You know I don't like violence," I tell her. A bird flies above us, letting out a cry.

"Does he look hot shirtless?" she asks, then laughs as I blush. "I knew it. I wish I could find a babysitter. I'd be in there to watch him in a minute." Her amused gaze meets mine. "Can you take a pic and show me."

"No."

"He's gotta be hot," she says. "I've never seen you blush like that before. Do you think he likes you?"

"He wanted me to stay til the end last night," I say, the words escaping before I can stop them.

"He wanted you to stay? What for?" Annie leans forward, her eyes gleaming.

"I don't know. I think..." I can't say the words. If I say them then I'll want them. And I hate wanting things I can't have.

I'd rather pretend I don't want them. The disappointment is always less that way.

"He wanted to have sex with you." Her voice is low.

"Yeah. I guess."

"Oh damn his brothers." She shakes her head, looking annoyed. "If they hadn't turned up you could still be tangled in the sheets with the hot doc right now."

I pick a blade of grass and roll it between my fingers. "I'm glad they turned up. It would have ended badly."

"So what are you going to do then?" she asks me. "You see him at work, you go to the hospital, you clean his damn house? It's not like you can avoid him."

"Can we go to the adventure playground?" Evan asks, stopping to catch his breath next to our blanket. There's no wheeze though. "The other kids are going. Please?"

Annie and I exchange a look. "Sure," she says. "Let's just pack up the picnic and we can head over there. Can you grab the plates, sweetie?"

"Okay, Mom." It's amazing how quickly a kid can help clean up when he has an ulterior motive.

And it's the end of our conversation about Holden. I can't say I'm sad about that.

Because she's asking me all the questions I don't have answers to.

———

HOLDEN

My hands are shaking as I lift my coffee cup, and from the corner of my eye I watch Myles frown. After last night's clusterfuck he insisted we all meet for brunch. Which luckily for me meant after noon because I needed the sleep.

I'm still not talking to Linc. Because the asshole put himself on the *Find My Friends* app on my phone that I didn't even know existed when he set the alarm to remind me to go meet them.

And when I didn't arrive at the restaurant they found me instead. At The Black and White Club. Where Linc, being the nosey bastard he is, wandered into the fighting area and worked out what was going on in there. And now I've had to explain everything.

Fuckers.

To top it all I'm still feeling wrung out. It's the kind of exhausted you only get from too many days on shift and not enough sleep. And from anger because the woman you want keeps running away.

I've been waiting for Blair to message me. To explain why she disappeared.

But my phone remains annoyingly blank. And I'm not going to message her, because I know Blair knows how to use a damn phone. I have the message she sent last night when she was looking for me to prove it.

Maybe she only wants you when she can use you.

Yeah, well I wanted to use her too. No, not use her. Bury myself in her. Lose myself. Find myself. I don't know.

"I don't get why you didn't tell us," Myles – my oldest brother – says. He looks hurt. He's obviously been thinking about my confession all night. Hence why we're here today.

"I told you, it's not a big deal." A bead of sweat rolls down my face and I blink it away. It's getting hotter in Manhattan. The streets are full of tourists, the restaurants full of Sunday afternoon patrons. I wish they'd turn the air conditioning up. I'm burning up in here.

"Of course it's a big deal," Liam, the second oldest says. He's the more laid back of our two oldest brothers. He and Myles work together in West Virginia. Right now I wish they'd stayed there. My head is pounding and I could do without the inquisition. "You're a doctor," Liam continues as

Myles beckons the server over to refill his coffee. "You know as well as we do that every time somebody hits your head you lose brain cells. You could end up injured. Permanently incapacitated. Why the hell would you do something like this?"

"Does Eli know?" Myles asks.

I ignore the question because Eli – the brother closest in age to me – isn't here to defend himself. I'm pretty sure he knows, but he also knows not to ask me about it.

"You're the one who taught me how to fight," I remind Myles, because it's true. Hell, every summer when we were teens we used to have the Salinger Olympics at our dad's place in Virginia. We'd compete for the gold medal; swimming, running, climbing trees, and fighting.

It was always the fights we loved the most.

"To defend yourself," Myles says. "Not to beat the living shit out of some guy for fun."

"We don't beat the living shit out of each other. It's a white collar fight club. We all have day jobs we want to protect. And can we change the subject now, please? I'm getting a fucking headache."

"You are a fucking headache," Myles mutters.

"Four steaks," the server announces. "Two medium, two rare." He places Myles and Linc's mediums in front of them, then gives Liam and me our rares. I take one look at it and my stomach tightens. I'm so not hungry.

"Jesus, I could eat a horse," Linc says, cutting into his. I look down at my own plate, looking at the juices swimming around on it. At the glistening meat staring up at me.

My stomach heaves again. Harder this time. And I know I'm going to be sick.

Shit.

"I'm sorry. I…" I shake my head. "I've got to go." I press my lips together as I stand, grabbing my wallet and phone from the table.

"Holden?" Myles stands, too. "What's going on? Liam and

I are leaving after this. We want to spend some time with you."

I want to spend time with them, too. They're annoying but they're my brothers. And I love them to the moon and back.

But I'm about to vomit if I don't get out of here.

"I'll call you," I promise. "I'm sorry." I run between the tables, causing more than one set of guests to shoot me a strange look. Keeping my lips clamped shut, I make it outside, and remember I didn't leave any money for my food.

I'll send some later. But right now I need to get home. I need my bed.

I need oblivion.

CHAPTER
ELEVEN

BLAIR

I've sent Holden two messages apologizing for my sudden departure on Saturday night, but he hasn't replied to either one.

It's a good thing I've learned to expertly lie to myself. So as I climb the steps to the huge brownstone apartment building where he lives the following week I'm telling myself he's probably overwhelmed at work, way too busy to tap out a quick message to me.

And even though he has no idea I'm the one cleaning his apartment, I vow to do it extra well today to make up for being such an ass over the weekend.

I walk through the lobby, nodding at the concierge who barely pays me any attention at all. Holden's apartment building has one of those old fashioned elevators that you'd see in a 1940s movie and I dump my backpack on the floor as the dial slowly ticks up to the penthouse.

I have a ring full of keys in my bag. They're all labeled but

I'd know Holden's anyway. Smooth and silver, it slides into his lock like a dream.

And then I step inside and get the strangest sensation on the back of my neck. For a second I wonder if Linc is here again, but honestly, the hallway looks too tidy. I check the living room and it's in the usual pristine state.

The kitchen, however, is a little worse for wear. More so than usual. I go to pick up the dirty glasses from the side and load the dishwasher when I hear a noise.

A groan. Coming from the bedroom.

My hackles are already risen, but they somehow lift a little more.

Is he here? I check my phone. No messages from my boss to tell me not to clean today, which I usually get whenever Holden is home.

Another groan. My cheeks flame because *what the hell is he doing in the bedroom?*

He's not...

Oh no...

Please God tell me he hasn't got a woman in there.

A sudden wave of jealousy washes over me. A jealousy I'm not entitled to have. I have no hold on him. He's a grown man, he can do what he likes.

Yet something pulls me to his bedroom door. I stand outside it, like some kind of masochist, waiting to hear a groan again. My heart is hammering against my chest, my cheeks so pink with heat you could cook an egg on them.

But maybe this is what I need to pull my head out of my ass and get on with my life. Knowing he has done that already.

No wonder he didn't reply to my apologies.

I take a deep breath in, ready to turn around and walk away when I smell it.

The funk.

It's distinctive. Not at all sexual. I've cleaned enough teenage boys' rooms to know the smell you get from one handed sex. And enough adults' rooms to know the smell you get from two or more.

No, this smell definitely isn't sexual, it's more like… somebody is sick.

My heart hammers a little more.

"Hello?" I call out before I think it through. Because on the other side of the door the man I've been fantasizing about for weeks could be pleasuring another person, himself, or… I don't know.

What the hell am I doing? Here? How did I let myself get into such a mess?

"Ahhhhh."

Damn it, I'm going in. I push the handle down and the smell immediately invades my nostrils. It's staleness and sweat and the dankness that comes from a fever.

My gaze immediately lands on the bed. Holden is laying on his side, his bare back facing me. The hair on his head looks drenched.

"Holden?" I whisper.

He groans again. How did I ever think that was a sexual noise? The man is clearly ill.

He rolls over in bed, exposing the curve of his muscles. His eyes are rheumy as they don't quite focus on me. Or the City Slickers uniform I'm wearing.

Walking over to his bed, I drop to my knees and reach out for him. As soon as my fingers land on his arm I feel the heat. God knows what his temperature is, but it's high.

"Holden?" I whisper. "How long have you been like this?"

"Blair?" he croaks.

There's no point in pretending otherwise. I need to get him some help. "Yes, it's me," I whisper. "What's wrong?"

"Been sick since Sunday." His voice is thick and low. "Head hurts."

That's two days. "Have you called anybody?"

He tries to shake his head but groans again. "Just need to sleep it off. All good."

I gingerly touch his brow. It's even hotter than the rest of him. "I'm going to get your medical case," I tell him. "So I can take your temperature."

"Don't mess it up," he says, his eyes closing again and I try not to smile because even when he's sick this man is anally retentive.

Still, when I grab his case and look for the thermometer, I take extra care not to move anything else. He's back asleep as I fit a sleeve onto the end and place it in his ear, pressing the button.

The display tells me he has a fever of one hundred and two.

I grab my phone and google fevers. According to the first page I come to, he's one degree short of needing to go to the ER. And really, one degree is nothing. He should be there now. Somebody should take care of him.

I look up from the screen to find him looking at me again.

"Are you really here?" he asks. He doesn't sound grateful. Just confused.

"Yeah." I nod, expecting him to ask me why I'm here. Or notice my uniform or something.

But he doesn't.

"How long have you had a fever?" I ask him.

"What day is it?" He frowns.

"Tuesday." Which is cleaning day this week. I don't remind him of that but all he has to do is look at my top and he'll know. But I won't leave him like this. If he asks me I'll confess everything. But right now I'm not sure if he'd hear it anyway. He's hardly coherent.

Still, if I end up losing my job so be it.

It's my fault anyway.

"A day I think. I was sick on Sunday." His voice slurs.

And then it dawns on me. "Sam," I say. "He had the flu. Do you think you could have caught it from him?"

A breath slowly escapes from his lips. "Intubation period is longer."

"You mean incubation," I say.

"That's what I said," he mumbles.

I google again and look up at him. "One to four days."

"I was feeling bad last week," he murmurs. "Thought it was a migraine." He trails off, his words disappearing into a long breath.

His eyes close again. There's a sheen of sweat on his face. And I know he's fallen asleep once more because he's not talking back to me. And anyway, he works in a hospital. He could have picked this up from anywhere.

I kneel and stare at him for a moment, then decide it's probably a good thing to let him sleep. While he does, I collect the water bottles and dirty glasses in his room, then pick up the clothes he must have stripped off before getting into bed, and throw them into the laundry basket with the rest of his dirty clothing.

He sleeps for another hour as I clean quietly. The kitchen, the hallway, the living room. I don't vacuum but I do everything else, and then I tackle the bathroom.

That's where I am when I hear him roll over in his bed.

"Hey," I say, running out. "Stay there, you're sick."

"I need the bathroom," he says, not quite meeting my eye.

Oh. "Sure." I nod. "I just cleaned it."

When he comes back his face looks as green as the grass. He stumbles back into bed. I grab a clean washcloth and dampen it with some cool water, then come back out and dab his face with it.

"That feels good," he murmurs.

"We need to get your temperature down," I tell him. "You're not far from me calling an ambulance."

"No ambulance," he tells me, and I'm immediately reminded of Sam. Except Holden can afford an ambulance and a hospital.

I'm guessing he just doesn't want to be the sick one. I can understand that. I hate it too.

"You want me to call somebody?" I ask him. "Your brother, maybe?"

"Jesus, no." His voice is hoarser still.

Well that was pretty emphatic. "I can't leave you here alone," I tell him. "If you get worse you're going to need to get to the ER."

He lifts a hand to his face. The same hand that took care of Sam. The same one that can lay a man out flat in the boxing ring. Except now it's trembling. "I'll be fine."

"Stupid stubborn man," I mutter, dabbing at his face again. He lets out a sigh as I do it, the same way our old dog used to when I was a kid and scratched behind his ears.

And that's when I realize I can't leave him. Not like this. Yes, the chances are he'll improve and be better by tomorrow or the next day, but what if he isn't?

I can't risk that.

There's only one thing for me to do. As he falls asleep once more I grab my phone and send half a dozen messages to Annie and the other students I'm supposed to be meeting with at school tomorrow to work on our final project.

But I'm not going anywhere. Holden Salinger needs me. And I'm weirdly okay with that.

———

HOLDEN

Every cell in my body hurts. My head throbs, my stomach grumbles, my muscles feel like I've just finished an Ironman triathlon. But it's my brain that's the most messed up. I drift in and out of sleep completely confused by whether it's day or night. And if it's day, *which day?*

What is a day?

Even worse, I keep dreaming of her. She's every damn where. So when my eyelids flutter open and I see pretty brown irises in front of me I'm almost certain I've died.

Not sure if I've gone to heaven or hell, though.

"Jesus." She puts her hand to her chest. "You scared me. I thought you'd stopped breathing."

"Blair?" I croak. It doesn't sound like my voice. But that's fine because this doesn't feel like my body either. *It feels like I've somehow transported into the body of an old man. Like in that movie... what's the movie?*

"*Big*," Blair says. "Or *Freaky Friday* if you're thinking about Lindsay Lohan."

I guess I said that out loud. *And I never think about Lindsay Lohan.*

"I do," Blair tells me. "I Googled her the other day. She's married to a banker, apparently. On the verge of a comeback."

I open my mouth to tell her I don't know who Lindsay Lohan even is, let alone why I should care. But all that comes out is a low groan because dammit somebody is drilling through my skull.

Blair scrambles up and reaches for something. It takes me a minute to realize she's holding out some pills.

I look at her and she looks at me.

"Just some painkillers I found in your cabinet. I'm not trying to kill you," she says. "Now open your mouth."

"That's my line."

She laughs softly, and even through the fog of my thoughts I like it too much.

"Shut up and open," she says, and I do as I'm told. She actually has to hold my head up as she puts a glass of water to my lips and I almost gag as I swallow down the painkillers.

"Not good with pills," I mutter.

She's smiling again. Damn she's pretty.

"You're hallucinating again," she says. Her cheeks are all pink and perfect.

"Again?"

"You've been talking gibberish for hours." She gently sets my head back down on the pillow and I turn to look at her.

"What time is it?"

She glances at her watch. "Four in the morning." She unstraps it from her wrist and puts it on the table next to the half-empty glass I've just drunk from.

"What are you doing here?" I ask. My ears are thumping. Is that the blood rushing through them?

"I came to clean your apartment," she says.

"That's very sweet," I murmur, my eyelids fluttering closed again. "But I have a cleaner."

———

My chest is hurting. Like somebody has put their hand in there and has a vice grip on my heart and lungs. I let out a groan, and feel a soft hand on my face.

"It's okay," she whispers. "You're okay."

I open my eyes and see Blair – or some kind of mirage that looks like Blair, staring into my eyes.

"Where did you come from?" I murmur.

"I've been here all along."

Of course she has. I like it. I like that I've somehow conjured her up with my fever. I like that I'm sick enough to feel her touching my face.

I fall back asleep, calmer now.

———

Hair tickles my bare arm. It's hard to open my eyes because they feel glued together.

"It's okay, go back to sleep. I was just checking your temperature."

Is that my mom? No. Sounds too young for my mom.

"It's Blair," she whispers. "Not your mom."

"Blair," I croak.

"Yes?"

But I can't say anything else, because sleep washes back over me like an ocean wave.

————

I'm not sure how much later it is when I wake up again. She's still there, sitting next to me. Not a mirage then.

I'm weirdly happy to see her. I just wish I could appreciate the fact that she's half naked on my bed, her bare legs splayed out in front of her.

She looks at the thermometer. So that's what woke me up. "It's come down a little," she says. "But not enough."

"Is that my t-shirt?" I ask, taking in the Salinger Bros slogan across the front.

Linc bought them for all of us as Christmas gifts last year. I'd thrown it at the bottom of my closet, because at some point I'll need to wear it to soothe his anal ass.

"Your brother is sweet," she tells me.

"He's a psychopath," I say hoarsely.

She exhales softly. "You should go back to sleep."

Her hand touches my brow. It's cool and I'm hot. There's something niggling at my mind but I can't grasp it. Like when I was a kid and I tried to catch fireflies. Enticing but just out of reach.

"Can you touch me again?" I ask.

"Sure. Where?"

"My head. My face."

So she does. And that's how I fall back asleep, with her soft hands soothing me. And I must be fucking feverish, because all I can think is how nice it is for the bed not to be empty for a change.

I enjoy having her here with me way too much.

CHAPTER
TWELVE

BLAIR

I try to stay awake so I can monitor Holden's temperature, but by five in the morning I'm fighting a losing battle. One minute I'm thinking about how I should probably go home once the sun comes up so I can change my clothes, the next minute I'm dreaming that I'm fighting with an angry customer who drags me into the ring at the club.

But instead of hitting me she throws flames at me. I'm confused because I don't know how she's making them – there's no sign of matches or a lighter in her hands.

But then Holden notices – how did he get there? – and he's throwing himself on me, using a soft voice to whisper in my ear that I feel so good.

It's only when my eyes fly open that I realize part of the dream is real. Holden is behind me, his body curved around mine, his arms around my waist. He's so hot I can barely stand it.

Did he really whisper in my ear?

I turn my head to look at him, but he's asleep, his eyelids fluttering, his lips slightly parted.

He's also naked. Sometime after I fell asleep he kicked the covers off. And his shorts, too.

And I can feel the long, thick length of him pressing into my behind.

"Don't go." He sounds like he's almost in pain. "Stay."

I have no idea who he's talking to in his sleep. But I twist in his arms and touch his face. "I'm here."

And now his dick is pressed into my stomach. And apparently I got hot, too, because the long t-shirt of Holden's that I borrowed is tangled around my waist revealing my panties.

Just one thin layer of silk fabric lays between me and the man I'm supposed to be nursing back to health.

Embarrassment washes over me. And so does desire. Which is wrong, so wrong, because he's sick and I shouldn't even be here.

Very slowly I scoot back, to put some space between him and me. Then I grab the sheet he's shucked off and gingerly pull it over him, but not before I get a glimpse of the part of him that's been pushing against all my neediest parts.

Dear God. I try to push the vision away, but it's still there behind my eyelids. Thick. Strong. Huge.

"Holden?" I whisper.

He slowly opens his eyes. They look sticky. "Blair?"

"Are you thirsty?" I ask him. It's too soon to give him more painkillers, even though he looks like death.

He nods and I sit up and grab the glass beside his bed, holding his head up so he can sip at it.

"What time is it?" he asks me.

"Just after six."

"Morning?" he croaks.

"Yep." I give him a half smile. But he's not looking in my eyes. He's looking at my stomach. Shit, I forgot to pull the t-shirt down.

"Sorry," I say, tugging at the fabric.

He's still staring. This time at my legs. And I let him, because let's face it, I just got an eyeful of his dick. It's only fair.

I take his temperature next. No change, but hopefully his fever will break soon.

"Do you think you're strong enough to take a shower?" I ask him.

He lifts his hand and then drops it again. "Soon."

"How about a bath?" I say.

"Not a cold one." He sounds almost scared.

"I wasn't going to make you take a cold one. Lukewarm, it'll be nice. And while you're doing that I can change your sheets. Put some fresh ones on."

"Lukewarm," he repeats. "Yeah, good."

And now I'm stupidly curious. "What made you think I'd run you a cold bath?"

"Mom used to make us take them when we were sick."

"Like cold-cold?" I ask. That sounds horrific.

He nods and I wrinkle my nose. "Ugh."

I leave him in the bedroom while I run the bath for him, adding some bubbles and laying out some soap, his towel, and a fresh bathrobe for him to get into. When I go back into the bedroom he's curled up again, the sheets sticking to him like saran wrap.

"Ready?" I ask.

"You need to turn around. I'm naked."

"I know." But I still do as he tells me.

He clears his throat. "What do you mean you know?"

"You've been naked for a while. Very naked."

There's a pause. Enough for me to turn to around to make sure he's all right. He's staring at me, an appalled expression on his face.

"Did I... do anything?"

"No!" I shake my head emphatically. "It's all good. I'll tell you what, stay there and I'll grab your robe, okay? Then I can help you to the bathroom."

He nods but still looks pained. "Just so you know, I'm hating every minute of this."

I give him the biggest smile. "That's good. Because I'm never going to let you forget it."

———

HOLDEN

Everything is still confusing. I think Blair is here but I'm not sure. Did she say something about going to the basement to get the laundry? Maybe. Or was that yesterday? And did I take a bath? I think I did, but right now I'm in my bed so maybe that was a dream.

Either way, when I hear a key in the lock a wave of relief washes over me. She came back. I try to push myself up to sitting in my bed that no longer smells of germs and sweat and fail miserably.

Christ, I hate being sick.

"Bro?"

As soon as I hear *that* voice I groan.

"Holden?" Linc yells. "You in here?"

"Yeah." My voice is too gruff and too small at the same time. "Now go away." Or turn into Blair. Whatever.

He either doesn't hear me or ignores me. Instead, he pushes the door to my bedroom open and looks inside.

"Jesus, what's wrong with you?" he asks.

Why the hell didn't I take the key back the last time he let himself in unannounced? If I could make a mental note to prise it from his grubby hands I would.

"I'm sick."

"Shit. You want me to do something?" He looks genuinely

panicked. And I'm completely regretful that I'm not well enough to enjoy it.

"I'm okay," I croak. "I just need sleep."

He tips his head to the side, eyeing me like I'm some kind of rabid dog he's not sure about. "You want me to call Mom?"

I have no idea if he's referring to his mom or mine. They were pretty much both of our moms for most of our lives. We have a weird family and despite them both divorcing our dad, our moms are the best of friends.

"No." I open my mouth to ask him what kind of grown man would want his mom when he was sick, but nothing comes out. I'm just so, so tired to the bone.

Like I could sleep for a year and still not feel awake. And I hate it. Hate being the sick one. Hate that Blair has to see me like this. Hate that I want her here with me anyway.

This morning I woke up with her in my bed and all I could think of was how soft her skin was and how good she smelled and how much I like seeing her in my t-shirt.

Fuck, I like it.

Maybe I'm not *that* sick.

"You're probably right," he says. "I think they're both on a cruise somewhere anyway." He pulls his phone out of his pocket and starts scrolling.

"Linc?" I say, my voice sounding groggier by the moment.

"Yeah?" He looks up.

"You going now?"

He blinks. "You want me to go?"

Like I want the sun to rise every day. I love my brother but he's... Linc.

"I just need to go to sleep," I say honestly. "You can go. I'll call you when I'm better."

He presses his lips together and for a moment he looks so much like Myles I want to laugh. Except he's carefree where Myles is careworn.

"Okay. You sure I can't order you some food? There's a great sushi place—"

"Linc!" My stomach turns at the thought of raw fish.

"Okay, okay. Feel better, dude." He slides his phone back into his pocket. "Call me if you need anything."

"I will." I won't.

And then he's gone and beautiful, peaceful silence descends. And for a minute I even stop wondering when Blair will be back.

———

BLAIR

I have my earbuds in and I'm listening to the lectures I've missed at double speed while I carry the clean basket of laundry out of the elevator. Two loads are packed in, all neatly folded, ready to go into Holden's dresser.

And then I really need to go home myself. Along with my laptop, Annie dropped off some clothes for me earlier so at least I don't stink, but she needs my help with Evan, too. I need—

Oof!

My body bounces off a thick wall of muscle, winding me instantly. I stagger back and two arms grab me.

And then I'm looking up into piercing blue eyes. Just not the ones I'm getting attached to.

And when I realize it's Holden's brother every part of my skin tingles. "Sorry," I say breathlessly, waiting for him to realize who I am.

"Cleaning lady, right?"

He doesn't remember my name. I don't know why I like that so much. No risk of him telling Holden who I am by name.

"That's right."

He smiles. "Gotta warn you, Holden's sick as a pig in there. Smells like one, too."

No he doesn't. He just bathed not to long ago. "I've already been in there."

"You have?" Linc looks almost disappointed. "I thought I was his savior."

The elevator pings and behind me I hear the doors slide shut. "I really should go in," I say, nodding my head at Holden's apartment door.

He gives me a beaming smile. "Oh hey, that Tux was perfect. Thank you for your help the other week."

"No problem." I shift my feet. "Well, bye, Linc."

"Hey, Blair."

So he does remember my name. "Yes?"

"If he gets any worse while you're here, can you call me? I feel kind of responsible for him."

"Sure."

He's still smiling. It's almost like Holden's but it's not. It takes me a second to work out why.

It's because his smile is easy. Constant. Holden's is rare and hard earned.

No guess needed on whose I like better.

BLAIR

Holden has kept his dinner down and it feels like a minor miracle. He's laying in his bed but he's more awake now than he has been. More talkative.

"What are you going to do once you get your masters?" he asks.

"Get a job," I tell him.

"You already have a job," he says.

He's talking about the bar. "A job where I don't have to watch grown men beat the shit out of each other."

He chuckles softly. It's weird how much I like that sound. "I thought you were getting to like it," he murmurs.

"The fighting? No." I'm not going to admit I kind of enjoy watching *him*. That the power in his muscles does things to me. "And anyway, I'm not staying in the city. We're moving out of the city."

"We?" There's a strange note to his voice.

"My sister and my nephew will go with me," I say. "We want to move somewhere more in the country. Where Evan can play in the yard and breathe easier."

"Evan's your nephew?"

I smile. "Yes."

"And he can't breathe here? Why not?"

"He has asthma. His doctor thinks it's exacerbated by all the fumes."

"There are fumes in the country," Holden says. His voice is even again. Low enough for me to feel it in my chest.

"And there are trees and grass and fresh air, too. And anyway, we'll get a lot more house for our money if we move."

He turns to look at me. Our heads are side by side. "You want the picket fence life?"

"I would kill for a picket fence," I admit.

His eyes flash for a minute. I can't read his expression at all. "I couldn't wait to get away from the picket fence and move to the big city."

"You haven't lived here all your life?" I ask.

"Nope. Brought up mostly in West Virginia. A bit all over the place. My family is complicated." There's a ghost of a smile on his lips when he talks about them. I like that.

"Complicated how?"

He coughs and winces. I turn to grab him some water but

he waves me away. "My father has a wandering eye. And hands. And dick. He's a serial husband."

"Like Rupert Murdoch."

He laughs and it turns into another cough and this time I panic. Somehow he gets himself under control, but there are tears in his eyes. "Yes," he says, nodding. "That's perfect. He's Rupert Murdoch. He keeps getting older and the wives keep getting younger. He's on his fourth, though we pretend she's his third because he doesn't like talking about the first."

"Four wives?" My eyes widen. "Is the man bankrupt yet?"

His gaze is soft as it meets mine. "Sadly not. He's rich as anything."

"You mentioned having two moms." I'm kind of fascinated now. And I stay fascinated as he explains his family to me. He's one of four brothers from his mom. Then there are two more from his stepmom – Lincoln and Brooks. And on top of that, they now have a little sister, Francine, whose sanity I worry for having six brothers like him.

"Wow. You weren't wrong about it being complicated. I bet Christmas is a blast."

"You don't want to know."

Actually I do, but I don't want to pry. "So is that what made you want to move here?"

"Some of it. I like peace. There's never any around my family. Not even at Misty Lakes."

"Misty Lakes?" I lift a brow.

"My dad's place. In the middle of nowhere. Just lakes and trees and a huge house. Plus some cabins."

"What kind of cabins?" I ask. I feel wistful, like I'm talking to the hero of a Hallmark movie.

"My brothers and I each have one. We got to build them when we were in our twenties."

"You have your own cabin?" I say, my voice lifting because I'm oh so jealous. "By a lake. With trees." I sigh at the thought of it.

"You make it sound better than it is."

No I don't. "I want a cabin."

"There's no picket fence," he teases. Yeah, he's feeling better.

"But there are trees and fresh air and you get to spend time with your family. How often do you go there?"

"Not as often as my family would like."

"The perils of being a doctor," I lament, and he lifts a brow in agreement. I turn so I'm fully on my side, my hand resting between my cheek and the pillow. He's turned, so our bodies are facing each other.

And for a moment neither of us speaks. He's looking at me. Not with the heat he had in his eyes when he was in the boxing ring and I was holding a tray of empty glasses. His gaze is softer. Warmer. Like a silk blanket wrapped around me.

It makes me breathless and achy. Wanting things I can't have.

He reaches out and slides his fingers over my jaw, my cheek, pushing my hair behind my ear. I breathe softly, unable to speak, because I like the way he touches me too much.

His hand turns, curls until he's cupping my face. Silence surrounds us. The kind of silence that sounds like blood rushing through your ears and desire melting in your stomach.

"Blair." His lashes sweep down as he blinks.

I don't think there's a question. But I nod anyway. His thumb traces the line of my bottom lip.

My stupid nipples go hard. My thighs clench.

And still we don't speak.

He must know how much he's affecting me, just with the touch of his hand. He traces the vein in my neck, then his fingers feather lower, until he's touching the dip in my throat right above another one of his t-shirts I'm wearing.

No, not a t-shirt. It's a tank. One of those ones you'd wear at the gym. It's hot laying in bed with Holden Salinger. It's the most I can do without being completely naked.

His hand traces the line of the neck. "So pretty in my clothes," he murmurs.

I inhale raggedly as his fingers dip beneath the fabric. His eyes catch mine. And I nod again because if he stops touching me I think I'll die.

The tips of his fingers brush the side of my bare breast. The fabric of his tank feels rough against my sensitive, peaked nipples. He moves his hand down further, cups my heavy breast.

I let out a sigh.

His eyes darken. Dip to where his hand is. Then he pushes one of the straps down until my breast is exposed to the air.

"Fuck." His voice is low. Raspy. His thumb brushes my nipple and I sigh louder. "You're beautiful."

My body is pulsing.

I'm so wet it isn't funny.

He leans his head toward mine, his gaze on my lips. I'm finding it stupidly impossible to breathe. I can't remember the last time somebody kissed me.

Can't remember the last time I *wanted* somebody to kiss me.

But I want this. Even though it's wrong and he's sick and I'm an idiot. I want this more than I want air.

Instead of pressing his lips against mine, he dips his head and captures my nipple in his mouth. Sucking, licking, scraping his teeth against me. The shock and the surprise and the sensation, *oh God* the sensation, makes my back arch as a cry escapes my lips.

My hand is in his hair. I'm tugging on the strands and he groans against my breast. The need between my legs is so thick it's making it difficult to think.

"Holden."

He looks up, his mouth still sucking me.

"Kiss me."

His lip quirks as he pulls away from my chest. And then he's brushing the hair away from my face. His mouth captures mine, and it's almost too much. He kisses like he fights. Hard and fast, then softer, teasing, making me lower my defenses. His hands hold my face, his fingers tangled in my hair, and then he rolls over me, sliding his leg between mine.

I slide myself against him to the rhythm of our kiss. He's hard against my stomach and I'm reminded just how thick he is. How much my body reacts to his.

How much I need him.

I reach down and trace the outline of him between us. He groans harder against my mouth. Then I'm holding him, moving my hand along him, and he's moving his leg between mine and I'm so close...

"Fuck." He pulls away, his eyes wide. "I'm sorry."

Cooler air breaks over my skin. My body's somewhere between the hope of ecstasy and the certainty of mortification. We stare at each other for a moment, and I hate the horrified look on his face.

"I'm the one who should be sorry. I shouldn't have done that," I whisper. "You're sick. It's all my fault."

He's probably having a hallucination. Thinks I'm somebody else. Can you get arrested for kissing someone with the flu?

"Are you worried you might catch my germs?" he asks.

I shake my head. "I've got a good immune system. And if I was going to catch the flu from you I'd have it already."

He runs his tongue along his bottom lip. "You don't need to be sorry." His smile is regretful and it hurts my heart. "I just... I can't give you what you need."

"What is it you think I need?" I'm genuinely confused.

"The white picket fence. I'm not..." He blows out a

mouthful of air. "I'm not that kind of guy." He glances down and I realize my breast is still exposed. I hurriedly pull the strap of my shirt up.

"I don't need a guy for the picket fence." I'm genuinely annoyed at the inference. "I can take care of myself."

He blinks again. "I know you can. I didn't mean that. I meant…"

"You meant that I'll think because we kissed that somehow we should get married and buy a house where I'll be barefoot and pregnant in the kitchen when you get home from work?"

His lips twitch. He can tell from my tone that I'm being sardonic.

For a second he says nothing. Just looks at me through those thick lashes. My body is calming down. Though I can still feel the sensation of his lips against my breast.

It's like he's burned himself into me.

I sigh and sit up. "I'm glad you're feeling better," I say, my voice low. "I can probably sleep in the guest room tonight."

"I meant to ask you how you knew I was sick," he says. "Did I call you?"

I exhale, because here's where I should come clean. But for the first time I'm scared.

I'm getting addicted to him. "I came to check on you."

"I'm glad you did," he whispers. "Thank you. But you don't need to stay." He looks at me carefully. Like he's afraid I might break.

I want to tell him I've faced worse things than rejection and kept it together. I'm not the breakable type.

"Can I get you another drink?" I ask him, all business like. "Something to eat?"

He swallows, and his Adam's apple dips. My eyes dip, too, to the hard planes of his chest.

This man is a mystery. Gentle and hard, soft and piercing.

"I'm good, thank you."

I nod and get up to leave.

"Blair?"

I turn to look at him. "Yes?"

He sits up without wincing. The man is definitely on the mend. "Thank you. For taking care of me."

I nod. "No problem. Now get some sleep."

CHAPTER
THIRTEEN

HOLDEN

When I get out of bed the next morning Blair is gone. There's a note from her in the kitchen telling me she has to get home and to call if there are any problems. And I already know I won't.

I'm an asshole. I hurt her. I was a few seconds away from moving down to taste her when common sense came crashing in.

And I'd like to blame it on being sick. Or being tired. Or being next to a beautiful woman wearing my clothes. But the truth is I wanted to touch her. I wanted to kiss her.

I wanted to feel her.

And that's the problem with me. I always want things I shouldn't.

I take a shower, feeling almost disappointed that she's not there when I emerge from the steamy bathroom with my towel wrapped around my waist. The whole apartment feels empty. Sterile. She's gone over the whole place with a fine toothcomb to make it look perfect.

I don't think I'm going to need the cleaning service this week.

When I've managed to eat a banana and drink some juice – and keep it down – I call Rose to check in on my patients.

She sighs as soon as she answers the phone.

"So you're feeling better?"

"Yes. I'll be back in work on Sunday." Truth is, if I didn't have what I'm almost certain is the flu, I'd be back at work now. But so many of the kids I work with are immunocompromised because of their treatment, and there's no way I can pass this damn virus to them. I'm lucky as hell none of them seem to have caught it before my symtoms got bad, but I still need to be super careful.

There's a silence. I think somebody's talking to her. Then I hear her breath again through the phone line.

"Mabel's had a bad night," she tells me.

Alarm prickles my skin. "What kind of bad night?"

"She was sick."

"Is it the flu?" Guilt pulls at my already weak stomach.

"I'm reading the notes now," Rose says. "No, not flu. They think it's a reaction to one of the drugs she's taking."

"Can you send me the details over? I'll take a look. We'll need to send her for some more tests."

"You're not on shift," Rose reminds me.

"I'm working from home," I counter, because if one of my patients needs me then I'm fucking going to be working.

She sighs. "Okay. But I'm going to run anything you say past the duty doctor."

"Who's on duty?"

"Nadia."

Good. I trained Nadia. She's good at what she does.

"Send it over as soon as you can," I tell her. "Now, how are the rest of them?"

I listen as she goes through each patient in turn. I make a few suggestions and she agrees. By the time she's finished my head is hurting again, but I ignore it. I'll take a couple of painkillers and work through it the way I usually do.

"So are you going to stop now?" Rose asks, once we've finished talking about my patients.

"Stop what?" I'm genuinely confused.

"The fighting. If it lays you out this low, you need to stop doing it," she says. "You're an idiot, but surely not that much of an idiot."

I open my mouth to correct her, but then I stop, deciding to let her assume the worst. "Just send me the details."

"I will." Her reply is short. And that's two people I've managed to piss off in less than twenty-four hours.

Rose will forgive me though. We fight and we make up. She's way too old and experienced to let her personal feelings interfere with our work.

Blair is another matter. And I feel like a complete asshole for saying those things to her. As I hang up with Rose I'm still thinking about the look in Blair's eyes when I told her I couldn't give her the picket fence.

She didn't look sad, that was the thing. She looked like she expected it.

I get the feeling that she's been let down a lot in life, and I don't want to be another person on that list.

This is why I should stay away from her.

And why I clearly won't.

———

BLAIR

"Don't forget you have that presentation for Evan's class this afternoon," Annie says a few days later, throwing me a banana as I rush into the kitchen.

"I've set an alarm on my phone," I tell her, even though

the last thing I want to do is talk about being in the Army in front of Evan's classmates. Yes, I'll be professional and explain the camaraderie, the travel, the feeling of doing something good.

And the way my time in the Army has paid for school.

But I'm a mess. And Annie knows it. She's been giving me a disapproving look for days.

"Are we going to talk about this some time?" she asks. I realize I've frozen again, caught up in my thoughts.

"Probably best not to." I shoot her a smile. "You don't want an insight into my world right now."

Her expressions softens. "Blair…"

"Please don't be nice to me. I prefer Angry Annie."

She exhales heavily. "I'm worried for you. You came home the other day a mess. You've been hiding in your room ever since."

"I've been working and trying to do my assignments."

"I know something happened," Annie says, refusing to be pushed away. This is what I love and hate about having a sister. We know each other so intimately it's impossible to hide away.

I know all her hopes and fears. I know her fierce love for Evan and her equally fierce hatred of his dad who walked away when she was pregnant and hasn't been heard from again.

And she knows me right back. I don't like that right now.

"Nothing happened," I say and she lifts a brow. I fold my arms across my chest. "Seriously, nothing happened, but it almost did and now I'm feeling all weird about it."

"For God's sake tell me," she says.

I glance at my watch.

"I have ten minutes, and you have twenty. If you talk while you eat we can do this."

My chest feels tight, the way it has ever since I walked out of Holden's house that morning. I haven't spoken to him since. He's tried calling, but I don't know what to say to him.

And if I'm honest I'm a little angry, too. I told him about my deepest dreams and he used them against me when I was at my most vulnerable.

Another reminder that I shouldn't ever expose myself in that way. Better to be closed up and safe.

It takes two minutes for me to give her the full run down of what happened at Holden's house. She's making Evan's lunch while we talk, because today is pizza day and Evan is the only kid in the continental US who doesn't like pizza.

When I finish she looks over at me, a knife still in her hand. She looks like a domestic serial killer.

"You're playing a dangerous game," she admonishes. "He's going to find out."

"I know." I nod. "Because I'm going to tell him."

"When?" She can't hide her look of surprise.

"On my last day working for him." I can't take the risk of telling him before then. I think I can trust him, but I also thought he wouldn't stop halfway through giving me the best sexual experience of my life.

"When will that be?" she asks.

"I'm already applying for jobs, so it shouldn't be much longer." I graduate this summer and the best library jobs are already being advertised. I've had to do a couple of first round online assessments. They're sought after but I have a good CV plus being a woman who was in the Army somehow makes me stand out.

I'll take every advantage I can get.

"As soon as I graduate and I have a job in a library I'll be done with cleaning and the club," I tell her. "And I'll explain everything to him." And then I'll leave and never see him again. The thought makes my heart do a weird clenching thing. It hurts.

She opens her mouth to respond but then Evan runs in,

wearing a pair of jeans that are too short for him along with a Captain America t-shirt we found at a thrift store.

"Looks like somebody needs to go clothes shopping," I say lightly. Annie catches my eye and I know what she's thinking. We can't afford it this month.

And that's why I won't be telling Holden Salinger anything about my jobs. I need them too much. A night's tips from The Black and White Club will pay for a new wardrobe for Evan.

And he's our priority. He always will be.

———

I have a tutorial this morning, in one of the meeting rooms at the back of the library. I say hi to the librarians behind the counter as I pass and one of them calls my name.

"Yeah?"

"Richards is on the warpath," she says. "I heard her saying your name."

Oh joy. Somebody else I've pissed off.

I'm trying to figure out what I've done wrong – *this time* – when I walk into the meeting room to find three of my fellow students there, along with Mallory Richards, the head librarian.

She looks nothing like you'd think a librarian should look. No glasses perched on the end of her nose, no hair in a bun. No dowdy but practical skirt suit.

She's all perfectly coiffed hair and designer pants, her makeup expertly done. A lot of her job involves meeting other people – faculty, publishers, donors. She's the public face of the library and I'd hate to have her job.

"So glad you could join us," she says as I take a seat at the end of the large table that dominates the room. She's at the other end and my fellow students are around the middle.

None of them will catch my eye.

"Sorry, I've been sick." That's the lie I told when I missed all my classes earlier this week because I was looking after Holden.

"I'm so glad you've made a miraculous recovery." Her smile is sardonic. I shift in my seat.

I've never been good with authority. Which is kind of ironic given the jobs I've done, but it's true. But I'm also a realist. I need to graduate and I also don't want to annoy one of the most influential university librarians in the US.

So I say nothing. I just nod, and try to ignore the stares of all the other students as I look at Mallory.

"You missed your turn at taking the children around the library," she says.

Shit. That was *this* week? We all have to sign up for three tours per term. Part of our academic outreach. I squeeze my eyes shut. "I'm sorry."

"That's not good enough," she says. "It was hugely embarrassing. One of their father's is a donor."

I'm so embarrassed. How could I have got that so wrong?

"I talked to your tutors," she says. "And they've noticed a downturn in your assignments as of recently, too."

From the corner of my eye I see one of the other students lift a brow. This kind of conversation shouldn't be taking place in front of them. Sure, ream me out but don't start talking about my work like this.

But I can't say anything. It's like an enormous weight is pressing down on me.

"I'm sorry," I say again.

"You're almost at the end of your degree," she says, and then she looks around. "This applies to all of you. There's no slacking off because there isn't long left. You need to be working harder. You're not colleagues anymore, you're competing against each other for jobs. And when I'm called by a library and asked for my opinion, I *will* give it. And honestly."

"There's another group coming today," Mallory says, her attention turned back to me. "Be there please."

I nod and then we thankfully get back to the tutorial. At least I'm prepared for this one. I even see a ghost of a smile on her lips as I talk through the presentation I've made.

And when it's over, I take a deep breath and walk to the information desk to find out the details of today's tour. I need to do that and then get to Evan's school before coming back here to finish my assignment that's due this evening.

I feel exhausted just thinking about it. So instead I try to concentrate on the light at the end of the tunnel.

———

It's almost nine by the time I put my assignment through the plagiarism checker and hit send to submit it. Every part of me feels exhausted. The tour with the kids overran, which made me late for Evan's class, and though his teacher was really kind about it, I could tell by the look on Evan's face that he was upset. I barely had time to talk to him, though, because I had to rush back here.

I head out of the library and into the evening air. I stop at the top of the steps, taking a deep breath before exhaling raggedly. I can't push the image of Evan's disappointed face out of my mind.

The kid asks for nothing. He didn't even ask me to present to his class. I volunteered, well *kind of*. I hate that he's learning disappointment at an early age. I hate even more that it's me who's teaching him it.

My eyes sting because I'm so tired of constantly trying to fight the tide. But that's what you do, isn't it?

Keep fighting until the fight is done.

"Blair?"

Holden is standing at the bottom of the steps. I look at him through my hazy vision, trying to work out what he's doing here.

Maybe I'm asleep. Maybe my subconscious decided it was time to make me feel even worse and throw the man I can't have into the forefront of my dream.

Thanks, me.

"What are you doing here?" I ask him. My voice sounds more tremulous than I intended. If he's here to tell me I'm an idiot I need him to go. I can't deal with anything else today.

But of course he doesn't. Instead he walks slowly up the steps. He's wearing a gray Henley and a pair of soft, faded jeans. His hair is mussed and it looks like he hasn't shaved since he got sick.

I weirdly like the scruff. It makes him look dark and dangerous.

"Are you okay?" His eyes are wary.

Those tears that have been threatening all day spill over. And I'm mortified. I don't cry. And I certainly don't cry on the library steps in front of the man who thinks I'm a walking advertisement for a picket fence.

"Never ask a woman on the edge if she's okay," I say, wiping away the tears. They keep on flowing though.

"Maybe you need somebody to ask you," he says. "Maybe more people should ask you. Let somebody else be the strong one for a change."

That makes the stupid tears roll harder. They blur my vision until he's an impressionist painting. I'm unable to see him close the gap between us, but I feel his arms lock around me, his thick muscles pressing against my arms. And I almost collapse into them.

"What are you doing here?" I ask him.

"I wanted to see you. Check your phone, there are a dozen missed calls."

"How did you know I'd be at the library?" I ask him.

"I didn't," he says, stroking my hair. "I just took a good guess."

I narrow my eyes. "How do you even know where the library is?"

Holden smirks. "I googled it."

He tangles his fingers in my hair, lifts my face until my eyes catch his.

"Blair…"

Soft lips touch mine. Our mouths part and I can taste the saline of my tears as he kisses me. My fingers tangle in his messed up hair, messing it up some more, and he holds me so tight, so close, that even though I'm feeling dizzy I know I am completely safe.

It's the sweetest, gentlest kiss. Not the needy ones we exchanged in his bed. It tastes of hope, something I've long since forgotten.

"You're an asshole," he says when we part.

My brows lift. I'm used to being the swearer. "You're the asshole."

He gives me the sweetest smile.

"Wait," I say. "Why am I an asshole? I nursed you back to health."

"Because you can give but you can't receive."

"What do you mean?" I wrinkle my nose and stare up at him. His gaze is so tender it makes my chest hurt.

"I mean you should let people help you. The same way you help other people."

"By people I suppose you mean you," I mutter and he smiles again. "You're looking better by the way."

"Thanks." He wipes a tear away from my cheek. "I had a good nurse."

"Are you back at work?" I ask him and he shakes his head.

"Not allowed until next week. Infection protocol."

It's my turn to smile. "I bet you're hating that."

"Completely." He nods. "But since I have time on my hands, why don't you tell me why you're crying."

"It's boring," I whisper. "You don't want to know."

"Actually I do."

"Okay, so maybe I don't want to talk about it."

His hands are rubbing my back, sending tingles down my spine. I may let out a little moan.

And he may look at me with those dark, narrowed eyes.

"So what *do* you want to do?" he asks. And when I answer, he takes my hand and practically drags me down the steps.

CHAPTER
FOURTEEN

BLAIR

Holden drives me back to his place, and every time we stop at a red light we end up kissing like hormonal teenagers who can't get enough of each other. He doesn't touch me anywhere but my face and back, yet I'm already on fire.

Somehow, he manages to get us safely back to the parking lot beneath his apartment without a fender bender, and we make it up to his apartment without dragging each others' clothes off on the elevator. But when the door closes behind me he leads me straight to his bedroom, which is exactly where I want to be.

He gives me that Holden half smile and pulls me to the bed and kisses me passionately.

I already know this is a mistake but I can't stop it. I don't want to stop it.

So much so that I practically pull the buttons off his shirt in my desperation to take it off.

The next to go is my jeans. We take turns tugging them

down my legs, and when they get caught around my ankles I start to laugh hysterically.

Am I losing it? I'm not sure. But I don't want to fall over and break my neck minutes before I finally get to feel this man inside of me. Luckily he hunkers down and untangles the denim, looking inordinately proud of himself.

"Come here," he whispers as he sits down on the bed, gloriously shirtless. I step toward him and he pulls me onto his lap. Then his lips claim mine and all I want to do is ride him like a bronco.

And yes, it's a mistake, not because it's bad but because it's good. Too good. Somewhere in my mind I've already told myself this is a one time thing.

A chance for us to scratch this itch we both have.

He tugs my t-shirt off and kisses the swell of my breast before moving his mouth lower, capturing my nipple through the fabric of my sports bra, moistening it, tugging me in. I arch my back and he pushes the bra down, until it's a truss, pushing my tits up. He groans and goes in for them again and I have to tip my head back to stop myself from calling out his name.

"I thought you didn't want this," I say breathlessly, as he scrapes his teeth against my sensitive flesh. "Because of the picket fence."

"I'll fuck you against the picket fence," he growls and somehow that image makes me feel even needier.

Holden Salinger fucking me against anything makes me needy. So I push him down until he's on his back and kiss his scruffy jaw, his neck, then flick my tongue against his nipples until he groans as loudly as I did.

And the whole time I can feel the hard ridge of him against me. I slither down, kissing the hard planes of his stomach. Seriously, I've never known anybody as hard as this man in every single way. He makes my stomach twist and my thighs tighten.

And my heart do a little dance.

When I reach the waistband of his jeans, I flick the button open and pull down the zipper. The outline of him against his gray shorts is impossible to ignore. I touch it in wonder and he groans again.

"Are you sure you're okay?" I whisper. "Are you still sick?"

He wraps his hand around my wrist in a vice grip and pushes my palm against him. "Do I feel like I'm sick?"

I look up and smile at him. "You're the one talking about fucking me against a picket fence."

His dick twitches against my palm. "Shut up and touch me."

So I do, with a smile on my lips, sliding my hand inside his shorts and curling my fingers around him. He lets out a strangled moan as I slowly move my palm up and down, giving him a taste of what I want.

What I need.

And then I tug down his boxers and wrap my lips around him.

"Fuck...Blair..." His fingers tangle in my hair as I snake my tongue over the plush head of him, before taking him into my mouth. He tastes of soap and man.

I pull my mouth up, swirling my tongue around him like he's my favorite lollipop. He grabs my hair and jerks my head up, until I'm staring at him.

"Take the rest of your clothes off," he tells me.

I might hate authority but I'm pretty good with commands. I shimmy off the bed and pull my bra off, then wriggle out of my panties until I'm bare in front of him.

"Christ." His voice is hoarse. "Get over here now."

His cock is jutting up as I climb on top of him. Instead of letting me grind against him he pulls me up further. It's only when I'm over his face that I realize what he's going to do.

He kisses me *there*. Just the softest of touches. But the

rumble in his throat is completely dirty. His fingers curl around my hip and I'm reminded of the strength of this man. But also of his gentleness.

It's a conundrum that I can't fathom. Maybe I don't want to, because he's licking me with long strokes that make me clench hard. I rock against his face and I feel that rumble of approval again. Even in my needy haze I worry that I'm too heavy on his face, but his hands pull me closer, as though he doesn't mind me smothering him.

Or breaking his nose.

"Relax," he whispers. I look down to see his eyes catching mine. They're dark again. Needy. "Let me make you feel good."

So I do. I let him lick me and suck me. And push two fingers in me. I have to lean forward and grab the rail of his bed to try to keep myself steady. He encourages my movement, his fingers sliding to my behind as I gyrate against him, the pleasure coiling, hissing. Exploding.

White heat flashes in front of my mind. I call out his name as I come and he grunts again. His hands grip me as I convulse, keeping me steady.

Keeping me safe.

Eventually I collapse, sliding down his body, feeling the hot steel of his cock against the cheeks of my behind. Holden looks at me, his face glistening from my arousal, lust making his gaze hazy.

I slide against him again. I'm so wet it isn't funny. He groans and rocks his own hips, kissing my neck, my breasts, my nipples.

"I need you inside of me," I whisper.

He gives me a smile that makes my heart do weird things. "Need that too," he murmurs. "Let me get something." He leans over to pull his top drawer open and then frowns. I'm about to tell him it's the bottom drawer he wants when he opens it himself and grabs an unopened box of condoms.

He rolls it on with his deft doctors hands and then he's holding me again, lifting me over him. His biceps flex, and I look at his tattoo, the snake curling around the stick. Thick desire washes through me, making me so tight that it's almost impossible for him to slide into me.

"Relax," he whispers again. He slides his hand around, circling me, and my body does as he commands, and then he's filling me completely and utterly.

Our eyes meet as I move back up again, creating a slow rhythm that feels so sweet I'm not sure how much longer I can last. He sits up to kiss me, his lips slow, his tongue long and teasing, and then he's sucking at my nipples again, sending a shockwave of pleasure to my core.

He's not fierce. Not hard and fast and violent. Instead his hands are all over me, like he wants to feel every inch. His lips worship my breasts as I rock, my own fingers tangled in his hair.

The pleasure is almost too much. My movements slow, stutter, and it's like he can read my mind because he lifts me once more, lays me onto my back, and then he's on top of me. No, inside of me, my thighs wrapped around his waist, his hands beneath my ass so he can angle me just right.

This time I kiss him. My breath is short against his lips and I feel him smile. I can feel his sweat, too.

"Holden…"

"It's okay," he whispers. "Let go."

And it's stupid because I don't need his permission. But it does something to me anyway. It makes my skin tingle and my stomach tighten and then I'm standing on the edge, teetering, tottering, feeling him slide against me in the most delicious way.

And then I fall, calling out his name, my nails digging into his muscled ass, his lips capturing mine as they mute my cries.

"Blair." He grunts loudly, then stills, surging inside of me, his cock pumping, his lips moving, his own hands sliding up to cup my face. "Jesus."

For a long moment our hands continue to explore as we both catch our breath. My head spins like I've been on a whirligig.

"I told you I'd make you see heaven," I tell him when I can finally talk. He laughs and I feel him move inside of me. Leaning down, he kisses me again, then withdraws, rolling onto his side and jumping onto the carpeted floor before going into the bathroom to do what he needs to do.

I grab my panties and bra, shimmying them back on a lot less elegantly than I took them off, then I pull my t-shirt over my head before stopping to take a breath.

When Holden comes out, a towel wrapped around his waist, he frowns at my semi dressed state. "What's going on?"

"I need to go." I smile at him, because I want him to know I don't regret this. "Thank you. You don't know how much I needed that."

I didn't know either, until it happened.

His eyes drop to my still bare thighs and back up again. "At least let me get you a bottle of water."

"It's okay, I'll grab one at home." I pull on my jeans and stand, rolling to my toes to press my lips to his. "Thank you."

He shakes his head, confused. "I should be thanking you."

"We can thank each other." I think my shoes are somewhere by the front door, so I don't delay my exit from his room any longer. "I'll see you around, okay?" I stop and tip my head. "Are you feeling okay now?"

"I'd say I'm a lot more than okay," he says gruffly.

"I mean after being sick."

His face softens. "I'm fine. Blair, I…"

There's a weird pull at my gut. I like the way he's looking at me. But I shouldn't.

It's been a horrible day and this has been the one good

thing in it. I'm not going to let myself regret it, and I don't want him to either.

"It's okay," I say, smiling at him again. "We promised no picket fences. We don't need to dissect what just happened or have a heart to heart talk. It was good."

"Good?" he asks archly and I try not to smile at his macho hurt.

"Great. Amazing. Thank you." My cheeks are starting to hurt with how hard I'm smiling. "Now I need to go."

I go to turn and he wraps his hand around my waist. "You're not catching the subway after I came inside of you."

"I was going to take the bus actually."

He doesn't let go of me. "I'll drive you."

I roll my eyes. "Isn't that a little too picket fence?"

Holden lifts a brow. "You know, I really am going to fuck you against that fucking picket fence sometime?"

"It'll have to be a high picket fence," I say lightly, but there's a weird warmth in me because his words tell me this isn't a one time thing.

I ignore it, because I'm an expert at guarding my heart.

"I'll get one custom made," he says, not looking amused at all. "Now stay right there while I get some damn clothes on."

I touch my fingertips to my temple. "Yes sir."

———

HOLDEN

"You know you don't have to do this," Blair says as we pull out of the underground parking. "It's going to take you forever to get back home and my bus stop is just over there."

"Shut up about the bus." I'm feeling grouchy. And I'm

also feeling grouchy about feeling grouchy. I just had sex, I should be feeling good.

And when I think about the sex I do feel good. Fucking amazing, in case you wanted to know. Being inside of her was better than I'd ever imagined. Kissing her as she came around me was like fucking heaven.

She wasn't wrong about that.

I take a right and let out a mouthful of air. "You could have stayed at my place. I wasn't going to throw you out."

There's still a smile playing at her lips. It's been there since she came the second time. If only I'd known how simple it was to make her soften.

Just a couple of orgasms and wham, she's relaxed. I wish I fucking was.

"You know sex is meant to make you feel better," Blair says, as though she's reading my mind. "Not worse."

"I don't feel worse." We come to a stop light. She's right, driving her home and back again is going to take all night. For some reason I don't seem to mind.

"You're grumpy as hell," she says. "You've barely said two words since you walked out of the bathroom."

"What is it you want me to say?" I ask, genuinely confused.

"I don't know. You could remind me that you don't do picket fences."

"It's very clear you got the message on that," I grumble. "But yeah, thanks."

She twists in her seat to look at me. The light is still red. "Have I annoyed you?" she asks. For the first time she's not smiling.

I swallow because we just had sex and I'm making her feel bad. The whole point of it was to make her feel good. "I'm not annoyed," I say, letting out a long breath. "I'm just..."

There's a moment of silence as I try to work out exactly

how I am feeling. But I can't. My emotional vocabulary needs some work.

A lot of work.

"You're just what?" she prompts softly.

"I just want to be your friend." It's weird how true that feels. I don't want to upset her or piss her off. I want to make her feel good. I want to see her smiles. But I can't figure out what that means.

She reaches for my hand and squeezes it. "We *are* friends."

I look at her and she looks back at me and it feels like my ribcage is too big for my skin.

"It's not unusual, you know, for men to get stupidly emotional after sex," she says. "Think of it as hormones. But semen related."

"Semen related," I repeat, shaking my head. "Semen doesn't contain hormones."

"No, but when you put it in someone else you must get a dopamine hit. And that does weird things to your emotions."

"I'm not emotional. I just want to make sure we're okay."

At last the light turns green. I take the left and head toward the bridge. Blair leans forward to turn my stereo on. Puccini blasts out and she looks at me askance.

"You listen to classical music?" she asks, her voice lifting up.

"Sometimes." I nod.

She looks away and I can't see her expression from the corner of my eye.

"What?" I ask. I don't like that I can't read her mood.

Blair turns to look at me again. I let out a low breath. "I just pictured you as more of a rock kind of guy. Not a sweet music one."

My lips twitch. "Tosca isn't sweet."

"This is an opera?" she asks, just as a low voice blasts through the speakers.

I turn the volume down because I want to hear her. "Part of it."

Her head tips. "I've never seen an opera. What's this one about?"

"It's a love triangle. Set in Rome in the early nineteenth century." I can feel the heat of her gaze on my face. "Everybody ends up dead."

Her mouth drops open. "What?"

"Seriously. He's a painter and she's a singer and the chief of police arrests him and tells her he'll release her boyfriend if she sleeps with him. She agrees but kills him instead. And she has a plan to save her boyfriend, but he gets shot so she kills herself."

"That's the most miserable thing I've ever heard." Blair sounds appalled. "No wonder you listen to it."

That makes me smile. "I just like the music."

"You're one of those then," she says. It's weird how much more talkative she is when we're not face to face.

"One of what?"

"Someone who doesn't listen to the lyrics, just the song," she states.

"Doesn't everybody do that?" I ask her.

"No. You're missing out if you don't listen to the lyrics. They tell a story. They're part of it. Take a left here."

"What?" Her sudden change in conversation jolts me.

"Left here," she says. "Ignore the GPS, my way's quicker."

I lift a brow and do as she says. "If I want to hear a story I'll get an audiobook."

Blair grins. "I forgot you don't read."

"I read. But I spend days reading test results and reports. I just prefer to rest my eyes on my days off."

"But not your fists."

"If I rested my fists we wouldn't have met," I say lightly. She doesn't respond. When I get a chance to glance at her she's staring out of the windshield, a faraway look on her face.

"Blair?"

"Uh, yeah?"

"Where do I go now?"

"To hell?" she asks, then laughs. "I mean, right here. You can drop me off at the end of the road. I can run down the alleyway to my building."

"You're not running down a damn alleyway." I wait for her to give me some more instructions and it's only a couple of minutes before I'm pulling up outside of her apartment. It's run down but not too badly. There are flowers in boxes outside of some windows.

"Thank you," she says, leaning across to kiss my cheek. I turn my head and capture her mouth with mine.

She lets out a little sigh and kisses me back, and for a minute I'm caught up in her mouth.

"I should go," she says breathlessly when she pulls away. "Before you get a ticket."

I don't give a damn about getting a ticket, but she's right. I climb out and walk her to the door despite her protestations, because my mom didn't bring up an asshole for a son.

"I'd invite you in but..." she trails off.

"It's okay. I need to get back."

"Thank you for coming to find me earlier." Her eyes are soft. And I want to kiss her again. I want to pull her back into my car and take her home. My bed is going to feel empty without her.

Like it has since she left the morning after she'd nursed me better.

"Mabel's been asking about you," I say. "Apparently she's finished the book. Says she loved it."

Blair's eyes soften. "How is she doing?"

"Had a few problems. Nothing major but everybody lost a few night's sleep."

She leans against the front door. "I bet you hate not being there."

I nod. "You could say that."

"At least you can go back next week." She shuffles her feet. "Do you think I can come in and see Mabel again?"

My mouth feels dry. "Yeah." My voice is a little raspy. "She'd love that."

Blair lifts her hand and presses it to my jaw. Cupping it. "You're a good man, Holden Salinger. You know that?"

No I don't. All I know is that standing beneath the porch light, her hair tumbling down her shoulders, her cheeks pink from the cooler night air, that she's the most beautiful thing I've ever seen.

"Good night, Blair."

"'Night, Holden."

CHAPTER
FIFTEEN

BLAIR

There's a woman's hair on Holden's bed. I've stripped the coverlet and the pillowcases and all I need to do is take off the sheet and carry it down to the laundry before I put fresh ones on. But instead of doing that I'm staring at the single long dark brown strand that's staring up at me accusingly.

Okay, it doesn't have eyes. But if it did it would be pissed with me.

The way I'm pissed with myself, because that's my hair on his sheets. My hair I'm cleaning up. And it feels weird. And wrong.

It was one thing keeping this hidden from him when he was just some guy at the club. Another now that I've been intimate with him. When I care about him.

And isn't that the stupid thing? He made it clear it's about picket fences. I even think he felt bad about it because he got all emo in the car on the way home. But he's scrupulously honest. I know that at least.

But my heart doesn't seem to get the message.

I pick the hair up and put it in the trash bag in the hallway, then finish stripping his bed before carrying the laundry down to the basement. I was surprised when I first started working here that there wasn't a washer in his apartment, but apparently it's some kind of rule. Nobody likes hearing a tumble dryer dancing along the ceiling above them I guess. Not in this part of Manhattan.

His apartment is a classic six. When it was originally built people had live-in maids, so it's comprised of a kitchen, a parlour, a dining room, two bedrooms, and a maid's room. It's been reconfigured since then, so the maid's room forms part of the kitchen and the original bathroom has become one of those jack-and-jill bathrooms, but it still has so much character to it.

Much like the owner.

I've finished cleaning the rest of his apartment before the laundry is finished. Way before. This is where I'd usually pull out my laptop and get some work done in the peace and quiet, but now that I know him I can't.

I'm stuck.

I think about baking him a cake, but he doesn't have the ingredients, and anyway, what the hell would he think if I did? My weird ass cleaner is trying to poison me?

No, I need to wallow in this mess of my own making.

When the laundry is done I bring it upstairs to fold it, sliding the clean linens and clothes into his closet, then putting his shorts and socks into the drawers beside his bed.

And I find the condom box. One condom missing. A few months ago, I'd have found this hilarious. Might have gossiped about it with Annie. The rich handsome doctor is getting some, although not a lot. Only one condom missing.

Hah.

I'm going to have to stop doing this. I should tell him. Maybe it would be okay.

And maybe you'll lose your friend and your job.

My phone starts to ring. I almost jump to the ceiling when I see Holden's name on the screen. I snatch it up, as though if I don't answer he'll start tracking me or figure out the truth.

"Hello?"

"Hey. You okay?" There's a frown to his voice.

Did I just snap at him? I take a breath. "I'm good. How are you?"

"Busy. Trying to make up for lost time at work. Listen, I was wondering if you're free to see Mabel some time this week like we talked about. She keeps asking me about you."

I laugh softly. "I'm free later today if that works? Around six?"

"That would be perfect," he says. "Thank you."

"Any time."

It's true. I'd pretty much do anything for him. Apart from give up on my picket fence.

"If I don't see you when you get here it's because I'm trying to mortally wound an insurance company," he says. "But hopefully I will."

There's a voice echoing. Then I hear the low rumble of his reply. "I gotta go. Blair?"

"Yes?" I respond, because I don't want to say goodbye and get back to my thoughts.

"Thank you." His voice is soft. It does things to me.

"Anytime, Holden." Because I'm going to make this up to him. All of it.

I just need to figure out how.

HOLDEN

It takes me half an hour to finish a meeting I didn't even want to have. With a drug rep who was way too pushy with Carter over the phone so he caved and arranged for her to come in to talk to us.

I don't blame him. Keeping drug company reps at bay is a learned skill, just like not taking no for an answer from insurance companies. I let him take the brunt of the meeting, just coming in at the end, and now he's going to have to work late to finish up his charting.

He'll learn, the same way I learned. And that's okay.

"You're in a good mood," Rose says as I emerge from the meeting room. "I don't like it."

"I'm just feeling better. Did I miss anything urgent?"

She shakes her head. "Everyone's quiet right now. Dinner was good."

It's amazing how a patient's day can rise and fall on what food they have to eat. Hospital food has a bad reputation for a reason. "Was it pasta?"

"Yep. As I said, a good day."

I nod and look over at the door at the end of the hallway.

"She's there," Rose says, as though she can read my mind.

"Who?" I ask, because yes, she's my right arm, but I'm not letting her think she can get the best of me.

"The pretty one. Blair. I scraped up a dinner for her, too."

"How long has she been here?" I ask, checking my watch. It's almost seven.

"Since six. Mabel's being demanding." Rose lifted a brow. After last week we both know she deserves a little attention.

"I'll tell her she can leave."

"You do that." Rose eyes me carefully. "She'd be a lot better for you than fighting, you know?"

"And I'd be much worse for her." I walk down the corridor, annoyed at how truthful those words are. And how even though I know the truth of them, I'm going to ignore them.

As soon as I open the door and see Blair's profile against the window my stomach tightens. The woman is beautiful. She reminds me of an Amazon. Strong, unbreakable.

Maybe that's why I lower my guard when she's around. I'm not afraid of breaking her.

"Dr. Salinger." Mabel's face lights up. Blair turns to look at me and when our eyes connect my body responds viscerally. Like somebody is actually kicking me in the stomach.

"Mabel." I glance at the book in her hand. *Catcher in the Rye*. "Aren't you bored of that one yet?"

"I've read it twice," she says. "And now that we've talked about it I'm going to read it a third time."

I can feel Blair's eyes on me. I like it.

"It was hard enough reading it once," I say. "I hate sharing my name with an asshole."

"Only your first name. Although, you share the second with the author," Mabel says, then she frowns. "Wait, did you say you've read it?"

"Yeah." I walk into her room and grab a plastic chair by the door. I'm supposed to be taking my dinner break but what the hell.

"Liar." Mabel rolls her eyes at me and Blair laughs softly.

"I did," I protest. "And I'm not wrong. Give me one redeeming quality about this kid."

Mabel tips her head to the side, her eyes narrowing. "He's just confused, that's all."

"He's a privileged jerk," I say.

Blair tries to stifle another laugh. I look at her and her eyes are so soft they feel like gossamer around my chest.

"What?" I ask, trying—and failing—not to smile.

"Nothing." She shakes her head, her own smile playing on her lips.

"Come on, you have something to say, say it." Weird how warm my blood feels.

"I just thought it was funny you saying he was privileged. Where was it you went to school again?"

"Virginia." I know where she's going with this. And I'm going to let her because I like hearing her voice.

"And was it a public school?"

I shake my head, still amused.

"And how did you fund your way through school?" she asks. "Did you get scholarships?"

"You know I didn't." I don't care that she's having a dig. It's so gentle it barely counts. And I like that she knows things about me. That she remembers them.

"Did you ever play hookey and come to New York to hang out in a hotel?" Mabel asks.

"Sadly not," I tell her.

She looks almost disappointed.

And then she looks at me once more, her brows knitting. "You're not him," she says. "You're the other one."

"What?" I frown and look over at Blair who shrugs. "I don't know what you mean," I tell Mabel.

"You're what he'd like to be. You're the catcher in the rye. You catch children who are going over the edge. You save them."

A strange shiver snakes down my spine. It makes my whole body turn cold. I swallow hard and can't look at her. Can't look at Blair either.

"No, I'm not him either." My heart is racing. Like I've just come out of the ring except there are no endorphins, no sense of freedom.

No sense of peace.

Just an itch that seems to cover every inch of my skin.

"I have to go," I say, taking an exaggerated look at my watch as I stand. "Mabel, you need to let Blair go, too. I'm sure she has things to do."

I'm all too aware that my voice is too terse. And I don't know how to turn that off. All I know is that I have to get out of here. I put the chair back where I found it, and glance over my shoulder.

Mabel is staring at me, looking confused.

Blair isn't looking at me at all.

Like the asshole I know I am, I walk straight out without saying goodbye to her. Even though I know I'm going to regret it later.

———

BLAIR

As soon as he walks out of the room Mabel looks at me, confused. "Did I say something wrong?" she asks. I can tell she's upset.

"No," I tell her. "You did nothing wrong. What you said was really sweet."

She wrinkles her nose. "In that case it's very wrong. I hate being sweet."

I catch her eye and smile at her. "Every teenager hates being sweet."

"You're not sweet, are you?" she asks me.

"I don't think I am, no," I say honestly. "Any sweetness potential was knocked out of me at a young age."

"Ditto," she says. Holden has given me a brief history of her time in the hospital. So I know it hasn't been easy. And Mabel has filled in all the blanks.

She comes from a broken home. Her dad left her mom for a woman he worked with. They've since had two kids and Mabel's mom is bitter. My heart aches for her.

Mabel glances down at her book. "Do you think Dr. Salinger's parents named him after the book?"

"Even if they didn't mean to do it deliberately, then subconsciously, yeah I think they probably did. It's too much of a coincidence."

"I wish he liked the book." Mabel sighs, putting it on the table that lays across her bed. "I like it."

"I do too. And I suspect he does. But he's right about

Holden Caulfield, isn't he?" I ask her. "He is a bit of a jerk." And I'm thinking that the other Holden is, too. But I'll deal with that later.

"Yeah. But he had a bad time. His family doesn't notice him, he hates school. Sometimes it feels like you're never going to fit in anywhere." Mabel sighs and I feel for her. I can't imagine what it's like to spend your teenage years in and out of the hospital. She has such a keen mind, it must be hell being alone so much. Especially with her family problems.

I know those all too well.

"Can I tell you a secret?" I ask her.

She nods.

"That feeling never really goes away. You just get used to it. Like it, even. Not fitting in is horrible at your age but at my age..." I smile at her. "It's like a gift."

"It is?" She frowns.

"It is. I promise. You'll see when you're older and all your friends are settled down with two kids and a mortgage and you're still studying while trying to make ends meet."

She gives a mock shudder. "I never want kids." Then she looks at me carefully. "Do you?"

"I love my nephew. And I guess if the time was right and the right man came along, maybe. But right now I need to graduate and get a job." I lean forward. "About a decade after everybody else."

"Well I think you're cool," she tells me.

"Right back at you, Mabel." I stand. "But Holden was right, I need to go."

"Will you come again soon?" she asks me, looking hopeful.

"Next week. I promise. You want to read something else this week?"

She grabs the book again. "I think I'll re-read this one."

"Okay then. But next week I'll bring something different."

Mostly because there's only so long it's healthy to read *The Catcher in the Rye* before you become depressed and nihilistic.

"It's a deal."

There's no sign of Holden when I walk into the corridor, even though I half-expected him to be skulking out there. Not that he has time to skulk. The man looks permanently over-worked and harassed, especially since he was sick last week.

But I should stop feeling sorry for him. He was an asshole to Mabel.

The head nurse is at the desk when I sign out. "Thank you for coming," she tells me. "Mabel really loves you visiting her."

"I love coming to see her too."

She looks at me like she wants to say something else, but then the phone rings and she sighs. "Have a good evening, Miss Walsh."

"It's Blair. And thanks."

I head out of the ward and toward the elevator. The doors open and I go to step in but Holden walks out, his expression still thunderous. Our eyes catch and I feel the connection deep in my stomach.

Somebody brushes past me and it makes me stumble.

"Hey, mind the lady," Holden calls out. But the other person has already gone.

"You okay?" he asks me.

"I'm fine." Our eyes catch again. And now all I can think about is how he felt inside of me. How I feel empty right now.

How I long to be full.

"You were an asshole to Mabel," I tell him.

He has the good grace to look embarrassed.

"She was wrong to call me the catcher in the rye," he says. "I don't want her thinking doctors are some kind of gods. We're not."

I look at him, surprised. "Of course she thinks you're a God. You're a grown up to begin with. And you're the one keeping her alive. You're her catcher," I say, my chest feeling tight. "Live with it."

He shakes his head. "I'm not her savior. I can't save her. I can't save most of these kids." There's a note to his voice that sends a shiver down my spine. He takes a step closer to me and I'm so aware of his height, his strength. The way he always smells soft and woodsy, like his house.

So aware of how he makes me feel whenever he's close.

"Did you really read the book?" I ask him.

"It was mercifully short," he tells me. "But yeah, I read it."

"And you didn't like it?"

He shakes his head. "What does that kid have to worry about? He needs to visit here to get a shock."

"He'd have to be a time traveler," I say, and the slightest hint of a smile hits his lips. I'm always so surprised by how lovely his smile is. How gentle it makes him look. And that's when I realize that I hated the way he responded in Mabel's room because he felt like the other Holden. The angry one.

The one who beats on people for sport.

"Doesn't everybody get to feel low sometimes?" I ask him. "It doesn't matter if you've got cancer or if you've been expelled or if you're recovering from the flu and hate that you can't be everybody's savior."

He leans in closer. Until I can feel the warmth of his breath on my skin. I also feel a pulse of desire between my legs. How is it possible to feel in danger and safe at the same time?

I don't know. But maybe I like it. Too much.

"What are you doing tonight?" he asks, his voice thick, his eyes dropping to my lips.

My pulse quickens. "Washing my hair."

"I finish at ten. Let me come pick you up. Come to mine."

I actually need to do some school work. But I'm an idiot for this man. "Okay. But I'll come to you. I'll be at the library."

"And you're staying."

"No I'm not." I shake my head. "I have a nine AM lecture tomorrow. And I'll need to shower."

"I'll drive you home early. But you're staying."

Our eyes meet again. His gaze is intense. So Holden.

"Okay," I whisper and he smiles.

And I'm gone.

He brushes his lips against mine and I feel it in my core. Sweet Holden is so very sweet.

And I can't help but wonder what version of him I'll get tonight.

CHAPTER
SIXTEEN

BLAIR

I knock on his door just after eleven, clutching my backpack to my chest like I'm hugging a baby. Or maybe like it's a shield.

Hopefully not both.

He knows I'm coming up – the concierge had to call him from the desk in the lobby. Luckily, it's the night concierge because I don't recognize him and he didn't recognize me either.

So when he opens the door right away I'm not surprised. What does surprise me – in a nice way – is how good he looks. He's showered and his hair is still wet, brushed away from his face. He's wearing a pair of gray sweatpants. Not too baggy, but hanging low on his hips. On his top is a black t-shirt that does nothing to hide the sculpted lines of his chest.

Without saying a word he pulls me inside and shuts the door in one easy movement. Before I can say hello my back is against the wall and he's cupping my face, his mouth smashing against mine in the most deliciously violent kiss.

I'm not going to lie. I usually like people who follow the rules of decorum. But this is hot. His tongue slides against mine and his hand feathers down my side to cup my hip. His body is pressed against mine in a way that leaves me in no doubt about what he wants.

And as he plunders my mouth I feel the slickness between my thighs. I kiss him back, my arms wrapped around his neck, and he groans into my mouth. My forearms rest against his shoulders, and I feel the muscles tighten as he slides his hands over the swell of my behind. He hitches me up against the wall until my legs are wrapped around his hips and he's pressed against me.

Between my thighs. Thick and hard.

His mouth releases mine and we both take hot, heavy breaths. He's still holding me up, still gazing into my eyes.

I feel like a feather in his arms and I'm nothing approaching that. Seriously. This man has strength.

"Hi," I breathe.

His lips curl. "Hi."

"So how was your day, darling?" I ask.

His smile broadens. "Fucked up. Yours?"

"I submitted my project draft. So it was pretty good."

His eyes soften, even though there's still that darkness behind them. He brushes a lock of hair behind my ear.

"Well done."

It's funny but I like those words as much as I like his body.

"Thank you, sir," I whisper.

His jaw tightens.

"You want to celebrate?" he asks.

"Definitely." I smile at him.

"Champagne?"

I shake my head. "You."

His eyes crinkle as he slowly nods. Still holding me, he turns and walks toward his bedroom. And it's not like in the movies. I'm scared because – hello – I'm not exactly light here. And if he drops me it's going to hurt. "Put me down," I whisper.

"Shut up."

"Seriously, you're going to get a hernia."

He stops dead and looks at me. There's not a sign of strain on his face. "Are you questioning my masculinity?" he asks, sounding amused.

"I'm questioning the ratio between the size of your muscles and the size of my ass."

"Your ass is perfect." As though to prove it he slides a hand over my behind, making my skin heat up. Then he closes the last few steps to his room, pushing the door open with his elbow before carrying me inside.

And then he throws me on the bed. I bounce a couple of times, but I kind of laugh too, because I can't remember the last time I bounced on a bed. Or got carried. I kind of like it.

"Take your clothes off."

I look up at him. The darkness is back. A thrill rushes through me. I keep his gaze as I scramble upright and pull my sweater over my head, then my t-shirt, leaving just a bra and my bare skin.

"And the jeans." His voice is low and lazy. It does things to me. The kind of things that make me want to do exactly as he tells me.

Maybe it's the old military training. Or the need to not think for a bit. To just do, just be.

Just be with *him*.

My shoes and jeans are off and I'm standing in front of him in only a bra and panties, feeling aching and needy. I can tell by the way he's pressing against his sweatpants that he's as excited as I am.

"Lose the bra."

I reach behind me and unclasp it.

For a moment there's silence. Then he lets out a sound – a

kind of rumble in his throat, and pushes me back softly with his flat palm until my legs hit the bed. He pulls them apart, his fingers digging deliciously into my flesh, and I wait for him to dip his head, the way he did last time.

But instead he kisses me. My mouth. Softly, slowly, like he's worshipping me. When I open my eyes he's staring into them and I feel my chest twinge. He's changed again. Hard to soft. Except where it counts, of course.

That's as hard as steel.

"Are you going to lose your clothes, too?" I ask him.

He gives me a smile. One that lights up the room. "It'll probably make things easier."

And then he does his thing. Taking his t-shirt off then the sweats, revealing his perfectly chiseled body to me.

I let out a long sigh, because the human eye loves perfection.

"Kiss me again," I whisper, because I need it. I need to feel him on top of me. There's something weird happening in my chest that I don't want to think about. It feels tight and wooly and needy.

His lips are warm, gentle. He pulls me up the bed as we kiss, until we're both fully on the mattress and he's between my legs. I wrap my legs around his, tangling my fingers in his hair, my hips moving because I need to feel him.

"Holden..." I don't have anything to say. I just want to say his name. Remind myself this is real.

He kisses my neck, making me shiver. Then he lowers his mouth to my breast, sucking at my nipple until I arch my back with delight. His fingers are on my hips, but they feather down, one of his hands dipping between my thighs.

Touching me where I need him the most.

"Jesus you're wet."

"I know. Do something about it."

He laughs, but does as I ask, sliding a finger along the core of me, circling, teasing, playing me. He lifts his mouth up again, kissing me, and I realize that this would be a good way to die. Being touched by Holden Salinger. Being kissed by him.

I reach down to slide my hand along the waistband of his shorts, before dipping my fingers inside, circling him. It's his turn to groan against my lips and I savor the taste of it.

"I thought you'd be rough tonight," I whisper.

"I thought about it, too," he says, his eyes meeting mine again. They're dark yet still warm.

"And?"

"Do you want me to be rough?" he asks.

"I want you to be you," I say. He blinks, those thick lashes sweeping down. His eyes scan my face, like he's trying to work me out.

"I don't want to be rough with you. Not today. I just want to lose myself," he admits. It touches me. "I want to be inside of you then hold you and sleep the sleep of the dead."

"Then do it."

We both tug at his shorts until he's naked, his thick erection jutting out, rubbing against me as he lowers himself over me. I roll my hips until he's there, touching me, pushing against me.

"Yes," I whisper in his ear. "Yes, please."

My breath catches as he pushes in to the hilt. It's delicious and stretching and everything I didn't know I needed. He waits for me to adjust, kissing me again, then pulls out in a long, sweet stroke that makes me moan loudly.

Damn this man knows how to make me feel good.

He reaches a steady rhythm, one that sends my senses into overload. I feel his breath against my ear, the soft sheen of perspiration on his back. His eyes are on mine, always on mine, as I feel myself tighten.

"So close," I whisper.

"Good," he murmurs. "I want to feel you coming around me."

He dips his head to kiss my nipple, and that's all it takes for me to explode around him, my cries ringing through the room as I clench repeatedly around the hardness of his cock. I scrape his back with my nails as white heat surrounds me, and all the time he holds me, whispering sweet words into my ear.

Sweet Holden. I definitely love him the most.

What? No. I shake that thought from my head.

"You okay?" he whispers.

I nod, even though my mind is reeling. I'm not going to get feelings for this man. Not beyond a kind of friendship and admiration that anybody would have for a doctor like him.

Thankfully I'm good at compartmentalizing, so I push all those thoughts into the box in my head, turning the key before I kiss him again.

"My turn," I whisper, pushing on him until he's on his back. He frowns at the fact we are no longer connected, but smiles as I straddle him.. I'm so slick it's easy for him to slide into me, and when he lets out a low moan it sends pleasure to the tip of my toes.

Leaning forward, I put my palms on his strong chest to steady myself. His own hands wrap around my waist as I start to move up and down. He lifts his head up to kiss me, his breath rasping as I reach a rhythm, his hands encouraging my movements, his mouth whispering promises against mine.

I'm going to come again. I feel it coil in my belly, hissing and flicking like a snake. My movements become erratic and he steadies me, taking over as his biceps flex and he encourages me up and down his cock.

"Holden…"

"Do it." His jaw is tight. Tense. Like he's as close as I am. "I've got you, Blair. Just let go."

My breath is ragged. My heart rate stupidly high. And as I crest, white heat sears behind my eyes as the pleasure takes over. I close them, hearing him call out my name. Feeling him surge inside of me.

This orgasm is longer. Even more intense. And it hits me in the chest. I look down at him and he's gazing up at me with the softest look I've ever seen.

It makes every part of me want things I can't.

Sliding his fingers into my hair, he pulls my head down until we're kissing again. "Blair?"

"Yes?" I'm still breathless.

"We didn't use protection."

My eyes widen. "Shit. I'm sorry."

He shakes his head. "No, it's my fault." There's regret on his face and I hate it. "I'm the fucking doctor."

"Literally."

He looks pissed with himself. "I'll arrange for some emergency contraception."

"It's okay. I'm on the pill." I swallow. "And I'm clean." One bonus of being in the Army. I've always taken my health seriously.

"I had a test last month." His lip curls. "Even so, it was stupid."

Yeah, it was. "If it makes you feel any better, I came like a steam train."

He shouts out a laugh, his hands soft on my face. "Me too."

"Okay then." I roll off of him. "I'm going to clean up."

"Let's take a shower," he says. "And then we need to get some sleep so I can get you across town at a stupid hour of the morning."

I smile at him. "Sounds good to me."

———

HOLDEN

. . .

Of course we have sex in the shower. Because when water is spraying down on you and a beautiful woman is staring up at you like you're God's gift to women, it does surprising things to your cock.

But then we get clean and I find an unopened spare toothbrush for Blair and we finally get ourselves ready for bed.

It feels weirdly good to know she's going to stay. Like I've tamed an anxious kitten that really would prefer to run away. I watch as she pulls on one of my spare t-shirts and climbs under the covers, waiting for me.

"How do you know what side I sleep on?" I smile because she chose the right side. The one I don't like.

"Because I've slept with you before, remember?"

Ah yes. My fever. The truth is I don't remember a lot of it. What I do remember is feeling safe. Warm. Taken care of.

It feels a little like that again as I climb in next to her and turn to look at her. She has the most expressive eyes.

"You comfortable there, Walsh?" I ask her.

"Getting there." She looks wary.

"Want me to make you more comfortable?"

"Is that a euphemism for more sex?" she asks. "Because I think I might have worn things out down there."

I laugh. "I was going to offer you an extra pillow, but whatever."

Her smile is fucking gorgeous. "I'm good. Thank you." She looks up at the ceiling, her brows pulling together. "I can't remember the last time I shared a bed with somebody."

I give her a half-smile. "Apart from me."

"Apart from you."

I'm kind of interested now. I reach out to touch her face. "How did you make it to your thirties without getting married?"

"Same reason you did probably." She smiles.

"Oh, you're a fuck up too?"

That makes her laugh. Her eyes crinkle and I like it. "Seriously," I tell her. "I'm a relationship avoidant. You must remember that?"

"The picket fence. Yeah." She tips her head to look at me. "Why?"

"I don't know." I do. I just don't want to talk about it.

"Come on. You tell me your deepest secret and I'll tell you mine."

I take a deep breath. She's easy to talk to but some things aren't easy to think about. "I was engaged once. During my fellowship."

"You were?" She doesn't look jealous. Just interested.

"Yeah. So I guess I wanted the picket fence, too."

"What happened?"

I shrug. "We got married. She should be home in about twenty minutes."

"Holden!" Her eyes widen. "Shut up."

She knows I'm kidding. I wrinkle my nose. "I was working in an oncology ward in Chicago. She'd followed me there. We had a nice apartment, she worked a few hours a day in a gallery, but mostly was at home. I think she got bored."

"Then she should have got another job," Blair says.

"Yeah. She found other ways to entertain herself." I clear my throat. "I had a bad day at work. Lost a patient I really cared about. And when I got home I found her fucking one of my fellow doctors."

Blair's expression is one of horror. "What?"

"And I beat him up."

"Oh…"

I give her a tight smile. "I nearly lost my job over it. One of the senior doctors pulled me aside and told me to find an outlet for my anger."

"That's when you started boxing?" she asked.

"Yeah. I got rid of the girl and got into the ring."

"What was her name?" Blair asks softly.

"Claire."

"Claire sucks."

I laugh, because she genuinely looks mad. Christ this woman would be easy to fall for. "Yeah, she did. But it's old history now. And I haven't heard from her for years."

"I hope her picket fence is up her ass."

I stroke her hair softly. "So what's your story? Why are you single?"

"I don't have time for relationships," she says honestly. "I'm too busy working."

"You work too hard."

"I work as hard as I need to." Her voice is soft. "My mom did the same thing. Our dad left us when we were little. Never sent any money."

"So you joined the military?"

"Yeah. I joined because I wanted the benefits. So I could afford college. And the pay I got from it was enough that I could help my sister get her education, too."

"You paid for your sister to go to college?" I ask, impressed.

"We did it together. She worked and I worked."

"What about your mom?"

She swallows. "She died a year after I joined the Army."

"I'm sorry."

She gives me this soft smile that feels like a blanket being wrapped around me. "Do you think we should go to sleep now?"

"Yeah, we probably should." I lean forward to kiss her, then pull her against me until her back is molded into my chest. Wrapping my arms around her waist I hold her tight.

She's an enigma, but I like that. I'm not sure I've ever met anybody as independent as she is.

And yet I feel this urge to protect her. To keep her safe from all the idiots that try to hurt her.

I really hope those idiots don't include me.

CHAPTER
SEVENTEEN

HOLDEN

Blair turns out to be the least restful sleeper I've ever met. She's a teeth grinder for one. I make a mental note to tell her to get a mouth guard made. She also turns, *a lot*. In the end I roll onto my side and spoon her again, wrapping my arms around her to keep her calm.

Miracle of miracle it works. She actually relaxes against me and her breath evens out. Finally I let my own eyes shut, feeling the sweet bliss of nothingness wash over me.

"You need to get up."

What the hell? I open my eyes to see her still in my arms, her head turned to look at me. "I just fell asleep," I tell her, fully intending to go back to it again. It was nice. Finally. Now that she actually calmed the fuck down.

Blair wriggles out of my hold and turns to her other side so she can face me more easily.

"Please don't tell me you're a morning person," I groan.

"The best time of the day," she says. "We need to leave in half an hour. I figured you'd want to shower first."

I reach for her, until her mostly naked body is pressed to mine, and slide my palm down her back to the sweet swell of her behind.

She looks up at me, her cheeks pink and cute as hell. "We don't have time for this," she warns. But she still arches into me, hooking her leg over my hip.

I can feel the dampness of her on the tip of my swollen cock. I'm not sure who hitches their bodies first – her or me – but the result is the same. I'm inside of her. Bare. The first woman I've felt like this.

It's heaven, even for a guy who hates mornings.

I rock against her, and she's staring up at me, her lips parted, her face flushed and damn, this woman is beautiful.

I brush her messy hair away from her face and dip my head to kiss her again. Her lips are soft and warm. I don't want to stop.

But I also want to feel her fall apart around me, so I reach down and touch her where I know it makes her gasp. My finger circles, my body rocks, and she's panting against my lips, until she stills and I feel her convulse around me.

So tight. So sweet.

So mine.

Fuck. I'm fucked. And I don't care because she's so tight and I'm so aching and desperate to come. My movements are erratic, I'm grunting against her lips, and even as I begin to tighten then surge I'm thinking about when we can do this again.

Because I know I want to. All the damn time.

If I was able to think straight right now, I'd probably be worried about that.

———

As I pull up outside of her apartment I notice it looks different in the daylight. Less dangerous but more shabby.

There's litter on the sidewalk, some graffiti on the wall, and a group of kids are playing at the bottom of a stoop.

I park in another illegal spot and climb out to open her door.

"You don't have to walk me to the apartment," she says, rolling her eyes.

"Shut up."

She smirks and climbs out, and I slam the door closed behind her.

"You working at the bar this week?" I ask her.

"Only Friday and Saturday. I have some assignments I need to get finished up during the week." She ruffles her hair but its still sticking out in a hundred different ways. I take her hand and she looks down at the way our palms are touching.

"What?"

"You're holding my hand," she says as though it's the first time anybody has done that in human history.

"Are you actually from this planet?" I ask and she laughs.

"Not sure right now." She sighs. "Thank you for last night."

"No," I say, pressing a kiss to the tip of her nose. "Thank you. I'll call you."

"No you won't."

I lift a brow. "Yes I will. I'll message you, too."

The hint of a smile pulls at her lips. I'm not sure she still believes me. But the stupid thing is I want to talk to her. I want to shoot the breeze with her. She makes me laugh and she makes me smile and she makes me...

"Hello stranger." A low voice brings me out of my thoughts. I look up to see a woman walking down the steps at the front of the apartment, a young boy next to her.

Blair lets out a groan and I realize this has to be her sister. *Interesting*.

I can't for the life of me remember her name, but there's definitely a familial resemblance. Her hair is a different color but it's the same thickness with the same wave. And they share a nose.

Well, not share exactly. They have one each. But they're the same shape.

"Who's that?" the boy asks, pointing at me.

"I'm Holden," I say, holding my hand out to him. The kid looks at it for a long, awkward minute, then holds his own up.

I high five it. Because I'm down with the kids.

"Are you Auntie Blair's boyfriend?"

Blair's sigh is audible. It makes me smile. "Yeah, I guess I am."

It's her sister's turn to make a noise. It sounds like she's choking.

"Well this is fun," Blair murmurs.

Actually, it kind of is. "You heading to school?" I ask her nephew.

"Yeah." He nods. "But I don't want to. We have math this morning."

I wrinkle my nose. "That stinks."

From the corner of my eye I can see Blair's sister gesticulating at Blair, as though they're having some kind of silent conversation.

"What else is on the school agenda?" I ask him.

"Sports. We're playing T-ball."

"I love T-ball," I tell him. "My favorite."

He looks at me askance. "You play T-Ball? I thought it was just for kids." He coughs. It sounds thick and phlegmy and I'm reminded of what Blair told me about his asthma. Poor kid.

"My hand eye coordination isn't the best," I tell him.

"I bet it is," Blair's sister says, looking completely amused. "I bet it provides complete satisfaction."

"Shut up, Annie," Blair says. Her sister laughs.

"Aren't you a doctor?" Annie asks. "I'd figure you'd need great hand eye coordination."

"I'm not a surgeon." And my hand eye coordination is just fine. I was making a joke, dammit.

"You're a doctor?" he asks, his eyes wide. "Wow. Do you like take care of sick people?"

"Mostly." I nod.

"And have you ever seen a dead body?" His voice is full of awe.

"Evan!" Annie chides. "Stop it."

"A few," I tell him. "But it's really not nice."

Blair catches my hand. Squeezes it. I squeeze back and she interlinks her fingers through mine, like she's finally gotten used to the hand-holding thing.

Weird how much I like that.

"We have to go," her sister says, giving me a wide smile. "It was lovely to meet you, Holden. I've heard so much about you."

I blink, surprised. "Thanks. Nice to meet you, too."

Evan starts coughing again.

"Did you give him his inhaler this morning?" Blair asks.

"Of course," her sister says.

Blair looks over at the demolition site on the other side of the road. There are bricks everywhere. Dust, too.

"Motherfuckers need to put better barriers up," she mutters.

"Language," Evan says.

"Sorry." She gives him a smile. Then she lets go of my hand and hugs him. "Have a good day at school."

"Thanks, Auntie Blair. You too."

She winks. "I'll try."

Her sister and nephew walk off, leaving the two of us standing on the sidewalk in front of her apartment.

"So you've met the family," she says, wrinkling her nose. "Sorry about that."

I lean forward and kiss her again. "I liked them," I tell her. She looks more pleased than I expected at that.

"I've got to go. Or I'll be late." She sounds reluctant.

"Okay." I smile at her, then brush my lips against hers. "I'll call you later."

Only once she's safely inside of her building do I go back to my car and drive straight to work.

And for once, there's a big smile on my face.

———

The next week is a mess. One of the other doctors is off sick and since they covered during my absence, I feel like I have to work all the hours to cover his. I manage to message Blair daily, apologizing for not being around, and she replies sounding breezy.

I like it and I hate it.

I've had my share of girlfriends who get pissed when I'm too busy at the hospital and miss dates or other important events. So I should be pleased that Blair doesn't want anything from me. That she isn't demanding a conversation about where this is going and whether I see a future between us.

But it annoys me, because maybe I want her to show more interest.

It's six o'clock on Friday when my phone rings. I'm sitting in my office, desperately typing up insurance requests so they're in the right place for Monday morning, and I smile as I grab it, looking forward to actually speaking to the woman who has occupied my thoughts.

Then I see the caller's name. It's my brother. My smile falters.

"Linc."

"Hey, how are ya?" he asks. "Feeling better?"

"Much. How are you?"

"Busy. I'm at Misty Lakes. Brooks is here, too. We wondered if you'd have time to join us."

Brooks is my youngest brother. He and Linc share the same mom. "Sorry, I'm overwhelmed at work."

"All work and no play…" Linc clears his throat. "So hey, how's your house cleaner?"

"What?" I frown. What a weird question.

"The one who takes care of you. Your cleaner, right? The pretty one. I like her."

"I've no idea," I say. "I never see her."

"Shame." He clears his throat. "So you can't join us?"

It's kind of sweet that he asked. Especially because the answer is always no. Of the six of us, I'm the one who spends the least amount of time at Misty Lakes. I'm also the one who spends the most time at work.

There's a correlation there.

"No I can't, sorry." I see the interns and fellows gathering for evening rounds. One of them is chewing gum. Another is scrolling through her phone. It's going to be one of those days.

"The air is fucking crystal clear here," Linc is saying while I'm half listening to him. The gum chewer catches me glaring at him. He swallows hard.

I don't know whether to laugh or cry because I'm pretty sure that gum is gone.

"I'd forgotten how good it felt to just breathe, you know?" my brother continues. "After the fucked up air in Manhattan."

It's weird how words can trigger a thought. Because I'm now back outside Blair's apartment, listening to her nephew wheeze. Why is it that kids like him can't have somewhere like Misty Lakes to escape to?

"I have to go," I tell Linc. "Give my love to everybody."

I hang up before he can respond. Then I walk over to the

interns, clearing my throat. "Sorry, am I interrupting you from your social life?" I ask Little Miss Scroller.

She looks up, her cheeks pink. "Sorry."

"Okay, we have a full ward today," I tell them. My voice is even because I'm not annoyed with them, just trying to keep them in order the same way I was when I was a student. "Carter, take the lead on the first one. Let's do this thing."

CHAPTER
EIGHTEEN

BLAIR

It's Friday night and Holden's waiting for me in the bar while I finish cleaning up. I've realized weekends are really the only time we can be together because it turns out we both work too hard.

Him because his patients are everything to him, and me because I'm coming to the end of my masters and there are a lot of assignments to hand in. My final assessment is project based, and I've been working hard with my tutors to get it into shape.

When I lock up – because it's my turn – we head to his car and he drives us to his apartment. He parks in the lot beneath his building and we take the elevator up. We mess around a little, kissing and laughing as the doors open onto his floor.

Once were inside he makes us both a drink, asks me if I'm hungry. Puts some music on the sound system he has running through his apartment. And all the time I watch him, my body thrumming with desire.

"You okay?" he asks as I squirm on the kitchen stool.

"Fine," I say through gritted teeth. It's nice that he hasn't tried to jump me as soon as we walk through the door, but I want this man so badly.

I always do.

He smiles and grabs a loaf of bread from the refrigerator, cutting some slices up before adding meat and cheese.

Seriously, how can making a sandwich be sexy? But it is. I can't take my eyes off the deftness of his fingers. Can't stop thinking about what else they can do.

What is wrong with me? I'm never like this.

I try to distract myself. "Tell me about the first time you stepped in a ring."

He looks up. "I thought you didn't enjoy fighting."

"I don't."

The corner of his lip quirks, like he's not sure what to say. "I can't really remember. I guess I started off sparring. At a normal gym."

"Normal gyms don't have boxing rings," I point out.

"Depends on which kind of gym you go to. But yeah, we'd fight and it was good. But nothing like the club."

"Why not?"

He looks up at me, and the intensity in his eyes pulls at my chest. "I don't know. It's just different when you're not doing it for exercise but to win."

"Doesn't the hospital frown on you being a boxer?" I ask. "You must lose a few brain cells from some of those punches."

"I dodge most of them." There's a boyish smile on his face. "And what they don't know won't hurt them."

"They don't know?" I ask. "Haven't they guessed?"

"Why would they? I don't miss work to fight. I don't mix my home life and work life at all."

Apart from me. He brought me in to meet Mabel. I swallow hard.

"What about when you get hurt?"

"I wear headgear. So facial injuries rarely happen. And they can't see the bruises on the rest of my body." He passes me a sandwich, lifting his own to his lips. "I think the head nurse at the ward has guessed, but she's good people."

"How does it make you feel?" I whisper. "When you hit somebody?"

He looks at me carefully, considering my question. "It makes me feel nothing," he finally says. "Like absolutely nothing. And when you spend all day feeling something, that numbness is just…" He shakes his head. "It's what I need."

"But not tonight."

Because for the first Friday night since I've worked there, he didn't fight.

He inclines his head. "No, not tonight. I know you don't like it."

"Does it matter what I like?" I ask him. I'm genuinely curious, but I'm also hoping for one answer. It's a dangerous path.

"Of course it matters."

"Why?" I breathe.

"Because…" He blinks. "I don't know."

My heart is hammering against my chest. He has that little boy lost look again. His sandwich is back on his plate, forgotten like mine.

"Holden?"

"Yeah?"

I open my mouth but no words come out. For somebody who loves books as much as I do, I feel like a failure not being able to articulate what I want.

But I don't know what I want. All I know is what I feel. I let it take over me as I stand and walk around the kitchen island to him. I cup his cheeks, feeling the roughness of his beard growth. Then I kiss him, showing him what I can't say.

What I'm too scared to even acknowledge.

And then I drop to my knees. He's already hard before

I've undone his zipper. I pull him out and wrap my lips around him, dragging my tongue across his tip, savouring the sound of his groan as I take him deeper.

He didn't fight because I hate it. Because my opinion matters to him.

For that he deserves the best blow job of his life.

———

"What's that?" I ask, leaning over to look at the tray he's carrying in. It's eight the next morning and he just woke me up with breakfast. Coffee and orange juice sit next to some glistening pastries. My stomach rumbles at the sight, so I sit up quickly, then groan because my ass hurts.

"You've bruised it," he tells me. "I've got some arnica somewhere. Don't move."

"I wasn't planning on it," I grumble as he puts the tray down on the table next to me and heads into the bathroom.

It felt like a good idea to have sex on his kitchen counter last night. It was unsurprisingly easy to persuade him to fuck me when he pulled out of my mouth on the edge of coming.

And neither of us had the patience to make it to his bedroom. So he lifted me onto the kitchen counter and dragged my jeans and my panties off before pushing inside of me.

It was heaven.

But now my ass feels like hell.

Holden walks out of the bathroom carrying a tube. "Roll over," he says. He has that sexy bedroom voice.

"No." I don't care how sexy he is, he's not rubbing ointment onto my butt.

"Blair." His voice is low. He sounds like he does when he's warning Mabel to behave.

"I'm not showing you my bruised ass," I tell him. "Some things are better left unseen."

"I've seen your ass," he reminds me. "And I'm the one who made the bruises."

"Technically, it was your kitchen to blame," I say. And my over enthusiastic response to my third orgasm. I was bouncing up and down on marble.

"Turn. Over." He's got that 'not taking any shit' expression on his face.

I sigh. "Don't look at my cellulite."

"I fucking love your cellulite."

I frown at him. "Are you saying I have cellulite?"

Holden laughs. "What's the right response here? Because all I want to do is take care of your owies."

"My *owies*?" I repeat. "What am I, six?"

"You're acting like you are." He lifts the sheet up. "Come on, let me do this and then we can eat."

I grin at him, then roll over like he asks. He lifts my t-shirt – his t-shirt – I'm wearing and then there's nothing.

He doesn't touch me. Doesn't say anything. I frown and look over my shoulder.

"Will I live?" I ask him, my voice trailing away as I see the intense look on his face.

"You have the most beautiful fucking ass I've ever seen," he tells me. "I'm just reasoning with myself."

"Reasoning?"

"Explaining to my libido why it's a bad idea to ravish you when you're bruised like this."

My cheeks pink up. He likes my ass.

Feminist Blair sighs loudly.

Before I can reply that he can ravish me if he wants, he's squeezing arnica into his hand and gently rubbing it against my skin. His fingers are soft but sure. I stare at the sheet in front of me and try to tell myself that this isn't supposed to be sexy.

But nobody has ever put arnica on my bruises before. And

nobody has touched me like this before either. Like I'm some kind of goddess to be revered.

I like it. Way too much.

His fingers splay across the globe of my cheeks, his palms warming my flesh. His thumb brushes me *there*. The final frontier. Where no sane man would go.

I jump like a cat.

"You okay?" His voice is low. A murmur. I look at him again and he's still staring at my ass.

"Yeah, I just…"

"Can I touch you there?" he asks thickly.

"Do you want to?"

A smile pulls at his lips. "Baby, every man wants to. It's just most of us don't get to."

I take a ragged breath in, as desire washes over me. A kind of dirty, needy desire.

"Yes," I whisper.

His thumb pushes against me. It's not hard. Still reverent, like he's trying to work out what feels good to me.

And the shameful truth is it does feel good. Too good. I drop my head against the pillow and sigh softly.

"You still with me?" he asks. His thumb pushes in. Not far, but far enough for me to feel the pulse of pleasure rush through my veins.

"Holden…"

"You want me to stop?" His voice is low. Gritty.

"Yes. No. I don't know." I take a deep breath and woman up. "Don't stop."

"Good."

I look at him again. There is darkness in his eyes. His lips are slightly parted, his thumb is pushing in further.

I can feel every inch.

"What do you get out of this?" I ask him. "Why are guys so fascinated by it?"

"Because it's the ultimate taboo." His gaze flickers to

mine. He's as turned on as I am. "Because we're told we can't have it, so we want it."

"Greedy boys."

"Yeah," he says, his voice low. "Very greedy boys."

He slowly pulls his thumb out. "You're so damn tight. If we ever did this you'd need a vat of lube."

I blink at the sudden change of conversation. "If we ever did what?"

He smirks.

"You're not getting my ass."

He shrugs. "I'm happy with the rest of you." There's a confidence to him. A swagger. Like I've given him something he's always wanted.

"Then come here and show me how happy," I say, turning over and reaching for him.

"You're still bruised," he whispers as I slide my palm down the thick, hard ridge pushing at his shorts.

"Then bruise me some more."

He leans over me, his lips capturing mine.

A wave of neediness washes over me. I feel on edge. I want him to ground me. I pull him on top of me, curling my thighs around him like I need something to cling onto. And as he slides inside of me I can't help thinking about what he'd done to me. What he'd touched.

It wasn't just about him soothing my bruises. Or about him touching a place that nobody else ever had.

It was that he asked first. And I felt safe when he did it. I'm not sure what to think about that.

————

Holden drives me home right before lunch time on Saturday. He's annoyed with me because we argued again. I wanted to take the bus. It's the middle of the day. It's safe. And it would save him an almost two hour round trip.

He has this whole knight in shining armor thing about taking a woman home after he's had sex with her. Part of me wants to ask if he's always like that, but then I'd have to acknowledge that there have been other women.

And I'm kind of jealous about that. Which is a brand new feeling because I've spent my life not being jealous of anything.

It's always been easy to accept what I have is what I need. That way I don't get hurt.

I put the radio on to cut through the silence in his car. Fleetwood Mac flows from the stereo and I start to sing along, mostly to annoy him. I get to the part where Lindsay Buckingham is accusing Stevie Nicks of only wanting to shack up and look over at him.

His knuckles are tight on the wheel. His jaw is tight, too. He doesn't look at me, just stares at the road.

The bus driver would probably have been more conversational than this, and that's saying something.

By the time we pull up outside of my apartment the tension is palpable. And I know some of this is my fault.

"I'm sorry," I say.

Holden looks at me, surprised.

"I'm just not good at this," I say, gesturing between him and me.

"At humans?" he asks.

"At non-transactional relationships. You offer me a ride and my head is immediately trying to figure out what I can do for you in return."

"I don't want you to do anything for me. It's just a ride, Blair. A little time out of my day. A chance to spend a little more time with you before you withdraw from me all over again."

"I don't withdraw." I frown, because I know I'm lying. "I'm just aware that you're a busy man. I don't want to make demands on you. Not when everybody else is."

"I'm a man," he says, almost repeating me. "I like you making demands of me."

Oh. My chest feels tight.

"Who made you like this?" he asks softly.

I blink. "What?"

His gaze catches mine. "Who hurt you? Who made you think you don't deserve to be demanding?"

His question feels like a slap to my face.

"Nobody. This is just me. Who I am," I say. "I've always been self sufficient."

His expression tells me he thinks differently. But wisely, he lets it go.

"I'm heading to my cabin next weekend," he says, completely changing the subject. And I realize what this is. A brush off.

I'm not going to lie, it hurts like hell.

And this is why I don't let myself be vulnerable. Because when you're not wearing armor the cuts go deep.

"Do you think Jimmy will give you the time off?" he asks.

"Sorry?" My brows pull down so tight my eyes squint. "Why?"

He looks at me as if I'm a moron. "Because I want you to come with me. Your sister and Evan, too. You said he could do with some fresh air, and it doesn't get much fresher than Misty Lakes."

"Your dad's estate?" I clarify. Where his cabin is.

"Yeah." He nods, half-smiling. "Do you want to come with?"

"Is your cabin big enough for all of us?" I ask.

"No, but there are six cabins. I can ask my brothers if we can use one for your sister and Evan."

"You barely know them," I point out.

"It'll give me a chance to get to know them better then, won't it?"

In my head I'm picturing a sparkling lake surrounded by

trees and grass. And Evan running and jumping into the water. It makes my heart clench.

"Are you sure?" I ask.

"I'm sure."

"Will I have to meet your parents?"

He smiles. "Sadly for you, everybody's there this weekend. So it'll almost certainly be just the four of us."

"Let me run it past Annie," I say. "But it sounds fabulous." And now I feel even guiltier for annoying him with trying to be so independent.

Even if this thing has a sell-by-date, I can at least throw myself into it until then. I like Holden. More than like him.

I'm getting attached. And it scares me.

He leans forward and kisses me softly. I kiss him back, wrapping my arms around his neck.

I have no idea what's happening here. But even though it scares me, it soothes me in equal measure.

CHAPTER
NINETEEN

BLAIR

Annie looks at me, her eyes a cloud of confusion. "I thought it was just a casual thing, you two."

"It is," I say. "We both know that."

"So why is he inviting us all on a family camping trip?"

We're sitting in the living room on Sunday afternoon. I had to work last night and Holden ended up meeting me again. And of course we went home together. He was as sweet with me last night as he was yesterday morning, insisting on rubbing more cream into my bruises.

Then touching me there again. Until I was blushed and breathless.

I push that thought away. "He knows that I worry about Evan's lungs. He was going anyway and I think he thought it would be nice. That's all."

"Will his family be there?" she asks.

"I don't think so. He says they're all there this weekend. They don't usually go two in a row."

She smiles. "That's a relief."

Yeah, I guess it is. "So what do you think? Holden says we can drive down on Friday evening after work, then come home Sunday night. Evan won't miss any school that way."

"How about you?" she asks.

"What about me?"

"Don't you have school work to do? Your final project is due in two weeks."

I smile at how thoughtful she is. "I'm ahead of schedule. And we'll be back on Sunday. That still gives me five days after the mini trip for the finishing touches."

Annie frowns. "What about the club? I thought you said they're short staffed."

They are. And when I asked Jimmy about taking some time off he down right refused. I told Holden it was a no-go and he'd nodded tightly then disappeared, coming back half an hour later, telling me that Jimmy had changed his mind.

I have no idea how he did it. And I'm not sure I want to know. But now I'm free next weekend and I'm going to Virginia and I want Annie and Evan to come with.

I look at her with a smile because she's out of excuses. "So what do you say? Wouldn't you like to get away?" The weather is heating up. It's getting stifling and it's not even the painful days of July and August yet.

Annie shifts on the sofa. "Evan would love it."

"And you?"

She pulls her lip between her teeth and looks at me. "A guy from work asked me out for Saturday night. I was going to see if my friend Ellie could babysit."

Ellie is one of her work friends.

It's impossible to hide the disappointment from my face, but I try anyway. "A date?" I say, trying to push my cheeks up into a smile. "With who?"

"One of the reps who comes into the office. He knows I have a kid, seems okay with it. It's nothing earth shattering, but I thought it would be nice." She looks me in the eye. "But, you're right. Evan would love a trip to a cabin by a lake. I can ask Darren if we can do it another time."

It's her turn to look disappointed. And she's not nearly as good at hiding it as I am.

"I can take Evan," I say. "You go on your date."

Annie's eyes catch mine. "I can't do that. He'd cramp your style."

"Evan never cramps my style."

"But you and the hot doc and a cabin." She shakes her head. "I bet he was imagining having sex with you against every wooden board."

I wrinkle my nose. "Sounds painful." And he's almost out of arnica. He seems to have a thing for rubbing it into me. "And seriously, you should go on this date. You haven't had sex for years."

"I'm not planning on having sex with Darren," she says.

"I know. But just in case he sweeps you off your feet, you'll have the whole weekend to rethink that," I tease. "Come on, it makes sense. Evan gets a great weekend, and so do Holden and I. And you get some child free time to enjoy yourself."

She looks torn. And I get it, because she and Evan come as a package. She's slightly better at taking help than I am – but only slightly. And that's only because she can't physically manage to keep a job and get Evan to school every day.

"Check if it's okay with Holden first," she says. It isn't a no and I grin.

"You're going to be having sex," I say, clapping my hands.

"Shut up. I'm not having sex with him. I'm just going to…"

"Have sex."

She rolls her eyes at me. "Sleep. I'm going to sleep."

"Whatever floats your boat." I jump to my feet. "Stay here, I'm going to call Holden right now."

HOLDEN

"So you're really doing this?" Rose smiles at me. "Taking some time off. It's a miracle."

"I'm leaving four hours early," I say dryly. "And I worked four extra hours yesterday."

Her eyes twinkle. "Still a miracle." She pats my arm. "You've changed. I like it."

"I haven't changed. I'm still an asshole. And don't let anybody think differently." She's right though. I feel lighter. Even Mabel says I'm smiling far more than before.

I can't wait to get home and shower then pick up Blair and Evan to hit the road. We're going to stop at a little diner in Virginia that I know Evan's going to love. It has those old-fashioned jukeboxes at each table, and you can press a button for a free soda refill.

"Oh my," Rose says and I bring myself out of my haze of thoughts to look at her. "You've gone all misty eyed. You like this woman."

I give her a look. The one I usually save for the third year medical students who come onto their clinic rotations and think they know it all. She just grins back.

"I'm proud of you," she says. "I haven't seen a bruise on you for weeks."

"You need to stop spying on me in the shower," I tell her. "I'll ruin you for all other men."

"You already have, sweetheart." She digs her elbow into my side and dammit, it hurts. But it's also true. I haven't got any bruises because I haven't signed up for any fights. I haven't had that urge. Plus I know Blair hates it.

She'll also hate it if she knew I agreed with Jimmy to get in the ring one last time in return for her getting the weekend off. So I'm not going to tell her.

I say goodbye to Rose, and then I leave some notes for the doctor on the next shift, asking him to call me if there are any problems. Misty Lakes is remote but I deliberately chose my cell provider because I know they have a tower nearby. I can't be out of reach when there are lives at risk.

Just before I leave I do one last check of the patients, saving the best for last. Mabel's stats are looking good. She's due to go home next week now that things are stable. After that she'll come in for outpatient treatment, and there's hope that she'll finally get into remission.

She hasn't got a book in her hands, which is a miracle in itself. Instead she's scrolling through her phone.

"I'm sorry, did you just wake up in the twenty-first century?" I tease.

She looks up, her brows raised. "Bite me."

"I'm heading out for the weekend," I tell her. "Be good for the other doctors."

"When am I ever good?" she asks.

"When you think nobody is looking." There is a pile of books on the table next to her. Some I know Blair brought in this week. I'm pretty sure she won't have a chance to get bored and into trouble while she's here. And Blair has told her they are hers to keep.

I'm hoping it will make Mabel feel happier about leaving the hospital. She's been fighting being discharged, mostly because she's still having constant arguments with her mom.

"Goodbye, doctor," she says, her voice dry. "Hope you get eaten by piranhas in the lake."

"Stop reading those horror books. They're bad for you."

I'm still smiling as I step into the warm early-summer sun, my eyes blinking to get accustomed to the light. It's going to be a good weekend.

Blair was so apologetic when she called to say that Annie

had a date and couldn't come. She was worried I'd be disappointed because Evan would have to stay in my cabin with us.

Truth is, I'm excited. I can't remember the last time I kicked back and had some fun. And I'm pretty sure that Blair hasn't had much chance to do that either.

Plus I want her to see my cabin. I built it myself when I was in my early twenties. It's had some upgrades since then but it's still mine. Still me.

And I want her to see me.

It takes just over an hour in the pre-rush hour traffic to get to Blair's place. She and Evan are sitting on the stone steps, a bag next to each of them. As soon as he spots me pulling up Evan shouts out and jumps up.

I climb out and walk over to them. The sun is still high in the sky. There are a couple of kids playing on the side walk. Not as many as when I was a kid, but if I would've had a hand held computer at that age I'd have spent most of my time holed up in my bedroom, too.

"Hey." I smile at her.

"Hi."

"Are we going now?" Evan asks. "When will we get there?"

"He's a little bit excited," Blair says, her voice low. "Sorry."

"If we leave now it should take around five hours," I tell him. "But I thought we could stop on the way and get some food. There's a diner about half way there. So if we stop we should be to the cabin by ten."

"That's late," Evan says, looking even more excited.

"Well you can go straight to sleep when we get there. The beds are already made up and it'll be pitch black so no point in exploring until morning."

"Can I swim tomorrow?" Evan asks. "I brought my trunks."

"You sure can."

I load their bags into the back of my car, then wrestle with the booster seat, all too aware that my car screams bachelor and it's not really designed for kids. "No wonder my older brothers drive SUVs," I mutter when it's finally attached.

"How many brothers do you have?" Evan asks.

"Five."

His mouth drops open. I point at the seat and he climbs in, buckling himself in easily.

"Are they all as big as you?" he asks.

Blair is already in the passenger seat. I catch her smirk in the reflection of the windshield.

"We're all tall," I chuckle, "Yes."

"Do you see them a lot?" Evan asks as I close his door. Blair turns to say something to him. He smiles at her and nods.

She's softer when she's with him. I've noticed it when she's talking about him, too. For one second I imagine what she'd be like with a child of her own.

And then I push the thought away.

"We used to spend more time together," I say, climbing into the driver's seat. "But we're all busy adults now. We try to get together every summer at the lake."

"The lake where we're going?" Evan leans as far forward as the seatbelt will let him.

"Yeah. We grew up spending every summer there. We'd swim, do some hiking. Have camp fires."

"Wow." Evan sounds wistful. "Like a summer camp. The stay away kind."

"I guess. Except instead of having a camp counselor we had Myles." I start the car up, the engine purring nicely as I pull away from the curb. From the corner of my eye I see Blair smiling at me.

"Who's Myles?" Evan asks.

"My oldest brother. The one who bossed us all around."

"Will he be at the lake?" Evan sounds excited. "Will your other brothers?"

"I don't think so." For the first time I feel bad about that. Maybe Evan wants some other kids around. Myles and Liam's kids are little but they're closer in age to Evan than Blair and I are. "But don't worry, we'll still have fun."

"Of course we will." Blair's voice is warm. "We get to go swimming, remember?"

"In a cold ass lake," I mutter.

Evan laughs and Blair shoots me a look that's not so soft. I reach over and squeeze her thigh.

Her breath catches.

I decide to take the interstate, driving through Pennsylvania, mostly because it's a faster route, and it has that diner I keep telling Evan about along the way. But getting out of New York proves to be harder than I planned, and I have to censor my language every time some asshole tries to cut in front of me.

Blair keeps biting down a smile when I turn shitbag into shootbag.

The sun is dipping behind the mountains as we near the Maryland border, casting an orange hue in the sky that reflects on Blair's face. She has her hair back, no make up on, but more than anything there's a sereneness to her that I so rarely get to see.

She's only this relaxed when she's asleep or as she comes.

She's staring out at the trees and fields as we pass them, her eyes darting this way and that as we drive through a small town or past some long-forgotten tourist attraction that would have looked at home on Route 66.

Evan snores. A glance in my rearview mirror tells me he's asleep. The road is clear and straight ahead, so I reach over and squeeze Blair's thigh again.

Damn it feels good to touch her. Her smile widens and she covers my hand with her own, interlacing our fingers.

"Hey," I say to her.

"Hi," she breathes back.

"You doing okay?" We've mostly been listening to music or talking to Evan since we headed out. I haven't had a chance to talk with her.

"I am. Thank you for being so sweet with Evan."

"He's a good kid. I like him a lot." It's the truth. He has this quiet enthusiasm. He's not an in-your-face kind of kid. He just asks questions and then considers them carefully. "He reminds me of you."

"Is it the high voice?" she asks and I smile because she has this low sultry voice that does things to me.

"That and the goofy smile."

"I do not have a goofy smile," she says, pulling her hand away from mine.

I grab it again. "You have the best smile."

"Don't try to sweet talk me. You called me goofy."

I lift a brow. "I think I called you a good kid."

She gives a little harrumph. "It's better than good girl, I suppose."

My lip quirks. "You don't like being called a good girl?" I murmur. The atmosphere between us feels thicker. More sensual. And I know there's a kid in the back of the car, but damn this woman does things to me.

"Depends who's doing the calling," she says lightly. There are pink circles on her cheeks. I've made her blush.

I live to make her blush.

"Me. From between your legs."

"Holden!" She turns to look at Evan, who's still sleeping. She doesn't have the advantage of glancing in the rear view mirror.

"He can't hear me."

"Maybe he can. In his sleep. I once had an entire dream about Tom Hanks flying a plane, and woke up to see my sister was watching *Sully*."

My lips twitch. "You dreamed about a plane crashing?"

"No, not quite. But Tom definitely got into my dreams. That's what I'm saying. And I don't want Evan dreaming about…"

"My head between your legs."

This time she slaps my thigh. I laugh.

"No sex for you," she says.

"Wasn't planning on having any," I say, keeping my voice light. That was one thing I had to let go of, knowing the three of us would share a cabin. It's one thing fucking her hard against the kitchen counter when it's only the two of us, another having Evan wake to see the scariest damn shit of his life.

"You weren't?" she asks, her voice lower now.

"Nope."

"But…" She sounds almost disappointed. "Isn't that why you wanted me to come away with you?"

"I wanted to go away with you because I knew it would be fun. Plus I thought Evan would like it."

From the corner of my eye I see her brows dip. Did she really think I was going to try to get it on with her knowing her nephew was sleeping in the same, completely un-noise proofed cabin?

And because I know her now, I understand exactly what's going through her brain. "This isn't a quid-pro-quo, you know." I don't expect anything from her. I don't expect payment. I'm enjoying this time with her as much as I hope she's enjoying it.

"You keep using Latin phrases and I'm going to want to jump you," she says. I laugh again, because this woman.

She makes me laugh and she makes me want. She makes me feel things I have no right feeling.

I like it.

"We're about a minute away from the diner. Want to wake Evan up now or wait until we're parked?"

"Let's park first," she says, then pauses. "This no sex thing…"

"Yeah?"

She inhales softly. "Does it include kissing?"

I glance over at her. She's blushing again. And I want her. All of her. "No, it definitely doesn't include kissing. I intend to kiss the fuck out of you every chance I get."

"And you can explain that to Evan," she says. But it isn't a no and I like that.

And if it means I get to taste her lips, I'll happily explain whatever the hell she wants.

CHAPTER
TWENTY

BLAIR

It's just after eleven when Holden turns left off the old country road we've been following for the last few minutes. Evan is asleep again. He had a sugar high from the ridiculous sundae that Holden bought him – after an adult size burger and fries – and then he crashed about twenty minutes later and has been snoring ever since.

I didn't eat much at the diner. I wasn't hungry and I kept getting distracted by Holden taking my hand in his, using his left hand to eat his own fries.

It seems like we're at the hand-holding stage of whatever this thing is between us and I like it.

Too much.

I'm so aware of him next to me as he drives down the tiny country lane toward his father's house. The road is bumpy and the trees form a dark canopy above us that shuts out any moonlight, making the car's headlamps the only illumination showing us the way.

Holden tells me about the house. About the cabins, and

how he and his brothers each built one. He explains that we'll park in the driveway at the house and then he'll take us to the cabin before coming back for our bags.

When we finally emerge from the tunnel of trees I see the silhouette of rolling hills against the inky blue darkness of the night sky. And on top of one of them is a house. It looks tiny from here but I'm guessing it's big.

Holden hasn't said it in so many words, but he comes from money. I try not to think about that too much because it makes me uncomfortable. His life experiences are so very different to mine.

It takes a little while longer to reach the driveway. He parks right outside his father's house. There are no lights on and for some reason that makes me feel more relaxed. I've never been good at meeting the parents. I'm too awkward and shy and it ends up being embarrassing.

Evan is still fast asleep when Holden switches the engine off. I walk around and pull open the back door, touching Evan's shoulder lightly as I whisper his name.

He groans but doesn't open his eyes. I'm going to have to be the horrible aunt and wake him up. It's not unusual. When Annie has to work super early I've been known to drag his covers off in an attempt to get him to school on time.

"I can carry him," Holden says, his voice low.

I turn to look at him. The moonlight shadows his face. His eyes are warm, meeting mine.

"He's pretty heavy."

"Are you questioning my carrying skills?" he asks.

"You want to impress me, go for it."

"I always want to impress you, Blair." His voice is so soft it makes me shiver.

I unclasp Evan's seatbelt and whisper to him that Holden's going to carry him, even though he's asleep because I still maintain that voices can get into your dreams, and possibly being carried down to a strange cabin in the woods can, too. He barely stirs as I talk to him.

It's probably a good thing Holden wants to prove his masculinity. Otherwise we'd all be sleeping in the car tonight.

Stepping away so Holden can lean in, I watch as he slides his hands beneath Evan's legs. That's enough to make him stir.

"Put your arms around my neck, buddy," Holden whispers. Evan does as he's told and Holden scoops him into his arms, my six-year-old nephew nestling his face into his neck.

My ovaries do a little happy dance as I watch them. I've seen Holden with Mabel, but she's barely a kid anymore. Watching him with Evan – the kid I love the most – is like a thick fist to my chest.

In the best way.

"Okay?" Holden whispers.

Evan nods sleepily, still not opening his eyes.

"You sure?" I ask Holden.

"I'm sure. Come on, let's go get him settled."

I follow him to a path through the grass. It's graveled and the stones crunch beneath our feet. "I keep saying we should get this paved," Holden says. I marvel at how un-breathless he is while carrying Evan. I gave up trying to lift him a year ago after I nearly fell and ended up with us both on the floor.

"The gravel is pretty," I say. "Or at least I'm guessing it is in the daylight."

"Try dragging a suitcase along it," he says. "Not so pretty then."

"I'm picturing you being annoyed at your Louis Vuitton cases getting scuffed," I say, teasing him.

"You should see what they do to my thousand dollar calf-skin shoes," he jokes. And I laugh because I've never seen him wearing anything expensive like that.

He's unpretentious. Just the way I like him.

We reach the edge of the lake and the moon is reflecting

against the water. Something must have either fallen from a tree or maybe an insect is moving along the water, because the smallest ripples distort the almost perfectly round yellow disc.

I hear the chirp of crickets. The sound of the light breeze as it ruffles the leaves. I feel it on my face too, like a gentle caress.

"My cabin is over there," Holden says.

Following the direction of his nod, my eyes land on the prettiest wooden cabin I think I've ever seen. It's a few steps back from the lake, with a pitched roof that's lit with solar lights, and a deck that has a rail around it. In front of it is a pier, with a boat tied up.

"It's beautiful," I whisper.

His lip quirks up. "Thank you."

When we reach the front door, he turns to look at me. "Keys are in my pocket. Could you grab them?"

"I've heard that one before." I smile, but slide my hand into his jeans anyway.

"Other pocket, Blair."

"Oops." I find them and slide them into the lock and it turns perfectly. It's completely like Holden to keep it well oiled. And when he opens the door I can see it's absolutely pristine on the inside, too. We step into the large living area, with an L-shaped sofa and a huge television fixed to the wall. There are easy chairs, too, and a small kitchen that looks full of high end appliances.

"Wow," I say softly. This was not at all what I was expecting.

"I'm going to take Evan straight to the bedroom if that's okay?" Holden asks. "It should be made up."

"Sure." I nod and follow him to a door on the far left of the living area. It opens to a large bedroom. Holden flicks the light on with his free arm and carries Evan to a carved wooden queen sized bed complete with what looks like a home made quilt on top.

I look around. "Is this your bedroom?"

He nods. "Yeah, I thought you and Evan could take this one."

"Where are you sleeping?"

"In the living room. On the sofa."

"You can't sleep on the sofa in your own house. Evan and I can take the sofa," I say.

He shakes his head. "It's a good sofa. I've slept on it before. And anyway, I kind of worry about the lake. That way I can make sure Evan doesn't go out there without us."

My throat tightens. "I hadn't thought about the lake. But he's a good swimmer."

"Better safe than sorry, though." We exchange a look and I nod. I love the way he thinks about these things.

If Evan stays asleep, this man may get a visit from me later.

He puts Evan down on the mattress, and my nephew immediately turns onto his side, nestling his head into the pillow. He's out for the count. I lean over to slide his shoes off and decide to leave the rest. I'll make sure he brushes his teeth extra well in the morning.

"I'm going to head back to get our bags," Holden whispers. "There should be drinks in the refrigerator if you want one. Snacks too."

"Put there by the maid?" I ask.

He shrugs. "Let's not look a gift horse in the mouth."

No wonder he feels comfortable having me clean his apartment, not that he knows it's me. He's been brought up with staff.

"I'll make us both a drink," I tell him. He smiles at me and leaves the cabin.

I listen as the footsteps on his deck fade to nothing, then pull the bedroom door closed and find my way to the refrigerator. It's full of food and drinks. I pull out a bottle of water and pour us both some, then find some cheese and bread and cut them up into a snack for us.

I'm feeling hungry now, thanks to my non-eating earlier. I check on Evan, and then I walk out onto the deck, setting my arms on the rail as I stare out into the lake.

This place is like a fairytale. I try to imagine what it must have been like growing up here. Spending every summer with family. Swimming and running and having fun. I picture Holden looking relaxed and tan, sitting on the deck with his legs dangling in the water.

I picture him building this place by hand. Wooden plank by wooden plank, nail by nail.

It's not that I begrudge him any of it, even though it's so far out of my range of experience it isn't funny.

It's just that I want that life for Evan, too. So badly.

I hear a scuff of shoes to my right and turn to see Holden emerge from the trees, walking along the path that leads to the cabins. His silhouette against the moonlight is tall and broad. Even from this distance I can see the cut of his jeans, the thick swathe of his hair. The way he carries three bags like it's nothing to him.

And deep inside of me I know that life doesn't get much better than this. I want this man so much. My insides clench at the sight of him. My body heats at the way he stares at me as he gets close enough for me to see his face.

My blood feels like honey as his lips curl into a smile just because I'm there waiting for him.

"Hey." He puts the bags down. For some reason even that is sexy. My body clenches again. I'm so needy for him it's not funny.

I say nothing. I just step toward him and incline my head, rolling onto my tiptoes until our faces are almost aligned.

When our lips touch it's like a match has been lit. I feel

like I'm on fire for this man. He puts his hands on my hips to steady me and I moan at the feel of his palms against me.

I have to go two days without feeling him inside of me. I think I might die first.

Our tongues slip and drag against each other as I press my hands on his chest, feeling the hard planes of his muscles. I flick my thumbs against his nipples and he groans.

That makes me smile against his mouth, because Holden groans are the best.

He's already hard against me. I roll my hips against him and it unravels us both. We're kissing harder, touching each other everywhere, getting rid of all the unspent lust that had been building up in the car.

He slides his hands beneath my ass and turns around, pressing me against the wall of his cabin, rolling his own hips against mine until my brain is a rush of stars.

Sliding my hand beneath his t-shirt, I feel the smooth warmth of his skin stretched taut across his back. Then I plunge my hand down, beneath the waistband of his jeans, until my fingers are feathering his peachy ass.

Yes, peachy. Definitely damn peachy.

"Fuck." He breaks the kiss, pulling his mouth away from mine. I'm panting and so is he. In a vain attempt to regain the pleasure, my hips hitch again.

He's still as hard as steel.

Our eyes are locked on each other. He's still holding me against the wall of his cabin. "Evan's asleep," I whisper.

"We shouldn't…"

"I know."

I drop my face into the warmth of his neck, letting out a warm breath. He twitches against me. I can feel how wet I am, how needy.

How much this man has control of my body.

"Just for one minute," he says.

I look up at him. His eyes are dark. I nod and he puts me down, and I go to pull his t-shirt off.

"No. Keep the clothes on."

My fingers are hot as I grab at the waistband of his jeans, releasing the button then pulling the zipper down. Jesus, this man is hard. I slide my hand inside his shorts and he groans as I curl my hand around him, feeling the thick wetness on the tip.

Then he's pulling at my jeans, dragging them down because we both know anything would be impossible with them on. He wrenches my panties to one side and kisses me again, his hands squeezing my tits through my t-shirt.

"Fucking beautiful."

He pulls one of my legs around his waist, grasping it with his hand. With the other he takes himself into his palm, sliding his cock up and down me twice before stopping.

And then he's inside of me and it's everything.

I'm breathless and hot and aching for him as he slowly fills me to the hilt. Our eyes are still on each other, and it's like something's twisting and turning in me. Like he can feel it, too.

"Blair..."

He pulls out and slides in again. My back is against the cabin. My bare ass too. He turns us slightly and it's only when I see him glance to the side that I realize he wants to see the front door of the cabin. Just in case.

He doesn't know that most people in our family sleep like the dead.

His head lowers to mine and he kisses me deeply, his hips reaching a rhythm that rocks my world. I feel him slide against the most sensitive part of me every time he withdraws, and my moans are getting louder.

Turning into a cry.

He puts his palm over my mouth, his rhythm not faltering. I lick his palm and he grins at me, brushing the hair from my face.

My body twists, coils, and my breath hitches. I pull at his t-shirt, clawing at him, muttering his name against his palm.

"Can you be quiet?" he asks.

I nod, though truthfully I'm not sure, and he releases his hold on my mouth and runs his hands down to my bare behind, lifting me.

Oh. My. God. This new angle... *oh*... I drop my head against his shoulder, digging my teeth into his t-shirt.

He fucks me harder. Faster, his fingers digging into my ass as he holds me upright. I feel like a rag doll in his hands. Not able to talk, just able to move, to feel.

I come, my teeth digging in deep enough for him to grunt. I grab at his back, trying to anchor myself, and he holds me tight, his hips surging as he joins me in my orgasm.

I'm still shaking when he lowers my feet to the ground. That's when I see the damp patch on his shoulder. The teeth marks.

Ouch.

I reach out to touch it and he winces.

"I'm so sorry," I whisper. But he's smiling.

"Six hours. That's how long we made it without breaking the no-sex rule. Six goddamn hours."

Our eyes meet and he's smiling. I am too. It's goofy and silly but damn I like it.

"It's going to be a very long two days," I agree.

CHAPTER
TWENTY-ONE

BLAIR

Holden and I are quiet as we tiptoe back into the cabin. I check on Evan who's still sleeping soundly, then we eat the cheese and bread before we take turns in the shower. I step out to find him in a pair of low slung pajama bottoms, brushing his teeth over the sink.

He looks up at me in the mirror. His mouth is covered in white foam.

It all feels so normal. Like this is how it's meant to be. And I have to remind myself that it isn't.

Not anywhere close.

"You look like a dime store Santa," I tell him. "You know you can spit, right?"

"I prefer swallowers."

Damn, he's dirty tonight. I reach across to grab my towel, letting my breasts brush his back. He groans and finally spits.

Once we're both clean and ready for bed, I help him make up the sofa bed in the living room. He wanted to curl up on it with a blanket but I insisted on putting the sheets and comforter on, since he's the one who gave up his bed.

He kisses me again and climbs in. "You want to lay with me for a bit?" he asks, holding up the covers.

"Okay." I smile and climb in next to him, marveling at the heat of his body. This man is always warm. Like a walking incinerator. He slides his arm under me and pulls me close, until my face is nestled against his shoulder.

Damn, I really bit him. There's a bruise there.

I reach out to touch it softly. "Did you see this?" I ask him.

"You marked me."

The corner of my lip quirks. "I didn't mean to. It was that or scream so loud I scared the wildlife." I lean over to kiss it. "Sorry."

"Don't be sorry. It was worth it."

"It was, wasn't it?" I kiss it again. "You can do the same to me."

"Do what to you?" He tips his head to the side. There's amusement in his eyes.

"Give me a hickey."

He laughs. "I've never given anybody a hickey."

"You haven't? Not even during high school?"

"I went to an all boys school," he says, reaching out to trace my cheek. "When did you give somebody a hickey?"

"Matthew Dawson. Seventh grade."

He blinks. "You started young."

"It was a dare. We didn't kiss or anything."

"Of course you didn't. Just sucked the life out of the poor guy."

"I didn't suck the life out of anybody," I tell him. "It was over very fast."

His eyes twinkle. Damn I like him like this. All relaxed and smiley. "The first time always is."

"When was your first time?" I ask him.

"You want to know?"

The weird thing is I do. I don't feel jealous, because we all have histories. I just want to know more about this man.

"Yeah, tell me."

"I was seventeen. Myles was back from college and had a party at the lake with all his friends while Dad was gone. It got a bit out of hand."

"Your first time was with a college girl?" I ask him. "Wow."

"I doubt she'd say it was wow. How about you? Who was your first time with?" He leans forward to kiss me softly. It sends a shiver down my spine.

"You."

The smile slips from his face and I can't help but laugh. "I'm kidding, I'm kidding…"

"Thank Christ. I was trying to remember if I was gentle with you."

"You weren't." I smirk. "And I liked it."

"So who was it then?"

"A guy named Damon. His grandma lived in the apartment below ours. We were both virgins. It was… yeah, quick."

"Did he give you a hickey?"

"Nope. Nobody's ever given me a hickey."

"I'm going to give you a hickey," he says.

My eyes lazily meet his. "Are you? When?"

He runs a lazy finger over my lips. "I don't know yet. It'll be a surprise when I do."

"Like a stealth attack."

His mouth captures mine again. My body heats at the thought of him marking me. I want to roll my eyes at myself, what am I, twelve?

I stop thinking about that because his tongue slides against mine, and I'm clawing at him again.

"Fuck." He pulls away. Why does this man have such self control? I'm impressed and annoyed in equal measure. "You should go to bed," he whispers. "Before I give you hickeys all over."

"Promises, promises," I tease, but I do as he says, because I feel it too. This constant need to be attached to him. To feel him inside of me. It's like the grandpapa of all itches that I can never soothe.

"Blair?" Holden whispers as I roll out of his bed and get to my feet, feeling the warm rug on my soles.

"Yes?"

"Thank you for coming with me."

I smirk and he rolls his eyes.

"To the lake, I mean. I'm glad you're here."

I give him the goofiest of smiles. "I am too. Good night, Holden."

"Good night, Blair."

————

I feel the warmth of the sun on my face before anything else. My eyelids are bathed in orange, and as soon as I open them I'm dazzled. There are no curtains in here and one of the windows must be east-facing. I sit up and look over at Evan.

But he's not there.

I jump up and look around, as though he might have crawled onto the floor to sleep but he's gone. It takes about a nanosecond for the adrenaline to kick in, as I run into the living room calling out Holden's name.

But he's not there either.

When I push open the front door to the cabin I find out why.

The two of them are in the lake, laughing and swimming. My panicked heart slows.

I walk barefoot down the dock that juts out into the water. They're in the shallows, where the surface laps against Evan's shoulders and Holden's waist.

Evan is saying something to Holden, who's listening carefully to him, the same way I've seen him listen to Mabel. Like there's nothing more important in the world than what Evan has to say right here and now.

The sun reflects on Holden's skin, casting shadows where his muscles rise and dip. I glance at his shoulder and see the mark I made still there. He doesn't seem to care.

Then they laugh again and Evan splashes his arms, as though he's pretending to be something. I want to listen in but I don't want to break the magical spell either.

Because there is something very magical about watching the man you can't get out of your mind bond with the kid you love the most. It's making every part of me ache in the best way.

"Auntie Blair!" Evan calls out when he finally sees me. His hair is wet and next to Holden he looks so tiny and skinny. I grin at him.

And feel the warmth of Holden's gaze on my skin.

"You couldn't wait for me, huh?" I say, my voice light because I really don't mind. Evan's been talking non stop about the lake all week. We're lucky he passed out in the car so we were able to get him to bed last night without him insisting on dipping his toes in.

"Sorry," Evan shouts, sounding anything but sorry. "I woke up early and you were snoring."

Holden coughs out a laugh.

"I don't snore," I say to Evan and he wrinkles his nose.

"You do," he says. "Mom says it's like a steam train."

Holden laughs a little more. I raise my brow at him and he slowly nods, as though telling me it's true.

Well okay then.

"Are you coming in now?" Evan asks.

"Not in my pajamas," I say. "How about I make us all some breakfast and then we can go swimming again later?"

"Do we have to?"

"Swimmers need fuel," Holden murmurs. "And I'm hungry."

"Yeah, I'm hungry too," Evan agrees. Funny that. I think he'd agree with Holden if he said the earth was flat.

"It'll be ready in twenty minutes," I tell them. "Make sure you're out by then."

"We will," Evan says, before he splashes his hands down on the surface of the water again. "Hey Holden, wanna play sharks and minnows one more time?"

———

HOLDEN

Evan's like a little perpetual motion machine. He can't keep still for a second. After wolfing down breakfast he insists on another swim, and the three of us dive into the lake.

Blair is wearing one of those swimsuits with cut outs in the middle. I have to swim out a little further to hide my immediate response. The woman is beautiful in whatever she wears, but seeing her in a swimsuit is something else.

Evan calls out her name and tells her to jump in like we did, but she refuses. Instead she lowers herself gingerly into the water, her toes barely skimming the surface before she lets out a yelp and pulls them up again.

"It's freezing," she says, wincing.

"Only for a minute," Evan tells her, his voice reassuring. "Then it's fine. Honest."

It takes her three tries before she finally keeps her foot in the water. I have to bury a grin because who would have thought the woman who's scared of nothing hates cold water?

I swim back over to where Evan is standing, the water up to his shoulders.

"It hurts more if you do it bit by bit," I warn her.

"Shut up." She dips her second foot in, and I swear her face crinkles in pain.

"Want me to carry you in?" Evan asks her. "I can help."

She looks at his tiny body and then at mine. "It's okay, sweetie. I can do it."

It takes about three days for her to finally lower herself in, where the water is reaching her hips. I try not to look at the way her nipples are as hard as pebbles.

Try not to think about how good they'd feel in my mouth.

Evan splashes her, taking her by surprise. Her mouth drops open as water drips down her face. I try to hide my laugh but she catches me.

"Just for that," she says, pushing her hands against the water. "You're getting splashed, too."

It's a poor attempt. And I've never been scared of cold water. Not that this lake is that cold. I shoot her an evil grin, then swim over and duck her under the water, to the sound of Evan's cheers.

"You mudderfudger!" she shouts once she emerges. "Now it's on."

She launches herself at me, trying in vain to push me underwater. Instead she kind of jumps up and down with her hands on my shoulder – on my bruise, I might add – as I stand there with an eyebrow quirked.

"Help me, Evan," she shouts. "Let's get him under."

Evan swims over – he's pretty good for a six-year-old – and splutters with laughter when I wrap my hands around Blair's waist and throw her under again.

"That's not fair," she shouts, water spraying everywhere as she jumps up. "You're too strong."

"Not too strong for me," Evan says, and the kid grabs my arm and pulls it. I catch Blair's eye and she watches as I let him pull me, pretending to stagger as I resist, before I go under.

"See, that's how you do it," he tells Blair, smugly.

She's smiling when I stand back up. Not so much when I shake my hair in her direction and she gets covered with spray once more.

And then I hear somebody clearing their throat.

I look at Evan, alarmed that our messing around might have caused an asthma attack. But he's still grinning. It takes me a second to realize that there's somebody on the shore.

Not just somebody. My brother, Myles. And his family.

My expression must change because Blair tips her head, as though she's trying to work something out. Then she turns to follow the direction of my gaze.

"Oh."

I hear it, but Myles doesn't. Shit, he didn't say he'd be here.

"Hi," he calls out, looking bemused as his gaze slides from me to Blair and Evan. "I thought we must have intruders or something."

Blair pulls her lip between her teeth. Evan looks over, interest pulling at his features. But he's too shy to say anything.

"I didn't realize you were coming," I said. "I would have told you I was here."

"Likewise," he says. His wife Ava is beaming at me. She's beaming at Blair, too.

My nephew, Charlie, is staring at Evan with interest. There's about the same difference in age between them as there is between me and Myles.

For some reason that makes my chest twinge.

"We should go over," Blair murmurs, elbowing me in the waist. I nod and we wade back to the pier, Evan holding on to Blair's shoulders so he can float behind her. I pull myself out of the water and onto the deck in one effortless movement, then offer my hand to Evan, who still looks shy.

Blair's the last to climb up. I reach for her, but she's

already wrapped her arms around her waist. She looks like a kid who's been caught with their hand in the candy jar.

I don't like that. She's allowed to be here. We all are.

"Hey." I reach out and shake my older brother's hand, trying not to get him wet because the man looks like a walking Calvin Klein ad in his stone colored pants and white linen shirt, his thick hair brushed back.

"Nice bruise," he says, looking at my shoulder.

From the expression on Myles' face he probably thinks I got it fighting. That's probably for the best, because I don't want Blair feeling any more awkward than she obviously already does.

I lean over to kiss Ava's cheeks and she whispers in my ear.

"Introduce your friend to us, Holden."

Shit. Yeah. "This is Blair," I say. "And Evan, her nephew. Blair, this is my brother, Myles, his wife, Ava, and their son, Charlie."

"Hi." Blair smiles at them, grabbing a towel and wrapping it around Evan before taking another to wrap around herself.

Ava is smiling widely. "Hi Blair, hi Evan."

Charlie walks over to Evan and tugs at his arm. "Do you like Pokeys?" he asks, his lisp thickening his words.

"He means Pokémon," Ava says. "He's kind of obsessed about them at the moment."

"Sure," Evan says, looking so much older now that he's standing next to my nephew. "I like them. They're cool."

"I got one," Charlie says. "Mommy?"

"It's in the cabin, sweetie," Ava says soothingly. "You can show Evan later." She smiles at Blair. "We were planning on grilling this evening. There's enough food if you three would like to join us."

"Grilling?" Evan says. "Over a fire?"

Ava's lips twitch. And I know why. She thinks it's hilarious that guys like fire so much.

"That's the plan. And later we'll make some s'mores. Do you like them?"

"I love s'mores," Evan says, his eyes wide.

"Great. Come over to our cabin at five," Ava says, and I kind of marvel at how at ease she's made everybody feel.

"Can we bring anything?" Blair asks.

"No, just bring yourselves," Ava says.

I look at Myles and he nods.

"Okay then," I say. "We'll see you at five."

CHAPTER
TWENTY-TWO

BLAIR

The sun is still blasting down as the three of us walk around the lake to Myles' cabin. The rays were too hot to play in the lake this afternoon, so we took Evan into the woods to search for Holden's old treehouse, which we found in a state of disrepair, much to the big man's dismay.

Evan was still impressed by it. Even more impressed once he learned that Holden and his brothers all built it together long before they worked on their own cabins. All day he's hung on Holden's every word.

I think somebody might have a little crush.

Not that I can blame him, I do, too.

I'm checking my emails as we walk into the yard surrounding Myles and Ava's upgraded cabin. According to Holden, they leveled the old structure and rebuilt it from scratch once Charlie was born. That way they'll have enough room for their expanding family.

Evan is chatting with Holden about T-ball as I delete the round robin emails from college, along with the ones offering me thousands of dollars to unlock a legacy I never knew I had.

And then I see an email from a library. One in Maryland. I'd applied to it on a whim, assuming that they'd want somebody from the alma mater since it's attached to a university. But when I open it, I see I'm being offered an interview.

It's scheduled for right after I hand my final assignment in.

My heart starts to pound against my chest.

I haven't thought about my degree all weekend. Nearly all my assessed work is already turned in by now. I still have to submit my final project – though we've been submitting it in pieces over the last few months for feedback – and then do an assessed presentation. And then that's it. It will be done.

Things are going to change. This beautiful, lovely time with Holden and Evan is only temporary. Everything is.

I quickly turn off my phone, trying to ignore my shaking hands.

"Everything okay?" Holden inquires.

"Everything's great." I push a smile onto my lips. I'm not going to worry about the future, not tonight. It can wait until tomorrow.

"Did you know that Holden and his brothers used to have an Olympics here every summer?" Evan asks me, looking excited. "They swam and climbed and fought."

I lift an eyebrow at Holden. He shrugs, looking amused.

I bet he got the gold medal at the last one.

"Boys will be boys," I murmur, as Holden reaches out to trace my bare arm with his finger.

And it's enough for my body to feel like it's on fire again. We've barely touched each other all day. And I'm not sure how much longer I can go without feeling his lips against mine.

It's like an addiction I'm unable to shake.

"Hi!" Ava walks across the shaded porch, wearing a long

white dress with a laced bodice. She's absolutely beautiful. "How was your afternoon?"

"We saw the treehouse," Evan says, his shyness gone. "Holden says we can repair it next time I'm here."

Ava looks at Holden with a question in her eyes. He doesn't look like he's planning on answering it. And I realize that we might not come back here at all. Not if we're living in Maryland or some other state by then.

"Why don't you come inside?" Ava says to Evan, holding out her hand. He takes it so easily I'm shocked. "Myles is trying to find something for Charlie to watch. And we have drinks and snacks."

"Cool." Evan nods.

They walk inside and Holden takes my hand, turning to look at me. "Okay?"

I take a deep breath. "I got an interview."

"For what?"

"A library job. After I graduate."

His smile is dazzling. He looks so genuinely pleased it makes me feel breathless. "That's amazing. Congratulations."

"It's in Maryland."

"Okay." He nods. The smile doesn't falter, but his eyes aren't crinkled anymore. "That's what you want, right? Somewhere outside of the city."

"Yeah. It's on a campus. Near some really lovely towns." The kind with houses that have huge yards and so many green spaces it's like living in the past.

"I'm glad for you," he says softly.

I try to ignore the lump in my throat.

"Can I get you a drink?" Myles asks me, appearing from inside the cabin. He's carrying a beer for Holden, who takes it gratefully and necks it.

Why is it that even him swallowing is sexy? Dear god, I need to take a dip in the lake again.

"Water would be great."

"We have wine if you prefer?"

I shake my head. I'm not a huge drinker and I'm in charge of Evan. "Honestly, water's fine."

"Take a seat," he says warmly. "I'll bring it out." He glances at Holden. "Can you come and help me with some prep?"

"Sure." Holden nods. I walk over to the swing seat. It's next to one of the windows and I can see Evan and Charlie sitting happily on a tartan sofa, the two of them watching the flat screen television fixed to the wall. I can't see what they're watching but it has their attention.

Normally I'd drag him outside, but he's had so much fresh air he could probably do with some rest.

"Mind if I join you?" Ava asks. She's carrying two glasses of water.

"Sure, go ahead." I shuffle to the left so Ava can sit on the seat next to me. She passes me a glass and I take a long sip.

"Thank you for having us over," I say. "It must have been a shock to find us swimming in the lake this morning."

"A nice shock," she says softly. "Holden doesn't come here enough. Myles misses him. We all do."

"Do his other brothers come here more often?"

"All the time," she says. "Especially in the summer. We almost didn't come this weekend but Myles has been stressed at work so I insisted."

"He doesn't look stressed," I say. "He looks like he has the whole world under control."

She laughs. "I won't tell him you said that. He's got a big enough head as it is."

She's so easy to talk to. I already like her a lot.

"Holden was saying you have an interview at a library?" Ava continues. He must have said it quick. They were only all inside for a minute.

"Yes. I'm about to complete my masters in Library Science.

I've been applying to jobs but this is the first interview I have."

"How exciting. I work with books, too."

I tip my head, interested. "You do?"

Ava nods. "I run a publishing imprint. Children's books."

"Do I know any of them?" I ask.

"Have you heard of *Dandy the Lion*?"

I beam, excited. "That was Evan's favorite book when he was smaller. I feel like I know Dandy intimately."

She laughs. "Sorry about that. He's kind of addictive."

"Who's kind of addictive?" Holden asks, walking out of the cabin carrying a tray full of meat.

"Not you." I smirk at him.

He lifts a brow back. "I beg to differ." He carries the tray around to the side of the cabin, where the grill is placed out of the way, just in case the kids run out without looking. Myles joins him and they light it up, the two of them holding beers and talking.

Ava sighs. "This is so nice. I can't remember the last time I saw Holden so relaxed."

"He has a stressful job," I murmur, unable to take my eyes off of him. He's a different Holden with his family. Carefree almost. It makes my thigh muscles tighten.

He glances over at me. Our gazes hold for way too long.

Myles puts some music on the outside speakers. The Four Seasons come on, singing "December '63". Ava is telling me about an outreach program she has with libraries, and I'm listening and nodding along while I watch the man I think I might be falling for.

It takes about an hour for the food to be ready. We all take turns going in and checking on the boys while the grill does the work. Charlie is curled up next to Evan, his head resting on Evan's arm. He doesn't look annoyed at sitting with the younger boy.

He looks as happy as I feel.

"Dinner's ready," Holden murmurs in my ear. A shiver snakes down my spine. This man could say the most inane things to me and sound sexy.

"That's good. I could do with some meat."

He splutters a laugh, and I turn to grin at him.

This is good.

Life is good.

It's time to start enjoying it.

———

HOLDEN

We spend the next couple of hours eating and drinking and laughing. Ava and Blair are getting along like they've known each other for years. They talk about books – of course – and raising boys, and then Ava regales Blair with stories of our escapades as teenagers.

Myles has a big mouth. There's no way my sister-in-law should know that I once got dared to streak naked through the school grounds.

"That's my cue to clean up," I say, because Blair really doesn't need to hear any more about me as a teenager.

"I'll do it," Blair says, jumping up. "You cooked."

"I'll help you," Ava says, her voice warm. At the same time Evan and Charlie start to yawn, so she takes them inside to watch one more movie before bedtime.

Myles and I are sitting on camp chairs, beers in our hands, looking at the sun setting over the lake. It's funny, but since I spend so little time here, I forget how beautiful this place is. How quiet.

I'm so used to noise, all the time that the quiet feels weird. But nice.

"So…" Myles clears his throat.

"She's a friend," I say. "That's all."

"Ava saw you touching her ass. That's not just friends."

I guess I'm not as surreptitious as I thought. And Blair has an amazing ass.

"Did I ever question you about Ava?" I ask him. The two of them met when they worked together at her publisher. They clashed from the start. Then he brought her here for a week when our Dad got remarried by the lake, saying something about them having a project to work on.

But it turned out the project was getting her pregnant. A long story, but Charlie was the eventual result.

"I got completely ripped apart by all of you about Ava."

"Mostly by Liam," I point out. My second oldest brother is the world's biggest gossip.

Myles chuckles lightly. "Probably." He takes a sip of his beer. "I like her a lot."

"Ava?" I ask, confused.

"Blair. She's good for you. And Evan, too."

I shift in my seat.

"You should tell her how you feel." He glances over at me. There's only kindness in his eyes. That's the thing about Myles. From a distance people think he's haughty, but he'd do anything for anybody. He's just had to build a wall to keep all the crap out.

The same way we all have.

"How I feel?" I repeat, mostly because I'm playing for time. I like her. No, I more than like her.

But I'm not supposed to.

"Don't let her slip through your fingers," Myles says lightly. "Ava says she's good for you."

It's my turn to laugh. "Thanks for the advice. But I think we both know my job and domestic bliss don't mix." I'm surprised she hasn't gotten pissed with my work hours already. It's only because hers are as messed up as mine are. For now at least.

But they won't be for long. She's going to graduate and then she'll leave. My throat tightens because that will be the end of us. I can't leave with her.

I won't leave my job, and I won't stand in the way of her picket-fence-dreams. We're at an impasse. Which is exactly why this wasn't supposed to be complicated.

Doesn't mean I don't wonder if we could make the long distance thing work. But she hasn't said anything about it. And I also worry that I'll mess things up between us if I try to talk to her about it. Things are good between us right now. I like her a lot.

More than a lot.

My chest tightens at the thought of that.

Myles gives me one of his looks. The same look he used to give me when we were kids and I'd borrow his Gameboy.

Without asking.

"It's nothing serious," I tell him. "Just a bit of fun." It's not true but I don't want to talk to my brother about this anymore. "Stop trying to make it into something it isn't."

"Okay, the dishes are done," Ava says, walking out with Blair. "Now it's time to relax."

I shoot a glance at Myles and he shrugs. Conversation over. It's a good thing, really. Neither of us like talking about emotions or love or anything like that.

Which was why we all spent most of our childhood beating each other up.

CHAPTER
TWENTY-THREE

BLAIR

It's almost ten by the time we get back to Holden's cabin. He carries Evan – *again* – because he was fast asleep on the couch, Charlie curled up in his lap like a dog, when we went in to tell him it was bed time.

Holden takes Evan straight into the bedroom and I grab his toothbrush and a washcloth then wake him up to get into his pajamas, but by the time he's under the covers he's fast asleep again.

When I walk out of the bedroom Holden is in the living room, looking at his phone.

"Hi." I smile softly at him. I like him so much, it's almost painful.

It's just a bit of fun.

That's what he said to Myles. I don't think I was supposed to overhear it but I did. He said nothing that was untrue, so I shouldn't be upset by it. I just want to enjoy this time together.

I want to push all the thoughts and fears away.

"Hey." He reaches for me and I walk into his arms. His hand cups my chin, tips my head up, and his lips softly touch mine.

All that not touching. Not kissing. Not being able to feel his skin against mine, it explodes in my chest. I kiss him hungrily, feeling his hands sliding down my hips, our mouths still moving against each other as we somehow stumble onto the sofa bed.

I can't get enough of this man. My fingers tangle in his hair as he kisses down my throat, to my chest, then pushes my dress up so he can kiss my breasts.

I let out a low groan as he captures my nipple in his mouth.

"Holden..."

He glances over my shoulder, his cheeks heated. "I know."

If we're doing this we need to be quiet. He pulls my dress down and kisses my lips again. And I somehow shimmy out of my panties. A moment later I free him from his jeans and boxers, feeling the thickness of his excitement rubbing against me.

Our kisses are softer now. More gentle. He reaches down to touch me, his hand dipping beneath the hem of my dress. He groans when he feels how wet I am.

Neither of us talk but we both know we can't stop this. Whatever it is, it feels bigger than us right now.

When he slides inside of me it feels so good my whole body clenches. Like I'm experiencing a little bit of heaven I don't deserve. We're both laying on our sides, facing each other, kissing, as he slowly hitches his hips against me.

His gaze is locked on mine. There's a rawness to it that I can feel in my own heart. My breath is ragged, our kisses uncoordinated, as I dig my hands into his behind, encouraging his thrusts.

I'm falling. I'm falling for this man. It's all I can think as I tighten around him, the pleasure making me groan against his mouth. And as I come around him, he comes apart too, surging inside of me, our mouths still attached.

As soon as I catch my breath he pulls out, but his eyes are still intense. On mine. For a long moment we just stare at each other.

I have so many things I want to tell him, but I'm scared.

"Stay here with me," he whispers.

"What if Evan wakes up?"

"I'll make sure you're back in bed before dawn." His gaze is a promise. I nod because I can't say no to him.

I don't want to. Ever.

We clean up and put our pajamas on, and I fall asleep in his arms.

And when I wake up I'm in bed with Evan.

The gorgeous, muscled idiot must have carried my sleeping body there.

———

As soon as I walk into the living room, I can sense something's wrong. Holden has his back to me, but he's on the phone, his voice low as he shoots questions to whoever's on the other end of the line.

"When did it happen? How did it happen?" he asks. "You can't just walk off a goddamn pediatric ward."

That's when I realize it's the hospital calling. I shift my feet, then decide to make us some breakfast because he could be on the call a while.

When I pull the cupboard open he looks over at me, but his eyes don't focus properly. He's definitely in doctor land.

"The police?" he asks. "Yes, of course."

My chest tightens. What the hell is happening? Why would the police need to be involved on a cancer ward?

"Aunti—" Evan runs out in his pajamas and I immediately shush him. Holden waves his hand and walks out of the cabin, the door closing behind him.

"Did I do something wrong?" Evan asks, sounding worried.

"No, sweetie. Holden just has a few problems at work." I think.

He's outside for at least fifteen minutes. Long enough for Evan to eat a bowl of cereal and take a shower. "Can I put my swim trunks on?" he asks, looking excited. "Can we go in the lake now?"

I offer him a quick smile. "I don't know. Let's wait for Holden to come back."

Evan shifts his feet, looking so disappointed it hurts my heart. When the door opens and Holden walks in, Evan runs over to him. "Can we go swimming now?"

Holden swallows hard. "Sorry, bud. I have to go back to New York."

"Now?" Evan says, sounding so disappointed it hurts my heart.

"Yeah, now."

Holden looks at me and I can tell from his face that something is very wrong. He looks almost panicked. My chest tightens, because he's an oncologist. The only conclusion I can come to is that one of his kids took a turn for the worse.

"Evan, pack your things up," I say, looking over at Holden. He's busy looking at his phone again.

"Why do we have to go?" he whines.

"Evan!" I immediately regret my sharp tone. "Sweetie, please do as I ask."

When he closes the bedroom door behind him Holden looks at me. "It's Mabel."

It feels like the floor is falling away from my feet. I saw her last week. She was fine. We laughed and talked.

"What?" I manage to whisper. "How bad is she?"

He blinks, as though confused. "She didn't take a turn for

the worse. She's run away. Somehow she escaped from the ward. They're looking at the security cameras now."

It takes a moment for his words to sink in.

"How do you know she escaped? Could somebody have taken her?"

"She left a note. It's her handwriting, apparently."

"So where did she go?" I ask. My heart is hammering against my chest.

He runs his hand through his hair. "On an adventure." The words come out as a monotone.

"An adventure?" I repeat. "I don't get it. She's supposed to go home next week."

"Yeah, and she doesn't want to. She and her mom…" He trails off and I nod, because I know that. She doesn't say a lot about her family but I've heard enough to know it's complicated. He clears his throat. "Rose thinks she got the idea to run away from reading that book."

My chest tightens. "*The Catcher in the Rye*?"

He nods.

"I gave her that book." I feel sick. Really sick.

"I can't find my other sock," Evan says. "Have you seen it?" I look at his feet. He has one sock on, the other bare.

"I'll come look." I shoot a glance at Holden. He's back on his phone again. His face looks pallid beneath the light tan we all got this weekend. I want to hug him. To touch him. To tell him it's okay.

But all I can think is that this is my fault. I gave Mabel the blueprint to run away in Manhattan.

———

Holden barely talks on the drive home. The atmosphere in the car is edgy. Even Evan must notice it, because he sits quietly in his booster seat, looking out of the window.

He asks if we're stopping at the diner again on the way

home, but when I tell him no, we have to go straight home, he doesn't complain.

And it breaks my heart a little bit.

It's lunchtime when we pull up outside our apartment. I messaged Annie earlier to warn her that we'd be home early and she'd replied that it was no problem, so I assume even if her date went well last night he didn't stay over.

"Are you sure I can't come with you?" I ask Holden. He's heading straight to the hospital from here to deal with what's happened to Mabel. "I could at least help search for her."

He shakes his head. "The board wants to talk to me. And the police are there, too."

"Will they want to talk to me?" I ask.

"I don't know." He frowns. "Maybe."

"Why do the police want you?" Evan pipes up from the back. "Have you done something wrong?"

I turn to look at Evan. His brows are pulled tight. We really shouldn't be having this conversation in front of him. "No, sweetheart. It's all fine. Just some work things that Holden has to do."

"Are the police sick?" Evan asks.

Holden's hands are still on the wheel. His knuckles are tight and blanched.

"Let's get you inside. I'll explain there."

I help Evan climb out and grab his booster as Holden grabs our bags. "I'm sorry," he says, his voice soft. "I just need to go."

"I know." I nod. "It's fine. We can talk later."

He flashes me the smallest of smiles. And that's it. He gets back in the car and I take Evan and our things up to our apartment, only looking back once, because Holden is already gone.

Annie is all smiles when we get up to the apartment. There's no sign that anybody was here, but I swear she has the same look on her face that I had on my own last night.

"How was it?" I murmur, when Evan is out of sight for a moment.

"I'll tell you later." She smiles. "How was yours?"

I take a deep breath. "It was good until it wasn't." I glance at the clock on the wall. Holden probably hasn't even made it to the hospital yet. I want to message him but I also know he probably needs that like he needs a hole in the head.

I can't help feeling anxious though. Like this is my fault. If I hadn't given her that book. If I hadn't thought it was funny because of his name…

"Tell me about the good bits," Annie says.

"Evan had so much fun. We swam and we hiked and we grilled and it was just perfect." I smile sadly remembering how fun it was.

"We met Holden's brother," Evan pipes up. I didn't even know he was listening. "Did you know he has five of them? And a little sister. She's smaller than me."

Annie smiles warmly at him. "Is that right?"

"Yep. And Holden says I swim like a fish. That's good, isn't it? Fish are good swimmers."

I nod and ruffle his hair. "They're the best."

"I met Charlie. He's Holden's…" Evan blinks.

"Nephew," I tell him. It's sad but Evan doesn't have the best grasp of wider family relationships. I should probably find a book about that to explain it all.

"Yeah. We watched a Pokémon movie. Next time you should come too, Mom."

"Next time," Annie repeats, giving me a concerned look. I shake my head slightly. We didn't make any plans for next time. It's just the hope of a little boy.

"When we move you'll be able to play like that all the time," I say to him. He nods, not looking that interested.

I glance at my phone again. No messages. It still hasn't been enough time for Holden to get to the hospital, let alone find out what's happening.

When I look up, Annie's eyes are on me. She looks worried. "Do you need to go?" she asks. "Because I have things under control if you do."

I nod, thankful that she can read me like a book. I can't just sit here and do nothing.

"Then go," she says. "Go and do what you need to do. Just call me if you need anything."

CHAPTER
TWENTY-FOUR

HOLDEN

The ward is in chaos as I walk in, and I'm keenly aware that I didn't shower this morning and probably look like I spent the weekend fucking.

The head of hospital security is in the meeting room, along with the police and two members of the hospital board. Mabel's parents are also here, and as I walk down the hallway I hear the high pitch of her mom's voice as she demands that they do something. Anything to find her.

I tap on the door and a deep voice tells me to come in. As soon as I push the door open the voices hush. Mabel's parents look at me like I'm some kind of savior.

"Do you know where she is?" her mom asks, the tiniest bit of hope in her tone. Even though she and her husband are divorced they're both here, and it's kind of ironic that it took this to get them to work together.

If Mabel was here she'd probably roll her eyes.

"I'm sorry, I don't," I tell her. "But I'll do whatever I can to help find her."

Dan Shawcross, the head of security for the hospital, stands and looks at me. I've only met him a few times. Once at a fundraiser for the hospital, and then a couple of times when we've had security reviews of the ward. Mostly I meet his officers if there's a problem that needs sorting.

"Dr. Salinger, can we talk in your office?"

"Why?" Mabel's mom asks. "Why can't you talk here?"

"I just need to bring him up to speed on events. I don't want to upset you by making you listen to it all over again," he says smoothly. Then he looks at the two police officers at the table. "Perhaps you can join us?"

I lead the three of them to my office. They pull up chairs and I sit down behind my desk.

"So here's what we've got," Dan says. "We believe she left the hospital right after two this morning. There was nobody else with her. The letter she left says not to worry, she just wants to be alone for a while and have an adventure. Our understanding is that she and her mom have been having a lot of arguments. They're moving and Mabel doesn't like it."

"Understandable," I murmur. "She's been through a lot."

"Can you think of anywhere she might go?" the older of the police officers asks.

I blow out a mouthful of air. "Have you tried the places in the book?"

"*The Catcher in the Rye*?" Dan asks. At least Rose updated him on that after our talk over the phone. "She took it with her."

"I have a copy here." I pull open the drawer in my desk and pass it over to them. "In the book the lead character runs away from school and comes to Manhattan. He goes to Central Park and a hotel and his house." I try to think where else that little shit went. Blair would probably know.

"Her mother mentioned something about a teacher coming in to read with her," Dan says. "Do you have her information."

"Her name is Blair Walsh," I say, hating that I have to bring her into it. "She's a librarian." No need to tell them about her job at the club. "She and Mabel have been studying the classics together."

"Could Mabel have gone to her?" the policeman asks.

I shift in my seat, aware of how bad it will look if they find out that Blair and I had been together this weekend. Neither of us are involved in this – for a start we were hundreds of miles away. But I know they'd spend a long time digging into her past, and she doesn't need that right now.

"I spoke with her on my way here. She hasn't heard from her at all."

It takes an hour for me to answer all of their questions. They want to know as much as they can about her diagnosis, her treatment, and every member of staff she's come into contact with. And when the police leave to follow up on my answers, Dan remains.

"We're completely in the shit here," he tells me. "Her parents are threatening to sue and they have every right to. This is a major security failure. I need you to make a statement as her physician. And we need to find her."

"Yes." I nod. "We do." I don't care how in the shit we are. All I care about is finding Mabel and protecting Blair.

Everything else can go to hell.

"And I need to talk to this Blair person. I'll need a statement from her even if the police don't. Can you give me her number?" he asks.

"I'll need to check with her first." I'm not going to let him call her without warning.

Dan frowns. "Okay, but get back to me soon." He stands. "What a shit way for us to spend a Sunday."

"It's even shittier for Mabel," I say.

"I don't believe that for a second," he replies. "I bet that kid's having the time of her life."

He opens the door to my office, and actually jumps when he sees someone standing on the other side.

My chest tightens when I see that it's Blair. She looks at me, her brows pinched. "I'm sorry," she says. "I just couldn't sit around and do nothing."

"Who are you?" Dan asks, then he glances at me. "Is this her?"

"Blair Walsh? Yeah."

"Who let you in?" he asks. "There's supposed to be a guard at the fucking door vetting everyone coming and going to the unit."

She blanches. "They called Rose. She let me in." She looks at me. "I didn't mean to cause any problems."

"You haven't," I tell her, all to aware that Dan's scrutinizing us both.

She shifts her feet. "Is there any news?" she asks.

"Nothing yet. The police are on it," I tell her. She nods, looking upset.

"Are they checking out the locations in the book?" she asks. It was one of the few things we talked about on the way back from Misty Lakes. She was insistent that they needed to check all the locations.

"I suggested it."

"I wrote them all down." She's holding out a piece of paper with a list of places, some with asterisks next to them.

"Can I have that?" Dan asks. "I can pass it on to the police."

"Not all of them are real locations in the book," Blair says as she lets him take the notepaper. "But Mabel's clever. She'll have worked out the places they're based on." She points at something on the paper. "This hotel for example, the Edmont, it's not real, but a lot of people assume it's located on West Fifty-Seventh Street, between Sixth and Seventh Ave."

"Great." Dan nods. "I'm gonna take this to them now. And

then I'd like to have a word with you. Get a statement from you. Can you wait here for me?"

Blair looks at me and then back at Dan, nodding. "Of course."

"Okay then." He steps aside to let her in, then walks out to the hallway, closing the door behind him.

"I'm sorry," Blair says. "I didn't know what else to do. I just knew I couldn't sit around and wait."

"It's okay," I tell her. "I was about to call you anyway. Dan was asking about you." I nod at the chair he'd been sitting in and she takes it. She's wearing the same jeans and white top she had on during our drive back, her hair pulled up into a bun, but she still looks beautiful.

"Do they think she'll be okay?" Blair asks.

"It's Mabel," I say. "If she left voluntarily she probably has a plan. And it's summer so it's not cold out there."

"That's good," Blair agrees. "I just wish she'd talked to me. I could have taken her to those places if she wanted."

"They don't really think it's about her wanting to see the locations. It's more about her family troubles. Her having to go home soon probably triggered this."

Blair's eyes catch mine. "Poor Mabel."

"Yeah, well I'm not exactly feeling sorry for her right now," I say. "The mess she's caused."

Her mouth twitches. "Shut up. We both know she's your favorite."

I pinch my nose because it's the truth. I'm furious with Mabel, but I'm worried sick as well. "When Dan gets back he's going to ask some questions."

"Okay." Blair nods.

"And I'd prefer if you didn't tell him about us." I've been thinking about this since Dan asked about her. If we admit the reality of our situation it will make him want to know more.

And I want to protect her. I don't want her being involved in any of this.

The tentative smile on her face disappears. "You want me to lie?"

"Let's just not make it complicated. We'll just give him the information he needs about Mabel, not us."

She opens her mouth to reply, but before she can, Dan walks back in.

"Okay then," he says to her, pulling up a chair. "Let's get this statement done so you can be on your way."

————

BLAIR

It takes a while for me to answer Dan's questions. They're mostly about my time with Mabel, as well as the books we looked at. He asks me whether we had any contact outside of my visits at the hospital, and I truthfully answer no. She doesn't have my number and I don't have hers.

He asks me briefly about my studies, and then when he finds out I'm ex-military he becomes a lot friendlier. It turns out he's from a military family. Two of his brothers have served overseas, and he originally was on the police force before moving into security.

Holden has to leave halfway through the conversation to give a second opinion on a patient. He glances back at me, his brows knitted, then strides out.

"Interesting man," Dan says as the door closes behind him.

"Yeah."

"How do you know him again?"

"I work part time at a bar to help pay the bills while I'm studying," I answer. "He's a customer." I deliberately leave out the name of the bar.

His lip curls. "Funny, I can't picture him chatting up barmaids."

"He didn't chat me up. We're just friends." There's a weird twist in my stomach as I say it. Partly because it's a lie. But mostly because it reminds me of what I overheard last night, when Holden was talking to his brother. When he told him that our relationship was just a bit of fun.

"And he asked you to visit with Mabel because of your studies?" Dan asks.

"He knows I love the classics." I nod.

"And in your opinion, what would have made Mabel run away?" he asks.

"I've no idea," I say truthfully. "I thought she was happy to be going home. I knew she has family problems, but we didn't talk too much about them. Mostly about books."

"This book," he says. "*The Catcher in the Rye*. You really think that's why she left?"

"I don't know," I tell him again, annoyed because there seems to be so much I don't know. "It was just a thought. She really liked it. A lot of kids do. They like the idea of running away from everything."

He looks at me one more time before nodding. "Okay, I think that's it. You can go home now."

"Can't I stay and wait for news?" I ask him.

"No." His reply is short. "The less people we have on the ward the better. I'll walk you out."

He's probably right, but I don't like it. And I don't like leaving Holden to face the music. But still, I stand up and follow him out, keeping my eyes open for Holden so I can say goodbye.

But he's not around. I do get a glimpse into the meeting room as I walk by though. At the table there's a woman weeping. It has to be Mabel's mother, the resemblance is clear.

Dammit Mabel, where are you?

I hate the way she's causing all this pain. I hate even more that I might have had a hand in it. But she's just a kid who's been dealt a shit hand in life. I can understand why she wanted to run.

"So you'll be graduating soon?" Dan inquires as we reach the door out of the ward. He really is taking escorting me off the premises seriously.

"Yes."

"And then?"

"Then I'm planning on getting a library job."

"Well good luck with that." He smiles and gestures for me to leave. "And keep your phone on, just in case we have any additional questions."

The door to the ward closes behind me, and I start toward the elevators, feeling frustrated that I couldn't do anything more to help. Even more frustrated that Holden looked so tired and worn out yet he's still being called to consult on emergencies. Maybe that's why I don't hear my name being called until I'm almost at the elevator.

But I feel his hand on my shoulder. And I also feel a rush of warmth go through me as I turn to meet Holden's bright blue eyes.

"Did everything go okay with Dan?" he asks.

"Yes." I nod. "He just wanted a few details, mostly about the books we've been reading."

"And you didn't tell him about us?" His voice is low. I notice him looking to the side to make sure we aren't being overheard.

"No. Nothing at all."

His expression softens. "Good. I just don't want to complicate things. We need to find Mabel, that's all. Plus I'd rather Dan didn't go digging into you. I know you like your privacy."

Oh. I immediately feel bad because I thought he was protecting himself.

But he wasn't. He was protecting me. Always me.

I stare back at him, so acutely aware that I'm falling for him. Or fallen. It feels like I'm on the ground staring up at him like nothing else matters.

He reaches out to cup my face. "Blair..."

Even his voice feels like a warm blanket. I want to bury myself in him. But then the elevator pings and he looks over my shoulder. It takes him a second too long to take his hand away.

But he doesn't look worried. He starts to smile instead. So I look over my shoulder to see who's walking out of the elevator. And every hair on my body stands up.

It's his brother. The one I met in Holden's kitchen in my cleaning outfit. And he's staring at me like he's seen a ghost.

Linc stops just short of us, looking from Holden then back to me. He's carrying a suit bag and a duffel. "Hey," he says. "Holden, Blair." He holds out the things he's carrying. "I got your message," he tells Holden. "I packed what clothes I could for you, man. Probably left your place looking like a tornado hit. I guess Blair can clean it up, right?"

Holden looks confused. "Why would Blair clean my place up?"

"Er, because she's your cleaner." The smile wavers on Lincoln's face. "I met her at your place, remember?"

I freeze. Because I should have told Holden this a long time ago. But I thought it didn't matter. Or that it shouldn't.

But right now I want to disappear into the ground.

"Are you talking about when I was sick?"

Linc looks at me, confused.

"No, man. I met Blair before that. When I borrowed your dinner suit and she had to put my mess away." He wrinkles his nose. "Sorry about that," he says to me. "If I'd known you two were..." he waves his hand from me to Holden, "seeing each other, I never would have asked for your help."

"My cleaner?" Holden says again.

The bafflement in his eyes is mixed with something else. It

looks scarily like betrayal. I open my mouth to try to explain. To tell him that no, I'm not just his cleaner. I'm also not just the woman who serves him water when he's thirsty after beating the hell out of somebody in the fight room at the bar.

But nothing comes out. Not a word. Not a squeak.

"Oh shit." Linc gulps.

CHAPTER
TWENTY-FIVE

HOLDEN

Blair's face is pale as she looks at me. Her lips are moving but no sound is coming out. Linc's still half-smiling but his shoes are scuffing against the hospital floor as he literally tries to back away.

And my own mind is fucking racing because I don't know what the hell is going on.

I take the bag of clothes from Lincoln and give him a nod. He understands immediately and starts to back away from us.

"I'll call you later," he says under his breath as he punches at the elevator button and by some damn miracle the doors open right away. He hightails it back in the car before they close again.

I look back at Blair. She hasn't moved an inch. With my bag in one hand, I take her hand with my other, dragging her down the hallway. She has to walk fast to keep up with my strides.

"Wait," she says. "Where are we going?"

"To talk." We stop outside an old storage room that used to be notorious among the staff for being the sex closet. We used to find interns and fellows in here all the time in various states of undress. But the janitor since put a keypad on the door and only a few of us know the code. I punch it in and push the door open.

Blair reluctantly follows me inside. Once upon a time we used to keep files in here, but most of them are either electronic or stored in a mountain somewhere else. Now there are only empty shelves.

When I flick on the light she blinks like she's about to be interrogated. And I'm all too fucking aware that at any minute my phone is going to buzz with another emergency and I'll have to go.

But I need to know what the hell is going on.

Why does she know Linc?

"Talk," I say. "And make it fast."

Her eyes fill with tears. "I'm sorry."

"Faster."

She inhales raggedly. And I'd feel sorry for her except I'm so damn confused.

"I've been your cleaner for almost two years," she says, swallowing hard.

It's like a slap in the face. I don't want to believe it's true. She's the person who's been cleaning up after me all this time and she never said a word?

"When did you figure out that I was your client?" I ask.

Blair looks like she's about to be sick. "I knew all along. From the first time I saw you at the club."

"You knew who I was before we met and you didn't tell me?" My heart is hammering against my chest. "Why not?"

"I didn't think it mattered."

"Of course it fucking matters," I say, loud enough to make her flinch. I need to get my reaction under control but all I want to do is punch my fists against the wall. "So it wasn't a coincidence, you meeting me at the club? Were you stalking me?"

"No." She reaches for me and I flinch away. "I found a card for the club in your bathroom. And then I was walking to the bus one day and I saw it. I got curious and went inside. Jimmy thought I was there for an interview."

"And then what?" I ask, my voice short. "You decided it would be a good way to get close to me? Was that your plan all along? You want my money or something?"

Was she planning on making me fund her picket fence?

"How could you say that?" she asks, sounding stupidly hurt. "Of course I don't want your money."

"Then why did you take the job when Jimmy offered it to you? You had to know that we'd meet?"

Blair takes a deep breath. "I needed the money," she says, shifting her feet. "But I wanted to earn it. From Jimmy. I didn't think it would be a problem."

"You didn't think it would be a problem?" I repeat. Is this woman an idiot?

No, you are.

"I didn't think you'd ever find out." She squeezes her eyes shut. "I'm sorry, that came out wrong. I mean, I didn't think we'd ever get close enough for it to be a problem."

"But we did. So why didn't you tell me then?" My voice is terse enough for her to flinch.

She won't look at me and I hate it. I reach out, trying to keep my hands as soft as possible when I tip her chin up. "Open your eyes," I tell her.

She does, and as they lift a single tear escapes them.

"Don't fucking cry." I'll be a goner if she does. And I can't be. I can't let this hurt me. I can't let myself be vulnerable.

She'll just take and take.

"I'm sorry," she whispers, wiping the tear away. I release her chin, because touching her hurts.

But not touching her hurts, too. It all fucking hurts.

"I should have told you," she says. "When we first had sex. I should have told you then. But I was scared that you'd react badly. That you'd think the worst of me. But I promise I wasn't stalking you, I just needed the job."

I want to believe her. I do. But this is way too much of a tangled mess. "I would have listened. I would have understood."

Her teary eyes meet mine. "Then try to understand now," she whispers.

My phone starts to buzz. Fuck. "I lied to Dan for you," I remind her. "To protect you."

"I lied to him, too," she says softly.

"And you lied to me. You're fucking great at it, aren't you? You're wasted in a library."

Pain flashes through her eyes. I grab my phone and see Rose's name on the screen.

"I have to take this." She nods as I slide my finger to accept the call, lifting the phone to my ear. "Rose."

"They've found her," she says. "She's safe."

"Mabel?"

"Yes, you idiot."

Blair's eyes open wider. She doesn't move her gaze from me.

"Okay," I tell Rose. "I'll be right there." I end the call and stuff the phone back into my pocket. A wave of weariness washes over me. Was it really only a few hours since we were in Virginia?

And a few minutes since I found out the woman I fucking adore has been lying to me all this time?

"Mabel's fine," I tell her. A half-smile pulls at her lips. "I have to go."

She nods. "Can I do anything—"

"Go home, Blair. If you want to do anything for me, just go home. Please just leave me alone."

BLAIR

Despite Holden's entreaties, I don't go home. Instead I find myself walking the streets, thinking about everything I did wrong. I should have told him, I know that.

It breaks my heart that I didn't.

But then my heart is broken anyway. It broke the moment I saw the look of betrayal on his face. After his experience with Claire, I know he hates being taken by surprise.

There's a reason why Holden's a fighter. He likes control.

I send a message to Annie telling her I'll be home much later, then I head to the only place I can think of to go.

I sit on a little bench just down the road from the huge brownstone building he lives in, watching as the sky slowly turns dark. It isn't until almost ten o'clock when I see his car slowly driving up the road. The indicator flicks on, and he begins to turn into the entrance of the underground parking lot.

But then he sees me, standing up and walking toward him in the half-light.

For a moment he just stares at me. I can't read his expression at all. Then he leans over to open the door.

"Get in."

I do exactly as he tells me, sliding into the seat and putting on the belt even though we're just going to his parking space. My hands tremble as I try to snap the buckle in.

Neither of us say a word until he's parked in his space. He switches off the engine and unbuckles his own belt, staring forward silently.

"Is Mabel okay?" I ask softly.

He doesn't look at me. "Yeah."

"Where did they find her?"

"At the natural history museum. The first place you put on your list."

I pull my lip between my teeth. I should have gone there myself. I could have prevented this whole mess.

"And she hasn't made herself worse? No injuries?"

"No worse than she was already. We checked her over, sent her for a hot shower and then ordered some food. Rose has her covered."

"That's good," I say. There's a drip coming from the pipes along the ceiling of the underground parking lot. It patters on the roof of his car. "I'm so sorry, Holden."

He slowly shakes his head.

"Please don't. I've had a shit day and all I want to do is go to sleep." He sounds exhausted. "I'm not in the mood for explanations."

"I wasn't going to give you one. Just an apology. I should have told you. I should have done a lot of things." My chest feels so tight it's hard to breathe. "You're the last person I wanted to hurt."

"But you did."

I wince. "I know." I turn to look at him. There's no kindness in his expression. Just a blankness. The same lack of emotion he shows before a fight. It's like he's put every barrier up he can find.

And I hate that. Because I thought we'd broken through them all.

"I thought you were different with me," he says. And those words hurt more than anything else.

"I was," I tell him. "I never let anybody in before you."

"You never let me in either." He sighs, running a hand through his hair. "I thought you did, but you didn't. I don't think you ever will."

Tears threaten again, but I blink them away because I know how much he hates it when I cry. "I did," I say. "I let you in. I fell for you Holden. I'm in love with you. I'll do whatever you need for me to make it up to you."

Disbelief pulls at his features. I hate that. I hate that he won't believe me.

"I don't want your love," he says, his voice flat. "I don't want to be loved by a liar. Now get out and go home, Blair. I don't want to talk to you anymore."

I try to think of something to say to make this better. But the right words don't come. Just a sob that I try to swallow because I can't pull the crying woman card.

"Okay." I nod. "I'll go."

He doesn't reply.

"But please give my love to Mabel." Because I know he won't let me contact her. He shouldn't either. "And I'm sorry for causing so much trouble. You didn't deserve it." I pull at the door latch, and it takes two tries before the door opens. I don't turn to look at him again because the tears are already pouring down my face. I love him. I didn't even realize that until I said it.

I love him so much and he's hurting and I hate it.

I stumble out of the car and close the door behind me, catching sight of his wounded look. And then I walk with as much dignity as I can to the parking lot entrance, because he doesn't need to see me break down.

I save that part for home, where I fall into Annie's arms.

Because I've messed everything up, and I don't know how to make it all better.

CHAPTER
TWENTY-SIX

BLAIR

"Eat," Annie says, pushing a bowl of soup toward me. We're in the kitchen and it's late. We should both be in bed, and we'll be paying for it in the morning.

"I'm not hungry." I shoot her an apologetic look because she went to all the trouble of opening a can and putting the bowl in the microwave. Which is quite a feat for her.

"Okay, if you're going to force me to do this." She pulls the bowl toward her and scoops up a spoonful and holds it out. "I'll feed you like we used to feed Evan if I have to."

"I'm not going to starve if I skip a couple of meals," I point out, aware that I haven't eaten the whole day.

"No, but you might fail your final assessment on Friday if you're not completely ready for it," she says. "And to be ready you need to eat and sleep. So do as you're told."

I do, taking the spoon from her because I don't need to be fed like a baby. It takes me a long time but I somehow manage to get through half the bowl without throwing it up.

"Seriously," she utters. "I'm not going to let him mess this up for you. You've worked too hard for this. Years."

"He's not the one who messed things up. I am."

She rolls her eyes. "You omitted one little thing. That's it. He doesn't get to treat you like crap without listening to your explanation. I thought he cared for you."

"He does. He did." Nausea pulls at my stomach because I'm not so sure anymore. "He thinks I'm untrustworthy."

"Then he doesn't know you as well as he thinks he does," she replies. She's pissed on my behalf which I appreciate, but it's causing me to defend him more. "I've never met anybody more trustworthy than you," she says. "You served in the military for years so that I could go to college. Then you waited even longer so you could do the same. You help me every day with Evan. You helped him with Mabel. You clean his fucking apartment and have done for years." She presses her lips together. "Without any thanks I might add."

"He pays for it."

"Not enough. Because you had to get a second job," she says.

I pick the bowl up and empty the rest of the contents down the sink, then load it into the dishwasher as though I'm running on automatic. She's angry and always on my side and it's sweet, but this time I think she's wrong. "It doesn't matter anyway," I mumble. "He's not going to forgive me."

"Then he's losing out." She shifts her chair, the legs scraping against the floor. "Can I ask you something?" she questions softly.

"Sure."

"If you're in love with him, what were you going to do? You're about to graduate. You have this interview out of state. You've always had this dream of leaving New York City. How would it have worked?"

"I don't know," I say honestly. "I've been too scared to

think about it. Maybe it's a good thing that I don't have to any more."

"I don't think it's a good thing. I hope he brings his scrawny ass around and begs you to take him back so you can tell him to take a hike."

"He's not scrawny and he won't be begging," I tell her. I know him too well. He's already closed up. He's done.

And it hurts like hell.

"Then promise me one thing?" I nod so she continues. "Don't let him mess this up for you. Go to class tomorrow and work your ass off the way you always have. You need to graduate, you deserve to."

My throat feels so full I don't say anything. Just nod and let the sadness overwhelm me again.

There are so many thoughts going through my mind. So many regrets.

But all I can really think of is him.

"I'm going to head to bed." My voice is thick with emotion. "Try to get some sleep."

She gives me a worried look, but nods anyway. "Sleep tight."

"Wait," I say, before I leave the kitchen. "Your date? How was it?"

She gives a little laugh. "Good but forgettable."

"Did you get any?" I lift a brow.

Annie shrugs. "A little. But it's going nowhere. Don't worry about it. Just go get some sleep."

———

HOLDEN

. . .

"Why did you say that to her?" Linc asks, shaking his head at me as he trails after me into the kitchen. "No wonder she left."

"Remind me why you're here again?" I ask, pinching the bridge of my nose because I have the world's worst headache and dealing with my kid brother is the icing on the cake I don't need. What is he doing here this late anyway?

I'd ask him, but I don't want to encourage conversation.

"Because you wouldn't answer your phone," he says.

"That's because I don't feel like talking to anybody," I point out, annoyed because I want to wallow alone.

Linc shrugs. He has this beautiful ability not to take a hint. "That's exactly when you should be talking to somebody. Is this a whiskey or a beer kind of talk?"

"I'm not thirsty."

He pulls the refrigerator open and grabs two beers, popping the caps and passing me one.

"I messed up," he says. "I'm sorry. I really thought you knew that Blair was your cleaner."

"I really didn't know." I lift the beer to my lips. It tastes good. "And it's not your fault. You weren't the one lying to me."

He wrinkles his nose. "It was just a little lie, though, right?"

"No, not just a little lie. She had all this time to tell me and she never did. I feel violated."

Linc splutters some beer out. "Violated? The woman cleaned your house, she didn't steal your jockstraps."

"How do you know that?" I ask.

"Is anything missing?"

Just a piece of my fucking heart.

"Only the things *you* steal," I say, because Linc has a habit of borrowing things without asking.

"And you forgive me, right?" he questions, giving me

puppy dog eyes. Do they work on anybody? I'm not sure, but they're definitely not working on me.

"There's nothing to forgive. You're my brother."

He actually smiles at that one. I guess it's kind of a compliment coming from me. Doesn't feel much like one though.

"And you'll forgive Blair, too," he says confidently.

"No." I shake my head. "I can't forgive her for lying to me."

His smile slips. He takes a mouthful of beer, his eyes on my face. "Why not?" he implores when he's finally swallowed it down.

"Because I promised myself I'd never let a woman do this to me again."

"After Claire," he says, nodding.

"Yep," I say curtly because I want to talk about that even less than I want to talk about Blair.

"But Claire slept with your buddy. Blair just cleans your house." He lifts a brow. "Claire and Blair. Hey, they rhyme. Maybe next time you can go out with a Stair."

"Fuck off."

The headache reminds me it's still there, pulsing at the center point of my brow. I sit down heavily on a bar stool.

"You okay?" Linc asks. "You look like shit, man."

"Just tired. I got a headache. Need my bed."

"You don't think it's that virus again? Because I'm not being your nursemaid." He looks appalled at the thought of it.

But now all I can think of is Blair. The way she slept – just slept – with me while I was sick. The way she took care of me.

I push the thought away. I don't need those. I need to be hard. It took a long time – and a lot of punches to get over being betrayed by Claire. But I did it.

And I'll do it again. But this time I'm not going to drag it out. I'm going to hate her, because if I think any other way it's going to crush me.

"So what are you going to do about it?" he asks. "I feel like I've messed everything up for you."

I soften, because I love this kid, even if he drives me up the wall.

"You've messed up nothing. And I'm doing nothing, except going to bed. It's over. She was going to leave after graduation anyway. This just ends it a bit earlier."

"And you're okay with that?" he asks, running his tongue along his bottom lip to catch a bead of beer.

No.

"Yeah, I am."

"Maybe you should talk to Myles," he says. "He's much better at this relationship shit than I am. He says he liked her when he saw her at Misty Lakes."

So the family chat has begun. *Wonderful.* I was never a fan even when I wasn't the one everybody was chatting about.

I hate it even more now.

"I don't need to talk to anybody," I say. "I just need to get some sleep then go to work tomorrow." And the next day and the next day. And eventually everything will be fine.

The way it used to be. When I didn't need anybody else.

"Is that your way of telling me to leave?" Linc asks. "Because I think it is, but I'm not sure."

He's looking unsure. He can be a cocky asshole but his heart is pure and I love him for that.

"I don't know," I say, because I don't want to be the asshole brother to him. "What do you want to do?"

He finishes his beer. "I think I'll leave," he says, patting my arm like he's the older one. "As long as you think you'll be okay without me."

"I'll survive," I say, deadpan. "But thanks for checking on me, I appreciate it."

He beams. "No problem. And next week we can talk about how you're an idiot for letting her go."

———

BLAIR

I'm at the library, trying to add some finishing touches to my presentation while trying not to cry when my phone rings. And for one stupid moment my heart leaps.

But then I see the caller. Georgie, my boss at City Slickers.

I think about rejecting the call because I'm almost certainly about to get fired. Which is good, really, because I was going to resign anyway. Even so, my hand shakes as I answer the phone.

"Hi," I say quietly. "Can you hold while I find somewhere to talk?"

"No problem," Georgie says, her voice echoing down the phone.

There are little break out rooms all around the perimeter of the library. Mostly they're for group work and the occasional seminar. The first two I come to are occupied, but then I find one that's free. From the electronic display outside it's been booked but whoever reserved it hasn't turned up.

As soon as I'm inside and the door is shut I unmute the phone. "Hi, sorry about that. I can talk now."

"It shouldn't take long," Georgie tells me, and I try to ignore the tightness in my gut. I feel physically and emotionally rung out. Annie gave me a pep talk this morning about getting through this a day at a time. She says I need to concentrate on my presentation for this Friday and my interview next week. I know she's right.

But my heart doesn't seem to be listening.

"I'll get straight to the point," Georgie's voice is sharp.

Chipper. "I'm afraid I have to take you off the Salinger Apartment. Dr. Salinger no longer needs our services."

My throat constricts. Even hearing his name makes me feel achy inside. "I'm sorry to hear that," I say.

I thought it felt like the end before. But now it feels like everything is crumbled around my feet. He didn't even call to tell me. Hasn't called me at all.

He wants to get rid of me in every way. I squeeze my eyelids shut for a minute, trying not to cry.

"I wouldn't be too sorry," Georgie continues. "Because he's offered to pay three months notice. Both to you and the company."

There's a long moment of silence. Enough for her to ask if I'm still here.

"Yes, I'm just surprised. I didn't realize clients needed to give that much notice."

"They don't, but he was very insistent. I suspect he's going with a competitor and feels bad. But we don't look a gift horse in the mouth, do we?"

"It's okay," I say softly. "I don't need the money. Please tell him thank you but no."

Georgie clears her throat. "He's already transferred it."

"Can you transfer it back?" I ask.

She sighs. She must think I'm being an idiot. But there's no way I'm taking any money from Holden. Yes, losing the cleaning job is going to dent our nest egg, but that's my problem, not his.

"I'm sorry, I just can't take it," I tell her. I don't want anything from him. Not this, anyway.

"I'll transfer your part back," she says, sounding unhappy about the whole situation. "But I'm keeping the agency's cut."

"Okay." I'm not going to argue about that.

"And you understand I don't have any work for you right now? All our slots are full. If I send back this money I can't pay you anything else."

"That's fine." I'm suddenly desperate to get off the phone, mostly because I want to scream at the world. I'm such an idiot. My heart is breaking and it's my fault. "But I'm sorry, I need to go."

"Okay then. Best of luck, Blair."

"And to you."

I hang up and lean against the heavy wooden door to the study room. I want to be angry about him trying to pay me off, but I can't be. All I feel is desperately sad. Because it's the end. He was only trying to make it easier in his own way. And that's the worst part of it all.

My melancholy is like a cloak that I hold around me as I go back to my work cubicle and fire up my laptop again, ignoring the interested looks from the students around me.

Because yes, my eyes are red. And yes, every now and then all I want to do is cry, but I have a degree to get.

I promised Annie I would do this and I will.

Even if it kills me.

CHAPTER
TWENTY-SEVEN

HOLDEN

It's been three days since I told Blair to leave, and I'm still feeling pissed. Everybody at work is giving me a wide berth. I heard two of the interns whispering because I told them off in front of all the staff.

And then Rose pulled me aside and told me to stop being an asshole.

It's funny, because that's exactly what I'm trying to be.

Assholes don't get lied to. And they don't get hurt. Maybe I'm a sadist at heart because I'd much rather be the one doing the hurting.

We've extended Mabel's stay by a week, just to make sure she's okay after running away. I spent most of Monday on the phone with her insurance company, because I wanted to run a battery of tests on her.

The results so far are good. If the rest of them come back the same she'll be able to go home on Friday. And this week she and her parents have been meeting with one of our psychologists to try to work through the reasons she bolted in the first place.

"Here," Rose says, walking into my office. "Mabel's been writing apology letters. We all get one." She passes me an envelope. I look at it blankly.

"Why's she written a letter to me?" I ask.

"Because she knows she's done wrong." Rose gives me a pointed look. I sigh and slide the flap open, pulling the hand-written note out.

Dear Dr. Salinger,

I'm sorry for causing so many problems. I thought I wanted an adventure, but really I wanted to be noticed. Not because I'm sick, (I'm tired of people noticing me because I'm sick) but because they love me more than anything.

It turns out, I'm as stupid as your namesake. I should have stayed in bed and read the books – they're always better than the movies. And real life too, sometimes.

Thank you for all you do to take care of me. And for introducing me to Blair. She rocks.

Anyway, I'd better finish this up, because I have TEN MORE to write. (That's why this is in big handwriting.)

Stay cool, Doc. And try to read some books. It'll do you good.

Your patient, Mabel.

. . .

I look at it for a minute. It's so Mabel it isn't funny. She obviously started off feeling emotional but then turned into snark.

I'll thank her for it later, because despite the way Rose is looking at me, I'm not a monster.

"Is there anything else?" I ask her, because I want to be alone. Which is almost impossible in this job, but I'll take five minutes where I can.

She sighs loudly. "There's one for Blair, too."

I try not to wince at the mention of her name. "Okay."

"So can you give it to her?" Rose asks. "I know you said she's not allowed on the ward anymore…"

"I said that there's no need to have her on the ward anymore," I correct. "Because Mabel's busy with her parents and then she's going home."

Rose has been trying to get the truth out of me, but I refuse to budge. I don't want to think about it and I don't want to talk about it.

She gives me one of her special, annoyed looks. "Whatever. You need to give it to her." She passes it to me. "I promised Mabel."

I push it back toward her. "I'll give you her address. You can mail it to her."

"Do I look like a mailman?" she asks. "She's your friend, you give it to her."

"She's not my friend." Something stabs in my chest. Probably my ice cold heart impaling itself.

For a moment she says nothing. Then she slowly slides it back to me. "I knew it!"

"Knew what?" I ask, aware that I'm taking the bait when I don't even want it. The letter stays in the middle of my desk like it's an island in the ocean.

"The reason you're a bear with a sore head. What did you do to her?"

I blink, annoyed at myself because I rose to her bait. "What do you mean?"

Rose lets out a long sigh. "Come on, Holden. I know you and she had a thing going. The same way I know you're an idiot and beat people up for the fun of it at a boxing club. I've known you for years and even though you can be a general ass…"

"General ass?" I repeat, my eyebrows raised.

"General ass," she confirms. "You're not usually this tetchy. So what did you do?"

"Why do you think I did anything? Why couldn't it be her?"

"She broke up with you?" Rose looks genuinely upset for me. "Oh, I'm so sorry."

Though I kind of like her sympathy, unlike other people I'm not a liar. "She didn't break up with me. I broke up with her."

"So it *was* your fault," she says. "I knew it."

My mouth gapes. "You're my friend, you're supposed to be on my side."

"I *am* on your side, Holden. Always. So why did you break up with her?"

My chest tightens. It's one thing for Linc to know the truth, another telling it to Rose. I just can't. I feel like an idiot. Like I've been duped. The sad sap who's a victim of a confidence scam or something.

"It doesn't matter," I say. "She's leaving anyway. She graduates soon and she wants to get out of the city."

"You broke up with her because she's leaving?" Rose looks confused. "Why?"

I mean I didn't, but whatever. I'm already over this conversation. "It doesn't matter. It's done, that's all you need to know."

"You're an idiot," she says. "I liked her."

Yeah, well I did too.

"Is that it, Rose?" I ask again.

This time she nods. "Give her the damn letter so I can tell Mabel it's done."

————

BLAIR

Evan is brushing his teeth when the intercom buzzes. Annie's in the kitchen, loading the dishwasher so I shout out that I'll get it, striding down the hallway to the receiver that's fixed to the wall by our front door.

"Hello?" I say, when I've pushed the microphone button.

"Blair." Holden's low tones echo out of the speaker.

Just hearing his voice makes my bones feel all wobbly. "Yes?"

"Can I see you for a minute?"

I blow out a mouthful of air. If this is about the three months pay he tried to give me, I'll probably end up whacking him in the face.

"Stay there. I'll come down." Evan doesn't need to see his aunt pitch a fit.

"Who is it?" Annie calls out from the kitchen.

"Just a delivery," I shout back. "I'm going down to get it." I slide my feet into my sneakers and check my reflection in the mirror. Why did I choose today not to wash my hair? It's a mess, and the rest of me isn't much better. I'm wearing an old pair of yoga shorts and a crop top because our air conditioning is on the fritz.

He's waiting for me outside when I pull the main door open. I don't stand aside to let him in, because I don't want him here. My heart still hurts too much.

It hurts even more when I see him standing there in his navy pants and white shirt, the collar unbuttoned, the sleeves rolled up. My body responds to him the way it always has. I feel sad and needy and I hate it.

He glances at my clothes and looks up at my face. There's a darkness to his eyes.

"I came to give you this." He holds out a white envelope.

"If this is about the money you tried to give me, I don't want it." I lift my chin up, trying not to look him directly in the eye. He's about a foot away but I can smell his shower gel. I'm assuming he came here directly from work and took a shower in the locker room before leaving.

It makes me think of the times I'd meet him at his apartment. And I hate that I miss those nights.

Instead I lay in my own bed, trying not to think of him at all.

"It's not money. It's from Mabel. She's written apology notes to everybody, including you."

"You could have put it in the mail," I say, taking the envelope, being careful not to touch him as I do.

Because I feel like I'm on the edge of something. And I don't want to fall over.

"Is there anything else?" I ask.

He looks at me for a long moment. "Are you okay?" he asks softly.

It's exactly the wrong thing to say. Because the edge I've been teetering on feels like it's crumbling beneath my feet. If I stay here he'll see me cry.

And I don't want that. I'd hate it. I don't want to appear weak.

My heart pounds against my chest as I clutch the envelope in my hand and turn away from him. "Goodbye, Holden," I mutter, pushing the door open and walking inside.

Annie is waiting with the apartment door open. She sees the tears in my eyes and her face hardens.

"Go in," she says. "Evan's ready for bed. Could you read him a story?"

I nod. I'll just wash my face first.

"Good, I'll be right back."

I frown. "Where are you going?"

She catches my eye, her voice warm. "To talk to the delivery man. Just come inside, it'll all be okay."

CHAPTER
TWENTY-EIGHT

HOLDEN

I walk across the road to my car, trying to shake off the feeling that I'm an asshole. I'm not. She's the one that lied to me.

But she was crying when she walked back into the apartment building. Because of me.

And that thought is currently trying to fracture the armor that I've been trying to build around myself.

"Hey, wait up!"

I turn around and see Blair's sister running out of the apartment building. Annie's wearing a pair of slides and shorts with a t-shirt. But unlike Blair her hair's down, lifting in the breeze as she runs across the road.

"Is everything okay?" I ask, frowning. Why is she looking so angry?

"No. You're an asshole."

"So I've been told," I say, turning fully toward her and bracing myself. Hell hath no fury like the sister of a woman scorned.

I kind of like that Blair has her to lean on.

She looks at my car like she wants to kick it. Then at me, like she wants to do the same.

"My sister isn't a liar," she says. "She's a good person."

It's an interesting tack. "I know she's a good person," I say.

"So why did you hurt her?" Annie folds her arms across her chest. It's my first real look at her. Her hair is darker than Blair's. Her face rounder. And her expression is exponentially more furious.

"She lied to me," I remind her. "I wasn't the one doing the hurting. Why is it that everybody thinks this is my fault? I've done nothing wrong."

She leans forward, her eyes scarily wide. "Because everybody is right. She made one little mistake. It's not like she deliberately tried to hurt you. And you didn't even hear her out. Not after she let you in." Her nostrils flare like a dragon's. "She'd do anything for you. And look how you repay her."

"I tried to pay her notice for the cleaning job," I say.

Annie rolls her eyes. "You don't get it, do you?"

"Don't get what?" I'm genuinely confused. My stomach growls like a bear. I can't remember the last time I ate, but it was probably at Misty Lakes.

"She told you she loves you and you threw it back in her face." Annie's own face is turning puce. She jabs her finger in the direction of my chest. The tip hits dead in the center of my shirt, and the impact makes her finger bend.

"Ow!" She winces, grabbing her wrist with her other hand. "Shit, shit, shit."

"You okay?" I frown, reaching for her hand, planning to check that she's okay, but she jumps back.

"What are you? Some kind of Iron Man?" she mutters.

"Can I take a look, please?" I ask.

"Why?" She sounds suspicious.

"Because I'm a doctor and I want to make sure your finger

is okay." I'm trying to keep my patience, but it's getting thinner.

"No," she says, putting her hand behind her back like she thinks I might try anyway. "It's fine. And we're getting off subject. Do you know what it took for her to tell you she loves you?"

I swallow hard at that memory. It's like a knife twisting in my gut. "No."

"She's said that to exactly two people since our mom died. "Me and Evan. Nobody gets in. Nobody." Her eyes flicker to mine. "Until you."

There's a twinge in my chest. I try to ignore it. "If she loved me she wouldn't have lied."

Annie's mouth drops open. "You really believe that? She would have told you the truth at some point. And somewhere deep inside you know that."

I mean, I don't. But whatever.

"She doesn't just throw love around. It's precious to her. You told her you'd take care of her. You forced her to fall in love with you."

"How?" I blink.

"By being all doctor sweetheart. All those rides home in the morning. Being her knight in shining armor when things went bad. Protecting her at the bar. You did that and you made her fall and then you let her hit the ground. She's devastated and it's all your fault. Do you know how much she didn't want to fall in love?"

I swallow hard. "I know she's had a hard life…"

"Hah! That's an easy way of putting it. She brought me up by herself while Mom was working. She gave up her teenage years to make sure I had the kind of childhood I'm pretty sure rich boys like you take for granted."

I say nothing. Because yeah, we had a good childhood.

"And then when she found out I was thinking about college, she joined the Army so she could put me through college first. Have you ever made that kind of sacrifice for somebody else, Holden?"

"No," I say gruffly. "I haven't."

"Then understand me when I tell you that you don't deserve her," she says. "Because you don't. You had your chance with her. She bared her soul to you. And now she's going to graduate and we're going to move to the country and she'll find somebody who will make her happier than you ever did." She narrows her eyes.

The twinge in my chest grows into the feeling of a fist squeezing my insides. I try to ignore it.

"Is that all you wanted to say to me?"

"No." She shakes her head. "I also want to tell you to never, ever come around again. Leave her alone. Let the people who love her take care of her, because you sure as hell haven't."

I say nothing, mostly because there's nothing to say.

"Her final presentation is on Friday," she continues. "If any of this messes it up for her, so help me…" She curls her left hand into a fist, presumably because the right one is still behind her back. "I'll mess every part of your face up until your eyes are fixed firmly in the back of your skull."

I believe it, too. Or at least she'd try. And if I mess up Blair's ability to graduate I'd probably let her.

"Understood."

"Good." She takes another step back. "Now get out of here and don't come back."

So I do. And all the way home all I can think about is what she said.

Blair never tells anybody she loves them.

But she told me.

———

BLAIR

. . .

I walk out of Evan's room at the same time Annie walks back into the apartment. Our eyes meet and she smiles softly at me.

"What happened out there?" I ask, because I might have been reading a story about a boy who invents a time machine to Evan, but my mind was firmly in the street outside.

"Nothing. He's gone. He won't be back."

I hate that my throat tightens in response. Of course he won't be. He didn't come here to repair our relationship. He came here to give me Mabel's letter.

"It's going to be okay," Annie says. "You'll get through this."

I nod.

"It'll be easier once we move away. All you have to do is ace that job interview, then I'll find a job too. A brand new start for all of us."

"I know." My voice is thick.

Once we leave New York there'll be no chance of ever seeing him again. I know that. There'll be no bumping into him at the bar, or going to the hospital to see Mabel and finding him waiting for me with that soft smile.

No meeting him at his place to feel his lips worshipping every inch of my body. It hurts, but I swallow that pain down, knowing that I'll get through it.

Or at least hoping I will.

"Remember what you said when I told you I was pregnant with Evan?" she asks. She takes my hand and squeezes it, then winces.

"What's wrong with your hand?" I ask her.

"It had an altercation with a certain doctor's chest," she tells me.

"You hit Holden?" My voice rises. Surely she didn't.

"I kind of jabbed him. And it hurt. That man has muscles on muscles."

"Yeah." I nod, trying not to think about that too much.

"Anyway, back to your wise words. Remember those?" she prompts.

"The future isn't something to be afraid of. Because we'll face it together," I say. I can still remember how scared she was. How she needed my support.

"Yeah. And we'll be making a new start together." She kisses my cheek. "It's going to be okay. You've got this."

I let out a long breath. She's right, I should be happy. I've waited for this moment for years. Worked so hard for it, dreamed of it.

But now it doesn't feel like it's supposed to. I'm just flat. Low.

And I hate it.

"I love you," I whisper.

"And I love you, too." She gives me the softest smile. "You take care of us so well. Let me take care of you this week."

I smile back at her, not because I'm happy, but because I want her to think I am. And I'll let her help me, not because I need it, but because I'm grateful she's here.

She's my sister and I love her fiercely, the way she loves me.

"Do you have work to do tonight?" she asks.

I shake my head. The good thing about trying to avoid heartbreak is that I spent the whole day making sure my slides are ready for the presentation instead of thinking about Holden.

Okay, I thought about him a bit. But not too much.

"Great. You go sit down and choose a movie. I'll grab some snacks." She walks to the kitchen and I head to the living room, looking out of the window to the street below.

His car is gone. So is he.

I will get through this. I will.

CHAPTER
TWENTY-NINE

HOLDEN

"I've got you down to fight tomorrow night," Jimmy says down the phone. He sounds like he has a cold. He's always nasal but this is next level.

When I don't respond he clears his throat. "You owe me this. You promised."

Yeah, I did. And it's kind of ironic that I said I'd do it so that he would give Blair the weekend off. That feels like a million years ago.

It's actually been less than a week.

"I'll be there." My whole body has been itching for days. Not an itch that you can scratch. It's on the inside, making my blood feel thick and viscous, making my muscles tense like they're trying to remind me there's only one way to get over this feeling.

And yeah, maybe it's also because I know she'll be there. She's on the schedule even though she has her presentation that afternoon.

Most people would go out and celebrate once that final test is done. Not Blair. She just works.

"You will?" Jimmy replies, sounding almost surprised. "Great. You'll be fighting Sean."

Sean is one of the few at my level. About twenty pounds heavier than me but the same height. They call him The Lawman for the exact reason you probably think. Jimmy isn't exactly inventive.

I end the call as I'm walking toward my car.

And that's when I see them, all standing there, looking like they're some kind of upper class mafia gang.

All five of my brothers are looking at me as I stop short of where they're standing. I don't even want to know why they're all here. Except I think I already know. There are a lot of unread messages and unanswered calls on my phone.

"It's Thursday night," I remind them. "Don't you all have places to be?"

"We do, actually. You're coming with us." That's Myles. Always the boss.

"Sorry, man. I have to wash my hair." I take my car keys out of my pocket, even though I don't need to because it opens automatically, but I'm trying to make a point here.

I love them. Desperately. But when they get you in their sights it's like being crowded by a group of gossiping grannies.

Before I can stop him, Linc takes the keys out of my hands. "You won't need these," he says.

"Actually I will," I tell him. "I need to drive to work tomorrow."

"I'll make sure it's delivered to your place," Myles says, and I know he means it. I don't bother to ask how. He'll speak to somebody who will arrange it. It's as simple as that.

And I could argue some more but I'm tired. I'm an asshole but I also know when people are trying to be kind. My brothers love me and I love them. So I take a deep breath and let them lead me along the parking lot, because I'm not sure I have much fight left.

There are two town cars waiting for us in the road. I climb in behind Liam and Eli, feeling kind of glad that Myles is riding with Brooks and Linc. Not just because it will give me a few minutes to get my head together, but because Brooks and Linc – god love them – are like a pair of vibrating bunnies. Always on.

"Where are we going?" I ask as the driver pulls away from the hospital.

"Out for dinner." Liam gives me a soft smile. I guess you'd describe him as Myles' lieutenant. That explains why they're all wearing suits.

"Shouldn't I go home and get changed first?" I look down at my jeans and Henley. They're lucky I showered before I left.

"We have a private room," Eli says. Which translates to: we don't trust you to go home first.

And they're right. I would have barricaded myself in.

I look at Eli. He's a retired hockey player, turned coach. We are the closest in age and we hung around together a lot growing up.

"Et tu?" I murmur.

He shrugs. "Sometimes you gotta be cruel to be kind."

It takes twenty minutes of driving through New York City to get to our destination. An expensive but understated Italian restaurant. The maître d' ushers us through the main restaurant to the private room at the back, and I'm all too aware that everybody is looking at us.

With their designer suits and matching dark hair my brothers look like they're in some kind of expensive gang. I feel like I'm their lackey, following along in my jeans.

"Sit," Myles says, pointing to the beautifully laid round table in the center of the room. The silverware is actually silver, there are flowers in the center that look more expensive than most people's wedding bouquets. And the wine is already open.

But I do as I'm told, mostly because the quicker I get this over with, the sooner I can get home.

"Would you like white or red wine?" the server asks. I put my hand over my glass. "Water please."

Once everybody's drinks are filled Myles takes a sip and then they all join in. Linc is sitting on one side of me, Eli on the other. Myles is opposite us.

"Is this like the scene in *The Untouchables* where Al Capone beats somebody's head in during the after dinner speech?" I ask. "Because if so, can we get it over with."

"I asked them to come," Linc blurts out. "I was worried about you."

"You need to learn how to use a phone," Myles' voice is low. "Didn't they teach that in medical school?"

"I've been busy," I protest. "It's only been a few days of ignoring you. Seriously, you all need to calm down."

"I hear you and Blair had a fight," he says.

"It wasn't a fight. We just agreed that things weren't working." I run my thumb along my jawline, wondering when I last shaved.

"Liar." Linc coughs the word out.

I should have taken the wine. "Look, I know you all love me. And under any other circumstances it would be great to see you. But this…" I wave my hand around at the table and their suits. "Don't you think it's too much?"

"We need to talk and we need to eat," Myles says, not unreasonably.

"But why are you all here?" I ask. "Don't you have jobs? Wives? Kids?"

"You know we do," he replies. "But we also have a brother who has some kind of masochistic tendencies."

I want to laugh, because it's the opposite.

"And we love you and want you to be happy," Liam adds. He's smiling at me. The man's always smiling.

"And our other halves would kill us if we didn't come and try to smooth things over," Eli says. "So we flew into town this evening. We leave tomorrow. So let's get straight to the point."

Yep. He's definitely on the dark side now.

Linc clears his throat. "You're an idiot who needs some sense knocked into him." He's looking stupidly pleased with himself.

"Agreed." Myles nods at the servers, who bring in the first course. I guess I don't even get to choose what's for dinner.

Whatever. At least Myles has exquisite taste.

"You want to tell us what happened?" Myles asks. "Because the last time I saw you, there was this woman who was staring at you like the sun shone out of your ass."

"And Ava says you were looking at her the same way," Liam adds.

I roll my eyes. "When did we decide to be the Waltons?" I ask. "I thought we were stoics. We don't talk about this stuff."

Linc tries –and fails – to stifle a laugh. "Since they got all loved up."

"Luckily, that'll never happen to you," Brooks says to him. "There's not a woman in the world foolish enough."

Linc lifts his brow. I'm so used to looking at my two youngest brothers like they're kids, but they're actually fully grown adults. In their thirties. Where the hell has the time gone?

"Can we get back to the matter in hand please?" Myles asks. And I realize we're not the Waltons. We're a board meeting.

I let out a long breath before responding. "I found out some information I didn't have before and ended our relationship," I tell him, trying to keep my voice even. "Not that it really was a relationship. Just some fun."

"Fun," Eli repeats. "You're never fun."

Myles clears his throat and looks at me, his eyebrow lifted.

"You must know all the sordid details," I tell him. "Linc has to have told you all."

"I know you think Blair lied to you about cleaning your house. But I don't know why it's a big deal."

"You don't?" I frown. "Seriously? If Ava had lied to you about something like that wouldn't you have lost it?"

Myles shrugs. "Probably. And I'd have been wrong."

"She lied to me," I say again, because it obviously hasn't sunk in the first time. I wrinkle my nose and decide to get it over with, so I tell them about all the sordid details. As I speak they're all deathly quiet.

They're still quiet when I finish.

"Ah, can somebody say something?" I ask. "Because you're supposed to be making me feel better here."

"Can you blame her for not telling you?" Myles asks, breaking the silence but not to my satisfaction.

"As soon as she told you the truth you blew it all up in her face," Liam points out. He rubs the scruff on his jaw. The man hates shaving.

"It wasn't even a lie," Linc adds in. "Just a little omission."

"And you'd know all about those," Myles says, his beady eyes boring into me. I shiver like we're kids again and I'm being told off. "You lied to us about fighting."

"I just didn't tell you," I point out.

"Exactly." There's a smug smile on Myles' face. "Bingo."

I take a mouthful of water, trying to keep my expression even. "Thanks for coming to see me, guys." I say sarcastically. "You're all making me feel much better."

"Our job isn't to make you feel better," Linc says. "It's to make you make better choices."

Brooks splutters out his mouthful of wine. "Make better choices?" he says to Linc, looking highly amused. "Like the one you made the other night?"

Linc blushes and shakes his head. "Another time, man. We're ribbing on Holden here. And we never get to rib on Holden."

"This is true." Brooks stabs a piece of melon from his plate with his fork and starts chewing on it.

"By the way," Linc says, pushing his elbow into my waist. "I didn't tell them the big thing."

I turn to him, my eyes wide. "No," I tell him shortly, shaking my head. "We're not telling them that."

It's like I'm mouthing the words but nothing's coming out. Because the next moment Linc turns to the table with a shit-eating grin on his face.

"She told him she loves him," Linc blurts out and I wonder if smashing his face in would result in jail time. Orange isn't my color.

"What?" Liam shifts in his seat. He's taken off his jacket because it's hot in here. "What did you say when she told you that?" he asks me, his brows pulled tight.

I blow out a mouthful of air, because this is where I am the complete asshole and I know it. "I told her I didn't want her love."

There's complete silence. All five of my brothers – the men who are supposed to be on my side – stare at me like I'm a monster.

I shift awkwardly, waiting for the silence to end. Then I take another sip of water. I should have ordered wine.

"She told you she loves you and you threw it in her face?" Liam finally says. "Is there a word for complete mother-fucking asshole whose face I want to smash in?"

"The word you're looking for is Holden," Linc says, and they all nod sagely.

"She lied to me," I say again. Weaker this time.

"She told you she loves you. What's wrong with you?" Myles questions. He looks down and I realize he has his phone in his lap, like a teenager.

"What are you doing?" I ask, alarmed.

"Telling Ava what an asshole you are."

My stomach twists. Because I don't mind these assholes thinking the worst of me. But I do mind Ava – and my other sister–in-laws – doing the same. Has he been messaging her this whole time?

There's a little beep and he looks up from the screen. "Yep, she thinks you're an asshole too. She says Blair worshipped the ground you walked on all weekend."

But now she hates me too. Great.

The servers come to take our first course plates away. I haven't even touched mine, but I allow him to take the plate anyway.

I'm feeling distinctly un-hungry.

"But the lie…" I say one more time, trying to focus on something. Anything. Because I'm starting to hate myself, too.

When the waiters have left Myles holds his phone up. "Ava wants to talk to you."

"At the dinner table?" I say, my voice rising.

He smiles. "I'll put her on speaker." He presses the screen. "Okay, babe, you're on."

"Can Holden hear me?" she asks softly.

"Hi Ava." I want to disappear into the ground.

"Holden." Her voice pierces the silence of the room. "Can I ask you something?"

I tense because she always talks rings around us Salinger brothers. "If you have to."

"I think it could help, that's all. Just to focus your mind on things."

And this is why I like her. She isn't being accusing or telling me I'm an idiot. She's trying to help. Maybe the rest of them could take some lessons from her.

"Okay then," I say begrudgingly.

"What reason do you think Blair had to lie to you?" she

asks. The door to the room opens again and the server starts to top up everybody's wine glasses but mine.

"Because she didn't want me to know she's my cleaner," I say. *Obviously*.

"Okay. Why didn't she want you to know that?" she continues. "I mean you're not an elitist. Why would she lie about that?"

I blink at the question, unsure I know the answer. "Because she planned this all along?" I say, aware of how stupid this sounds. This is Blair we're talking about. She doesn't have a devious bone in her body. "Maybe she was after me for my money."

"She's not Claire," Myles says.

I shoot an angry look at Linc because we had this conversation. He must have repeated it verbatim to them all. "I know that," I tell him.

"But do you?" he continues. "Because you're treating her like she's Claire. Has she ever indicated that she wanted you for your money?"

"No," I admit. The truth is, she works harder than anybody I've ever met. "She was in the Army to put herself and her sister through college. She has two jobs."

"And she's studying," Ava adds. "Doesn't exactly scream gold digger."

My stomach twists. "She's not a gold digger," I say softly.

"Then why do you think she didn't tell you?" Myles asks.

"Because she was embarrassed, probably," Linc says. "Not that she needs to be. I think she's fabulous."

I side eye him.

"What?" His voice rises. "She helped me choose a tux. She sewed your button back on after I pulled it off. Jesus, the woman's a keeper."

I open my mouth to tell him that I lied to our head of security about her. Said she was all above board.

And then I remember that I asked her to lie, too.

And it's like a cold bucket of ice water is thrown over me. It takes my breath away because, *fuck*. I'm a liar too. Worse than that, I accused her of doing something I actually asked her to do.

Goosebumps erupt over my skin. All I think about is the way she looked at me when I told her to get out of my car. I open my mouth to say something but nothing comes out. It's like I'm frozen. Or paralyzed.

Christ, I think I'm going to be sick.

It's like I've been anesthetized and I'm suddenly coming back to life. And it hurts. But not because somebody's operated on me, but because I hurt myself.

Even worse, I hurt her.

Myles says something into the phone and switches it off. I'm aware of the servers putting our main courses in front of us. Mine is a steak, done exactly how I like it. The smell makes me nauseous.

"You okay?" Linc murmurs.

I exhale heavily. "No."

I haven't been okay since I made her walk away. Truth be told, I haven't been okay for a long time. But she made it better.

She made everything better.

"You think we should do something?" Brooks asks. "Give him the Heimlich maybe?"

"He's not choking," Myles says. "He's having an epiphany."

Is that what it is? Whatever it is, I don't like it. I want to hit something. I want to run.

I want to see her.

"Shit," Linc says. "Maybe somebody should slap him."

"I'm okay," I croak. "Don't touch me."

"You love her, don't you?" Eli asks next to me.

My chest feels so tight I can't breathe. "Yeah, I do. I love her." Why didn't I say it when she told me?

Why do I have to make things so difficult?

"That's good," Linc says. "Because if you don't love her then I will. The woman cleans your house, takes care of you when you're sick, and puts up with your bullshit. Seriously, she's a saint and you're an asshole. You don't deserve her."

There's ringing in my ears. All I can think about are all the times she's been there for me. I hate to admit it, but Linc's right. She put up with way more than she should have. The fighting, the stupid hours. She came in to see Mabel because I asked her to, and then she gave the police the blueprint to find her.

And when I told her to leave on Sunday she waited for God knows how long until I came home.

Then I pushed her away. Completely.

I look up at my brothers, stricken. "I fucked everything up."

"Halle-fucking-lujah," Linc mutters. "Now can we talk about how you're gonna clean up this damn mess?"

CHAPTER
THIRTY

BLAIR

"Thank you, Miss Walsh. You're free to leave now." The head examiner gives me a nod.

I start collecting my things, sliding my notes, pen, and laptop into my backpack. It's over. The last eight years of my life have led up to this moment.

Longer, if I think about it too much.

"Thank you for your time," I say, blowing out a mouthful of air. The adrenaline is thick inside of me. I think I've been riding on it for days. But now that I've given my presentation and all of my assessments are in, the only thing left is to find out if I've passed my masters.

In all truth, I think I have.

A few students I know are waiting outside the room. Two of them still have presentations to give, but the others have completed theirs over the past few days.

"How did it go?" one of them asks.

"Good, I think."

"We're all heading out to celebrate later. You coming?"

I give her a smile. "I have to work."

"That sucks."

I shrug. Because keeping busy is also keeping me sane. I have to spend this weekend preparing for my interview next week. Plus I'll need to apply for some more jobs in case this one doesn't pan out.

And yes, I don't feel better yet. But I will, I really will.

Cuts heal. Hearts mend. It's basic medicine.

The heat of the early evening hits me as soon as I walk outside. The muggy kind of New York heat that comes from the concrete and blacktop on the ground as much as the sun in the sky. I'm not going to miss that.

"Blair."

My stupid heart skips a beat at the sound of his voice. I turn to see him standing at the bottom of the library steps. "How did you know I'd be here?"

"I asked your sister. She says hi, by the way. And also says you should knee me in the balls."

"That sounds like Annie." I take a deep breath. "It's been a long day, Holden, and I have to go to work now. I don't want to argue with you." It's hard to look at him, because every time I do my heart feels weird. Like I can't breathe.

And I need to breathe.

"I'm not here to argue. I thought I'd give you a ride to the club if you'd let me."

"It's fine. I can catch the bus."

"I'm going there anyway. And I need your advice on something," he tells me. And I hate that his words give me a little shot of hope.

So I dash them myself before he can. "You're a doctor. I'm an ex-cleaner. I don't think there's any advice I can give you."

There's a little sound from his throat. It makes me look at him again. The sun is shining on the side of his face and body, casting a long shadow to the side of him. I can see the sharpness of his jaw, the growth of beard that he hasn't shaved off.

It's like I can feel them against my hand without even touching him.

Why can't you just turn love off, like a television program you no longer want to watch? My body still feels drenched with it.

"You're Blair Walsh. I should always listen to your advice. But if you'd rather take the bus, I'll take it with you."

From the corner of my eye I see his car in the road. Parked where it shouldn't be, *again*. "We always argue in your car," I say.

The corner of his lip quirks, like he knows I'm on the edge of agreeing to go with him. "I know. What if I promise not to be an asshole for once?"

Truth is, it's hot. And his car has the best air conditioning. Even though I want to punch his face in then kiss it afterward, sitting next to him will still be more comfortable than sitting next to a sweaty passenger on the bus.

"If I go with you it means nothing," I tell him.

"I understand." He holds his hand out. It takes me a minute to realize he's asking for my bag. I shrug it off my shoulder and give it to him, because, hey, it means nothing.

Absolutely nothing.

When we get to the car there's a parking ticket under the windshield wiper. He pulls it off and stuffs it in his pocket, completely nonchalant.

"If you don't pay they won't let you graduate," I murmur.

He smiles. "That would be terrible." Then he opens the passenger door and I slide into the most comfortable seat in the world. He walks around, sliding his sunglasses back onto his face and my whole body clenches at how gorgeous he is.

As soon as he's inside he switches the engine and air conditioning on. It's like a balm to my soul. I lean forward and turn it to as cold as it can go and unbutton my shirt a little, letting the ice cold air kiss my skin.

There's another sound from his throat. Deeper this time. I turn to look at him, but I can't see his eyes.

Stupid mirrored aviators.

"I start at seven," I remind him.

"What?" He sounds almost dazed.

I like that he's looking at me. I like that I've affected him. Because it's mutual, buddy.

Even if I don't want it to be.

"You need to put your foot on the gas pedal if you want this thing to move," I tell him.

A smile ghosts his lips. But he puts the car into drive and we're off.

It's a beautiful early evening and there are people everywhere. Cars, too. "Can I have your phone?" I ask him.

"Why?"

"Because I want to listen to some music."

He pulls it from his pocket and passes it to me. "Two two one one two seven five," he says.

I punch it in, all too aware that most people don't give their passcodes out so easily. Even if they have nothing to hide. We've grown attached to our phones like they're a part of our anatomy. Not to be touched unless in an emergency or we're fully committed.

Don't read anything into it. He hurt you.

It opens to a screensaver of me and Evan sitting on the pier in front of Holden's cabin last weekend. My chest tightens because I remember that moment. How happy I was. How I was thinking this was what I wanted.

The fairytale.

"Did you know I'd see this?" I ask, flashing him the photo even though his eyes should be on the road.

"Figured you would at some point."

"Smooth," I say.

He gives an embarrassed laugh. "Thank you."

I hit the music icon and scroll, finally choosing the song I was looking for. The gorgeous harmony fills the car.

"The Beach Boys?" Holden asks, looking surprised.

"They were my mom's favorite." I shrug.

He says nothing, but there's a smile on his lips like I just gave him something precious.

"So what did you want to talk to me about?" I ask him, turning the volume down enough for him to hear me over the Wilson brothers.

He's tapping his fingers against the wheel to the rhythm of the song. I can't stop looking at them. Fingers that hurt and fingers that heal.

That's Holden Salinger. A strange but beautiful mix.

"I'm supposed to fight tonight."

My chest tightens. "Okay."

"And I know you hate it. So I don't want to do it. But I also owe Jimmy one last one."

"Why?" I ask.

He lets out a mouthful of air. "Just a bargain I made with him. I have to do it, but I don't want to upset you."

We hit a red light. He turns to look at me and I can see my face reflected in his lenses.

"Why are you asking me?" I say. "It has nothing to do with me."

"Everything I do has something to do with you." The light turns green. He puts his foot on the accelerator but then somebody walks out in front of the car and he hits the brake. We both jolt forward.

"You okay?" he asks.

"Stupid New Yorkers," I mutter, sitting back in the seat.

"We're stupid New Yorkers," he points out. "Or at least I am. Stupid, I mean. And I don't want to fight, but I don't want to owe any debts. I want to end this fighting thing, Blair. I want to deal with my problems and stress like a grown up. Not take them out on grown men... or grown women."

I don't say anything. There's a shiver running through my spine. Holden Salinger is opening up. I don't want to jinx it.

He wrinkles his nose, staring out at the road ahead. "I started fighting because it took the pain away. The pain of losing a patient, or losing a girlfriend. I hit people because I thought it would make me feel better," he says. "And I guess sometimes it did. Until it didn't."

He takes a left. We're about ten minutes away from the club. For the first time I wish the drive was longer.

"And then I found you," he said. "And the pain wasn't gone, but it had numbed. But when I was with you I was different."

I swallow hard.

"And yes, you made me different. But I think I did, too. I felt like a better person. Like I was more than a doctor or a fighter. I was finally somebody who got up in the morning and looked forward to the day. And the night. Because you were there and you're everything, Blair. Every fucking thing."

"Can you pull over?" I ask him.

"You want to get out?" His voice is thick.

"No. I just want to look at you as you talk." I think I need to. I'm shaking a little. I want to hear everything he has to say.

Wanting more.

He pulls into a space that's not a space, but that's Holden. He keeps the engine on because the air conditioning is completely needed right now.

I lean forward and take his glasses off. He's looking at me with those blue eyes. They're not dark or angry. There's a softness to them that I like to think has been there for this entire car ride.

"I'm sorry I lied to you," I whisper.

He shakes his head. "You didn't lie. You just didn't tell me."

"There's something else I should tell you," I say. "Your

apartment is way too neat and tidy. I spent most of my time there studying and not cleaning."

His lips curl into a smile. "Please don't ever tell my brothers that. I'll never hear the end of it."

I want to touch him. To feel him. But there's still the little ache, too.

"How's Mabel?"

"She left today. Gave me this." He lifts up a paperback that's in the plastic pocket of his door. I take it from him.

Jane Eyre.

"She says I should read it. Apparently I have a lot in common with the hero."

"She thinks you're Rochester?"

He shrugs. "Says something about me being blind. That I need a woman to save me."

I laugh because that's so Mabel. And then he's smiling, too.

"Tell me not to fight and I won't," he says.

"I can't tell you that. If you owe Jimmy, you owe him. I hate not paying debts and I think you're the same," I tell him honestly.

"Will you let me drive you home afterward?" he asks.

"I don't know." I run my tongue along my bottom lip. "You hurt me, Holden. And I think I hurt you, too. I don't know what we can do about that. And I have my interview on Monday. We're hoping to move soon. There's a lot going on."

"I know. I'm not asking for anything at all. Except to drive you home." There's an honesty in his voice that touches me.

"I'll probably have to work late." I don't know if I'm being too easy or too hard. All I know is that life is complicated and yet when he's here it seems less so.

"That's okay," he tells me. "You're worth waiting for."

From the way he looks at me, I'm not sure if he's talking about tonight or something else.

"Table five," Katrina says, passing me the tray. I lean over the bar and grab it, winding my way to the door to the fight club. I haven't seen Holden since I started work two hours ago. I assume he's in here somewhere.

I also got a message from my sister apologizing for telling Holden where I was, but she got a trip to the cabin with Evan in return, all expenses paid, so she thinks it's a fair deal.

And I think I'll forgive her.

I hand out the two beers and three whiskeys, then look up at the ring in the center of the room. If I get this job at the library, I'll only have a few weeks left to work here.

I haven't given Jimmy the heads up about me leaving yet, mostly because I no longer have the cleaning job and I need the money from this one. Plus, I don't think he'll have much trouble replacing me.

I'm about to walk back to the bar when I hear Holden's song come on. It's time. I think about leaving but I also want to stay.

He asked me what I thought. I told him he should follow his conscience. He's doing that and it feels churlish to be annoyed at him for fighting one last time.

When he climbs into the ring he looks around, his eyes alighting on me. There's no expression on his face. Just a hardness that I recognize. It makes my breath catch.

I'm a sucker for soft Holden. But hard Holden is also very attractive.

His opponent climbs in. A man who looks like a walking barrel of muscle. He looks at Holden who stares back at him as the referee talks quietly. They both nod and then the referee steps back.

The bell rings.

His opponent starts to do that stupid dance that so many

boxers do. There's nausea brewing in my stomach as I wait for Holden to do the same.

But he doesn't. He's standing in the center of the ring. He turns until he's fully facing me. Somebody shouts that he needs to swing a punch.

There's a little uncertainty in his opponent's movement now. He's still circling but slower. Holden's eyes catch mine and he's mouthing something.

No, not just something. *Everything*.

"I love you."

I'm not sure I can breathe anymore. Which is kind of unfortunate because I have everything to breathe for.

I love this man, too. Like the idiot I am.

He's still staring at me. And I'm smiling.

Then there's a sickening thud. Holden is punched in the head.

The glove ricochets off his cheek. I can see spittle and blood flying through the air.

And he goes down.

He isn't moving and my whole body turns cold. I drop the empty tray I'm clutching to the floor and push my way to the ring. People are booing, because Holden never goes down. And there's no movement from him.

"You're not supposed to hit his face," I scream as I hoist myself up, clinging to the ropes as I clamber over them. I used to climb ropes every day, but this is hard.

Holden is face down. His hands are splayed out above his head, gloves still on them. There's a cut on his cheek and lip. Neither of them are protected by his headgear. I'm trying not to cry as I reach for him.

"Get out of the fucking ring!" Jimmy shouts. "The fight hasn't ended."

The referee starts to count him out. I scream at him to shut up. I must be more vehement than I intend because he actually backs up, looking shocked.

Yeah, take that, mother fucker.

"Holden," I say, dropping to my knees next to him. "Are you hurt?"

"Huh?"

Relief washes over me. Along with anger. "You're supposed to fight, not let him hit you without defences."

He turns to his side. Without thinking I reach to take out his gumshield. He blinks up at me as though I'm the most beautiful sight he's ever seen.

"I decided I didn't want to fight," he says. "I just wanted to look at you."

My bottom lip trembles. "You're an idiot."

"For you," he croaks. "I'm an idiot for you."

"Somebody get her the fuck out of there," a guy at the front table shouts. He's got money in the center of the table. I'm guessing he's regretting betting on Holden.

"Can you get up?" I ask Holden.

"Yeah." There's a crooked smile on his face. "I just don't feel like it yet. I want to look at you."

The man must have a concussion. "Come with me and you can look at me in the locker room," I tell him, unlacing his gloves. There are now more people surrounding the ring. There are shouts and whispered conversations but we ignore them all.

When his gloves are off, I thread my fingers through his. "Promise me you'll never fight again."

"I promise." He gets up. I don't let go of his hand. I don't think I can.

It makes it a lot more difficult for him to take his headgear off single handed. But he manages. And then I'm climbing over the ropes and he's following me, though I insist on helping him and he laughs about that.

We walk through the crowded tables. Some of the men are shaking their heads at Holden, others are looking at me as though I caused all the problems. But neither of us care. I'm holding his hand and he's holding mine.

And when we walk through the door to the locker room we leave it all behind.

Or most of it.

Jimmy rushes in. "What the hell was that?" he asks Holden. Then he looks at me. "You're fired. Get out of here."

Holden puts his arms around me. "She's not going anywhere," he tells Jimmy. "Until I leave."

"Then you both can go," Jimmy huffs. "I'm done with you."

It's funny, because a few hours ago I wanted to keep this job until the bitter end. But there are better jobs out there. Better things. Annie and I have already saved enough to cover our move. As long as I find something within a few weeks we'll be fine.

"You ready?" Holden asks, his breath close against my ear.

"I'm ready. Let's go."

And we do.

CHAPTER
THIRTY-ONE

HOLDEN

"Stop squealing," Blair says, as she wipes my cheek with some alcohol.

"It hurts," I complain, kind of liking the way she's looking at me so intently. As soon as we got back to my place she insisted on sitting me down while she cleaned my face up. And to be honest, I only agreed because I want her to touch me.

I could probably have cleaned myself up in half the time. And with half the pain.

"How come you can take a massive punch silently, but you can't take a little sting on a cut?" she murmurs.

I grab her wrist. "I only took the punch silently because people were watching. It hurt like hell."

She smiles as I tug her closer, until she's sitting on me, straddling my legs. Damn, this woman is beautiful. Taking the blood-stained wipe from her hands, I throw it into the sink and cup her face.

"I love you," I tell her. Because it's true.

"I love you too," she says back, and it's the sweetest sound in the world. Like laying on the grass on a glorious, sunny day and hearing the birds singing overhead. I lean forward, pressing my lips to hers.

"You're hurt," she murmurs, looking worriedly at my mouth.

"Not any more." I kiss her again, and sure it stings. But it would hurt more not to kiss her. Her mouth is as soft as she is. Pliant against mine. I slide my hands down her sides, pulling her harder against me as we get lost in each other.

All the blood rushes to my groin. She wraps her arms around me as though she can't get close enough. Which is good. I can't either.

Did I really almost lose this? I'm such an asshole.

"I'm sorry," I say when we part.

"Why? That was a good kiss." There's a smile on her lips.

"I'm sorry I hurt you. I won't do it again."

She runs her tongue along her bottom lip. I'm absurdly distracted by it. I want to suck that lip. Kiss it until it's swollen.

"You can't say that," she says, stroking my face. "Because people hurt each other. That's what they do."

She's right and I hate it. "I'll try really hard not to again."

She smiles. "Ditto."

And then, because I can't stand not kissing her, I pull her against me. This time it's more frantic. We're a tangle of lips and tongues and stroking hands. I get her top off and bury my face in her delicious cleavage. She pulls mine off and takes a long time inspecting me for damage. With her tongue.

I worship her breasts, sucking each one in turn, until her face is pink and delicious. Then I'm pulling her jeans off, followed by her panties, until she's naked in front of me and I'm more than admiring the view.

"You're the most beautiful thing I've ever seen," I tell her honestly. I lift her onto the bathroom counter, using my middle finger to part her. She's glistening. Pink. I kiss her and she sighs.

"Your lip…"

"It's okay," I murmur, sliding my tongue along where I know it will make her body clench. "You have healing juices."

And then I do the thing I planned on doing since we got home. Maybe before then. I scrape my teeth against her hip, right below where her bone shapes her curves, then I close my mouth and suck her in.

"Ow," she says.Then she looks down at me. "Did you just give me a hickey?"

"I did." I smile at her. "Now I'm not a hickey virgin anymore."

I can't think of anywhere else I'd rather be than here, my mouth kissing its way between her legs, her fingers tangled in my hair.

I give her a long, slow lick, circling my tongue until her thighs tighten against me. I slide two fingers inside of her, curling them until her grip on me tightens, and as I push my face forward to suck her in, I'm starting to wonder if I'm actually going to be able to get enough oxygen.

But she's my oxygen. And if I die here it's a noble cause.

"Ohmygod, Holden!"

I feel her tighten around my fingers and scrape my teeth against her before sucking at her again. And then she's folding her body around me, clinging on for dear life, calling my name again like a mantra.

My dick is so hard it's almost painful.

I hold her as she rides the wave, and she kisses me hard, her hands feathering my face like she wants to memorize every inch.

And I love this woman. I love her.

And when she's done, I carry her to bed, laying her down in front of me so I can stand and admire her for a moment. She's all sated and smiley and gorgeous.

"Come here," she says, her voice gritty. "I need you."

I like the way she says it, although I know she doesn't need me. She wants me, which is better. So much better.

I want her too. All the time. Just like this. I unbutton my pants, sliding them down until I'm in my boxers which are embarrassingly tented.

And when I crawl over her, resting my weight on my hands, she's still smiling. "I've missed this," she says, running her finger down the length of my cock. It jerks against her touch.

"Not as much as I have," I say gruffly. And then I'm silent because she slides her hand inside my shorts and grips me in a way that makes me see the most beautiful stars.

"Fuck." I grunt.

Together we get my underwear down, and I kick them to the side. Then we're naked and I'm on top of her, marveling at the wonder of this woman. And I slowly push myself inside of her.

But she's also inside of me. In the cold dark place where I now realize my heart is.

"Kiss me," she whispers. And I do.

And I'm not sure I ever want to stop.

———

BLAIR

I spend the weekend at Holden's, even though most of my time there is taken up with preparations for my interview on Monday. We don't talk about what will happen if I get the job and we're hundreds of miles apart. I think he's avoiding the subject because he's worried that he might influence me.

But for the first time in the last eight years, I'm starting to wonder if staying in New York would be so bad.

Holden insists on being my emotional support sex god all weekend. While I pour over my laptop, making notes, he brings me coffee and chocolate and kisses when I demand them.

And on Sunday night I go home, because he has work in the morning and I have to grab an early train from Penn. Of course he insists on driving me back to the apartment, and I'm amused to find him listening to an audiobook of *Jane Eyre*.

"I'm trying to educate myself," he tells me. And I laugh because he's the most educated man I know.

It actually hurts to leave him, so he comes into the apartment with me. We're holding hands when Annie sees us stride into the kitchen.

"I see he still has his balls," she says.

"Hi Annie." Holden smiles at her.

"Hi Asshole."

"Mom!" Evan walks up behind us, his skin covered in water droplets like he's just got out of the shower. He makes Annie jump. "That's a bad word," he tells her.

"One you weren't supposed to hear." She ruffles his hair. "I thought you were still in the bathroom."

"I heard talking." He looks at Holden, his face beaming. "Hi Holden."

"Hey bud." Holden winks at him and I think my ovaries are doing a little dance in my abdomen. "How are you doing?"

"I'm good. I finished first grade on Thursday. I start summer camp next week. We're going looking for bugs."

"That's cool," Holden says. "I remember hunting for bugs with my brothers. We used to make each other eat them."

"Eww, gross."

"Don't get any ideas," Annie warns Evan. Then she looks at Holden. "You're a bad influence."

"Sorry." He doesn't look it though.

He stays for another twenty minutes. Then Annie conveniently steers Evan into his room to get him ready for bed and we kiss for another ten before he leaves. And when he's gone – without a ticket on his windshield from what I can see from the apartment window – she walks back into the kitchen with a smile on her face.

"You look annoyingly happy," she says.

"I am."

Her face bursts into a smile. "Then I'm happy too. You could have ripped one ball off."

"You're the one who told him where I was," I point out, because she's trying to be all tough but I know she's a marshmallow underneath.

"Yeah, well everybody deserves a second chance. God knows I did." She leans forward and hugs me. "So, what does this mean for tomorrow?"

"What do you mean?" I ask, my brows knitting.

"I mean your interview. Are you still going? What if you get the job? I assume Holden isn't leaving New York any time soon. Are you two going to do the long distance thing?"

"I don't know," I tell her honestly. "We haven't talked about it. I guess we will if I get a job offer."

"You'll get the offer," she says, sounding certain.

I swallow. "I hope so."

"Will you take it?"

"Auntie Blair?" Evan yells from his bedroom. "Can you read me a story?"

I let out a long breath. "Yeah, I think I'll take it. If you'll come with me."

"Wherever you go, we go. You know that."

———

I'm as quiet as a mouse as I leave the apartment the next morning. It's barely five and the sun is just rising, but it hasn't made it over the high roofs yet, so it still feels like the middle of the night. I check one last time that I have everything I need. My laptop, my purse, my phone. And then I check the bus times, because I need to get to the train station.

Luckily for me the bus will be to my stop in five minutes.

"I brought you a good luck gift."

I blink when I see Holden standing across the street. To his left, his car parked further down. I guess he couldn't find a space closer.

"What are you doing here?" I ask him.

"I figured you wouldn't have time for breakfast," he says, holding out a coffee cup and brown bag. "My mom always says you can't perform your best on an empty stomach."

"She obviously didn't see you last weekend," I say and he grins. He passes me the cup, his fingers touching mine, sending electricity sparking all through me.

"This is very sweet of you. I didn't know there was anywhere open this early."

"When you're a doctor you get to know all the twenty-four hour places."

I smell the sweet aroma of muffins through the bag. Damn it, now I'm feeling all weak in the knees and wondering if this interview is a good idea.

I look at my watch. "I have to go."

"Want a ride?"

"To the station?" I clarify. "It's okay, I can get the bus."

"I mean to your interview."

"It's in Maryland, you doofus," I say, a smile pulling at my lips.

He shrugs. "I know. I feel like a drive today. And Maryland is calling me."

"What does it sound like?" I ask suspiciously.

"Like the sweet voices of angels." His expression is completely serious. "You coming or what?"

He isn't joking? I really thought he was. "Don't you have to work?"

"I swapped."

"You swapped the other day."

"I'm owed a lot of favors. I've been the bachelor doctor. I filled in for everybody. It's payback time."

I look at him, my chest feeling tight. "You took the day off and you want to spend all of it in the car?"

"I want to spend it with you. Making sure you're relaxed. You need to ace this interview." He reaches for my free hand and we walk to his car. Like the gentleman he is – when he's not being a non-gentleman – he makes sure I'm comfortable with my coffee and muffins before he walks around to the other side of the car.

He starts the engine up and I take a sip of coffee.

"You want me to shoot some questions at you as we go?" he asks. "So you can practice?"

"Um, yeah. Okay." He knows what I've been researching for this interview. He heard all about it this weekend. But this still feels weird.

And it also feels like he wants me to get this job. Which makes me feel torn, because if I get this job what will it mean for us?

What does he want it to mean?

I try to push those thoughts away. I need to concentrate.

"Okay, Miss Walsh," he says, his voice low and smooth. "Can you tell me why you want this job?"

———

HOLDEN

I hate seeing Blair nervous. She's attempting a smile as she stands at the top of the library steps. I smile back at her, my eyes crinkling because even if she doesn't realize it, she's got this.

She'll do well. And if she doesn't get this job she'll get one of the next ones. She's too good a prospect to miss out for long.

There was no way I was going to let her come here alone. Not when I know she's worried about what's to come. I know how much she's dreamed of this. How desperate she is for Evan to move somewhere more suburban.

I'll never stand in front of her dreams. I just want to be in them with her somehow.

I find a coffee shop around the corner and order an Americano, grabbing my phone to reply to some messages. First, I call the hospital and check that everything is okay – my friend Craig has stepped in on short notice for me, and he reminds me I owe him a drink sometime.

And then I make some more calls. To my brothers. To Ava who wants to know everything that's happened since the last time we talked. And then the woman behind the counter of the half empty coffee shop asks me if I want to order lunch, which I do, because I don't want to move from here.

By the time I'm finished, and on my second coffee, my phone is buzzing. I see Blair's name flash up.

Interview is over. I think it went well. Where are you? I'll come meet you. – Blair

I tap out a quick reply letting her know that I'm around the corner, then I order her a coffee and some iced water because I'm pretty sure she'll be parched after talking for so long.

"Hey." There's relief mixed with anxiety on her face as she walks through the door. I pull her into my arms and she melts into me. God, she smells good.

"Well done for getting through it," I say. "Go sit down. I

got you some drinks. I'll grab you a sandwich, too. Anything in particular you want?"

She looks at the coffee and smiles. "If you keep doing this I'm going to get used to it."

"Good." I want her to. I want her to get used to the fact that I'm not going anywhere. "I'll be right back. And then I want to hear all about the interview."

Five minutes later, she's biting into an egg salad sandwich. It's one of those big ones that splurge everywhere and are almost impossible to eat, but it's fun watching her try. She swallows a mouthful, unaware that she has crumbs all over her lips.

I kind of want to lick them off.

I listen as she tells me about her interview. She sounds excited but not too excited. "There are downsides," she says. "They seem a little resistant to new ideas. A lot of them have been there for years."

"I guess they like working there."

"Yeah." She nods. "I guess."

I shift in my seat, because there's something I want to ask her, and now I'm feeling nervous. "Are you dead set on Maryland?"

She looks at me, surprised I'm being so straightforward. But if the clusterfuck of the last week has taught me anything, it's to be honest about what I want.

Her expression softens as she looks at me. "I don't know," she says. "I just… I think… I know you're in New York. And I want to be with you. But I want this kind of environment for Evan."

"That's not what I'm asking. Because, honestly, I want this for him too. I'm just wondering if it has to be Maryland or if you've thought of any other smaller towns or cities."

"I've applied to a job in Pennsylvania," she says. "And a couple in upstate New York."

"Have you considered West Virginia?"

She blinks. "That's even further from New York than Maryland is. Are you trying to get rid of me?"

I shake my head slowly. "Not at all. I'm trying to find a way for us to be together. There's a vacancy coming up at a hospital in Charleston. And I spoke with Ava and she has some contacts with a couple of libraries in the city. I know you don't know the area, and maybe you don't want to, but it's green and it's leafy and it's surrounded by my family."

"Evan loved spending time with Myles and Ava and Charlie," she murmurs. "He keeps asking when he can see them again."

Warmth rushes through me. It feels like hope and love all mashed into one. "We could have all of our family in one place."

She beams at me. "Isn't it too soon to mix them up?"

"I don't know. I don't think so. All I know is that I want to be with you. And I'll do whatever it takes to make it happen."

"Even leave the job you love?" she whispers.

"I love you more." It's the truth.

"If you keep sweet talking me like that, I might say yes." She reaches her hand across the table. Our fingers slide against each other until our palms are touching. She's staring at me like I'm some kind of God.

And I like it. Not because I am – I'm only human – but because I want to be the one to make her happy. To make her safe, to make her smile.

I've spent a lifetime fighting against making myself vulnerable like this. Now I want nothing else.

"Ava said we can visit them next week and look around the library and town. Maybe Evan and Annie can come, see if they like it?"

"What if they don't?" Her brows knit.

"Then we'll find somewhere they do like. That all of us like."

"We?" she whispers.

"If you'll have me. I want to be where you are." It's as simple as that. "Maryland, Pennsylvania, West Virginia. It doesn't matter."

It's not a proposal. But if I have my way that'll happen before too long. It's a request. To be part of the dream she's had for so long. I rub my thumb against her wrist and she blushes.

"Yes," she says, her voice strong. "Yes, I want you with me."

And I don't think I've ever heard sweeter words than that.

EPILOGUE

BLAIR

"What do you think?" Holden asks, his hand squeezing mine. We're standing in the driveway of an old, run down house right outside Charleston, West Virginia.

It's set on an acre of land, but is still close enough to town for me to get to work within half an hour. I stare at it, taking in the weatherworn brickwork and the cupola on the roof. It's a dream house, if I'd ever dared to dream.

"Say something," he says softly, turning to look at me. "If you hate it, we can look some more. Maybe at something more modern."

I shake my head. "I love it," I whisper. A rush of emotions go through me, making my breath ragged. "It's perfect."

He gives me a boyish smile. "Good. I love it too."

"Can we afford it?" I ask him.

"Yes we can afford it. But it's going to take a lot of work to make it the way we want it." We walk up the driveway together, and I take in the porch that surrounds the house. There's a dilapidated bench swing hanging from the roof.

That's the first thing I'll tackle so we can have somewhere to sit at night once he's home from the hospital and I'm home from work.

"There's more," he tells me. "Come with me."

We walk around the side of the house and I realize what he means by *more*.

Another house. A little cottage. "They remodeled that one already," he says. "It has three bedrooms and two bathrooms and a kitchen that's bigger than most apartments in New York. I thought Annie and Evan could have it."

Okay, if I wasn't crying before I am now. He watches, alarmed as the tears pour down my cheeks.

"Shit." He wipes them away. "You're supposed to be happy."

"I am. It's just too much." I look at him, the man who wants to give me everything. The one who wants my smiles and my happiness, but knows how to deal with the fear, too. "I'm trying to take it in. When I talked about moving into the suburbs I meant a little bungalow that we could squeeze into."

His smile is crooked as he cups my face. He brushes his lips against mine and my heart does a stupid hammer against my chest. "The only thing I want to squeeze into is you."

"Nice segue," I say, shaking my head at him.

"Thank you, I thought so." He kisses me again, then looks excited. "There's something else I want to show you."

He pulls me around the side. That's when I see it. It's old and it's falling down but it's there.

A white picket fence.

I'm going to fuck you against that white picket fence.

I remember him saying it to me. I remember laughing. But now I'm feeling stupidly horny.

His eyes catch mine and he smirks. "I'm going to get it repaired," he tells me. "So it surrounds the property."

"And my sister and nephew will be here, so don't get any ideas."

"They won't be here all the time." He reaches for me again, pulling me against him. It's stupid how much I like the heat in his eyes. "And I will fulfill my promise."

"You always do."

His eyes soften. "That's because you're worth it."

This time when he kisses me it's hard enough to take my breath away. I'm clinging to him, my body arched into his, his hands holding me because I think I might fall over if he doesn't.

And when we part he's still smiling. I am too.

I officially graduated last month. Though I was only supposed to get two tickets to the ceremony, I got three so that Holden, Annie, and Evan could all be there. And afterward we went to the cabin for the weekend to join his family for a massive party. I'm slowly getting used to how many of them there are.

And Evan is in heaven whenever we all get together. Holden's brothers make a big fuss over him and Charlie thinks he's some kind of hero. Annie loves it because she finally gets a break.

She's already got a job offer from three different banks in Charleston. She got the third the same day I got an offer from a private university right on the outskirts of town. It's smaller than the other libraries I applied to, but it's a great opportunity to get some experience while settling into a new life.

And Holden already has a job offer from the children's hospital in the center of town. He's working his notice out in New York, and I can tell he's finding it difficult to say goodbye. It's not a job that you easily skip from one place to another.

He's doing it for me. And that fills my heart.

Another thing he's doing is jogging every day.

He runs before I even wake in the morning, usually

bringing back coffee and pastries which we don't eat and drink fresh because I follow him into the shower and we forget the world together.

Who knew that running and sex were a good replacement for the high he used to get from the boxing ring?

And who knew that I'd love them both in equal measure? On weekends we try to run together, though I can tell he holds himself back for me.

The same way he does in bed. I'm a lucky woman.

An hour later we're walking out of the house, and I'm more in love with the place than ever. It's so beautiful and so neglected. It almost feels like a duty to make her pretty again.

"So what do you think? Should we put an offer in?" Holden asks me.

"Yes. I say yes."

He smiles at me softly. "I like it when you say that."

"I say it a lot when you're around."

His eyes flash. "I know." He pulls me lazily against him and we look at the house again. My heart does a little leap to think it could be ours.

Annie and I have already agreed that if we find the right place our nest egg is going all in. I know Holden will fight it, but that's a worry for another day.

"You want to?" He has that excited look on his face again.

"I do."

He kisses me softly. "Then let's go buy ourselves a house."

———

HOLDEN

"Are you sure you don't want me to drive you?" Annie says as she and Blair fuss around Evan, making sure he's got his bag, his shoes, and his lunch.

"No, Mom. I want to take the bus," Evan says. His eyes catch mine and he shakes his head. I want to laugh because I know exactly what he's thinking. He hates the fuss.

He just wants to go to school.

Blair is a little better at hiding her emotions about his first day at his new school, even though she's got a vice grip on my hand. The four of us are standing at the bus stop at the end of the lane. Evan spots one of the friends he's made from playing in the street and waves at them, looking excited.

When the yellow bus arrives, Annie's lip wobbles. She hugs him tight and makes him promise to come home safely, then the three of us watch as he walks up the steps.

And now my chest is tight. I fucking love that kid. I spend a lot of time with him. We've been trying to tackle the back-yard together on my days off, and we're making good progress. His latest idea is that we should get a dog, and that we need a great backyard for that.

The bus door closes and Annie stifles a sob. Blair hugs her tight, and I put my arm around them both.

Truth is, I'm a little emotional here, too. My throat constricts as I hear the air brakes release and watch the little yellow bus trundle up the street.

"You think this is what Neil Armstrong's family felt like when they watched him go up the steps to the rocket?" I ask Blair.

Despite the emotion in her eyes she smiles at me. "Probably."

As soon as it's out of sight, Annie rushes to her car because she has to get to work. She's still new and is saving all of her paid time off for the school vacations. She tells us she'll see us tonight, and then she's gone.

Neither Blair or I are working today. She's scheduled for a Saturday this week, and I can build my own around hers. So we walk back into the house and she mentions maybe going out for breakfast, but there's something I want to show her first.

"Come outside," I say, opening the kitchen door. The house still isn't completely repaired. So far we've mostly tackled the big things. Knocked some walls down to have a bigger kitchen, put in new cupboards, appliances and counter tops surfaces, plus two new bathrooms.

And though the kitchen and bathrooms are modern, the rest we're planning to keep to the original character of the house. Everywhere you look there are wallpaper catalogues and paint samples and mood boards for the rooms.

I love how much she's loving this. It's something we're building together.

But now there's something I want to show her. I slide my hand in hers as we walk across the grass to the far end of the yard.

"Oh my God," she says, laughing when she sees it. A twenty foot stretch of picket fence. The whole thing will be there soon. But I wanted to tackle this part myself.

And yeah, it's behind some trees and out of view. I chose my position wisely.

She runs over to it and touches it, still laughing. I love it when she laughs. Then she turns around to look at me, and I see the blush on her cheeks.

I love that too.

"What are you waiting for?" she asks me.

I run my tongue along my bottom lip. I'm so in love with this woman it hurts. "You. I was waiting for you." I tell her.

"Then come and get me."

So I do. And while we awkwardly take as little clothing off as possible – because yes, this is private property, but it's also eight o'clock in the morning and I'm pretty sure there are laws against this – we kiss and laugh and I wonder if there are picket fences in heaven.

If there aren't, I'll build one just for her.

"I love you," she whispers, her hand cupping my face. Happiness shines out of her eyes, the same way it radiates from mine.

"Not as much as I love you." I take her hand and we walk back to the house we're making our own.

And begin the rest of our lives together.

THE END

DEAR READER

Thank you so much for reading STRICTLY NOT YOURS. If you enjoyed it and you get a chance, I'd be so grateful if you can leave a review. And don't forget to check out my free bonus epilogue which you can download by typing this URL into your web browser: https://dl.bookfunnel.com/1wdqer7yxr

The next book in the series is Linc's story - join him and all the Salinger brothers in STRICTLY THE WORST.

I can't wait to share more stories with you.

Yours,

Carrie xx

ALSO BY CARRIE ELKS

THE SALINGER BROTHERS SERIES

A swoony romantic comedy series featuring six brothers and the strong and smart women who tame them.

Strictly Business

Strictly Pleasure

Strictly For Now

Strictly Not Yours

Strictly The Worst

THE HEARTBREAK BROTHERS NEXT GENERATION SERIES

A steamy and emotional small town / big family romance series, set in West Virginia.

That One Regret

That One Touch

THE WINTERVILLE SERIES

A gorgeously wintery small town romance series, featuring six cousins who fight to save the town their grandmother built.

Welcome to Winterville

Hearts In Winter

Leave Me Breathless

Memories Of Mistletoe

Every Shade Of Winter

Mine For The Winter

ANGEL SANDS SERIES

A heartwarming small town beach series, full of best friends, hot guys and happily-ever-afters.

Let Me Burn

She's Like the Wind

Sweet Little Lies

Just A Kiss

Baby I'm Yours

Pieces Of Us

Chasing The Sun

Heart And Soul

Lost In Him

THE HEARTBREAK BROTHERS SERIES

A gorgeous small town series about four brothers and the women who capture their hearts.

Take Me Home

Still The One

A Better Man

Somebody Like You

When We Touch

THE SHAKESPEARE SISTERS SERIES

An epic series about four strong yet vulnerable sisters, and the alpha men who steal their hearts.

Summer's Lease

A Winter's Tale

Absent in the Spring

By Virtue Fall

THE LOVE IN LONDON SERIES

Three books about strong and sassy women finding love in the big city.

Coming Down

Broken Chords

Canada Square

STANDALONE

Fix You

An epic romance that spans the decades. Breathtaking and angsty
and all the things in between.

ABOUT THE AUTHOR

Carrie Elks writes contemporary romance with a sizzling edge. Her first book, *Fix You*, has been translated into eight languages and made a surprise appearance on *Big Brother* in Brazil. Luckily for her, it wasn't voted out.

Carrie lives with her husband, two lovely children and a larger-than-life black pug called Plato. When she isn't writing or reading, she can be found baking, drinking an occasional (!) glass of wine, or chatting on social media.

You can find Carrie in all these places
www.carrieelks.com
carrie.elks@mail.com

Made in the USA
Monee, IL
19 April 2024

57185067R00187